ALSO BY TINA FOLSOM

Cain's Identity

Scanguards Vampires – Book 9

Tina Folsom

Cain's Identity is a work of fiction. Names, characters, places, and incidents are the products of the author's imagination and are used fictitiously. Any resemblance to actual events, locales, or persons, living or dead, is entirely coincidental.

Cover design: Elaina Lee
Cover photo: Shutterstock
Author Photo: © Marti Corn Photography

Printed in the United States of America

1

If sin were a woman, there would be no doubt what she'd look like.

Long dark hair cascaded over her bare shoulders and caressed the strapless, elegant dress she wore, a dress that accentuated her voluptuous breasts. Nipping in at her waist, the red silk flowed to the bottom of her legs and over pretty toes that peeked out from high-heeled golden sandals.

When she made a motion to kick them off, Cain commanded, "Leave them on." He paused. "Take everything else off."

A gentle laugh as delicate as a whisper in the wind came from her. "Oh, Cain," she drawled in a soft southern accent that instantly sent a flame to his groin and filled his entire body with desire.

"You know how much I love it when you strip for me." He tossed his dinner jacket onto an armchair and glanced around.

The suite of rooms was large and opulent, and consisted of a bedroom and a sitting room connected by large double doors that stood open at present. The absence of windows made this the ideal place for a vampire's residence, providing safety as well as privacy. Priceless works of art adorned the walls, and elegant furniture provided an atmosphere fit for a king. This was no cave dwelling despite its underground location. It was an impenetrable fortress.

The seductress made a step toward him, her body moving with the grace of a tigress approaching her prey. And Cain might as well have been her prey, albeit her very willing prey. Just as she was his.

When her lips parted, he caught sight of her fangs elongating.

"Starting without me, my love?" he asked, and gave a shake of his head, a gentle reprimand, while at the same time the beast inside him delighted at her primal reaction and readied itself to react in kind.

A vampire showing his fangs had only two reasons: hunger for blood or for sex.

And he was certain this beautiful specimen, who now brought her hands behind her back to lower the zipper of her dress, wasn't hungry for blood. Although Cain wouldn't mind biting her while he impaled her on his cock. The memory of it now manifested on his tongue. So sweet, so rich, so full of passion. A strange sense of longing and loss slammed into him, but the latter feeling vanished just as quickly and made way for more pleasurable thoughts.

His gums itched, and he allowed his own fangs to descend, readying himself for what was to come. Anticipation heated his body from the inside, dispelling once and for all the false belief that vampires were cold. Parting his lips, Cain made her aware of his desire for her, though he was certain that the red glow in his eyes had already given him away.

Blood pounding in his veins, he watched her peel the red fabric away from her torso. His breath hitched in his throat as she bared her rosy nipples, already hard and standing to attention, her hands casually stroking her skin as she pushed the dress lower past her hips. The dress bunched there for a moment, getting caught by her generous proportions, which, these days, were perhaps less common. Women with hourglass figures like hers were rare, and maybe that was one of the reasons Cain was so fascinated by her. So drawn to her.

He imagined his fingers digging into those hips, holding onto her as he pounded into her softness. The knowledge that he could take her as hard as he wanted, because she was nearly as strong as he, made his fingers want to turn into the claws of the beast that lived inside him. But he pushed back the urge, not wanting to mar the flawless skin that stretched over her tantalizing flesh. Nor did he want to remind her of the violence in her past, the pain she'd endured at the hands of a cruel master. Never again would he allow anybody to hurt her. Not even he himself.

"More!" Cain demanded now and noticed the change in his voice. The hoarseness in it attested to his aroused state. He dropped his lids, glancing at the front of his pants. The bulge there was hard to overlook. He wasn't trying to hide it from her. He wanted to show her what she did to him, what the extent of her power over him was.

"Oh, I don't know if you can take any more." A saucy smile underscored her words.

He took a step toward her, while his hands got busy ridding himself of his bowtie and shirt in vampire speed. He threw both on the armchair to keep his jacket company.

"Impatient much?"

"Do as I say!" Cain ordered, his chest heaving with the effort it cost him to keep a modicum of civility when inside him the vampire raged with the need to take her, to make her his.

Elegant hands pushed the dress over her hips, making the garment fall to the floor with a soft *whoosh*. But Cain didn't look at what lay at her feet now. Instead, he stared at the dark triangle of hair that guarded her sex.

Mouth watering, his eyes lifted to her face. "You weren't wearing anything underneath."

She acknowledged his observation with a sinful smile.

Stepping out of the dress, she strode toward him, her high heels clicking on the hardwood floor, echoing in the vast windowless space.

His cock was rigid now, pressing painfully against his zipper. Instinctively, his hand went to it, but she was faster. The warmth of her palm engulfed him instantly, sending a thrill through his entire body that made his control dance on a blade's edge. Lust impregnated the air and made it hum.

"You have a present for me?" she murmured, and rubbed her body against him, while her hand squeezed the hardness in his pants.

"A present that keeps on giving." Cain slid his hand to her nape, pulling her face to him so their lips were only a fraction of an inch apart. So close, yet so far away. "I missed you."

Her breath bounced against his when she opened her mouth. He inhaled it, allowing her scent to fill his lungs and drug him. "What did you miss most? My lips on your cock? Me riding you? Your cock thrusting into me?"

Though he loved all of her suggestions, he countered, "I think you forgot something." His fingers caressed one side of her neck, tracing the plump vein beneath her skin. Her pulse beat against the pad of his fingers, as if to signal him her acquiescence. "My fangs in your neck."

An intake of breath pressed her chest firmer against his. "I didn't forget. I always keep room for dessert."

On her last word, Cain captured her lips and kissed her. There was nothing tentative or hesitant about the kiss, nor her reaction to it. He tasted her sweetness on his tongue as he delved into her and showed her who her master was. Yet she was no submissive. Her response to his kiss was that of an equal, a strong vampire female who knew what she wanted. He sensed it with every stroke of her tongue against his, with every glide of her lips against his mouth—and every thrust of her hips against his groin. She wanted him, and that knowledge only added to his desire for her.

Cain's fingers fanned, sliding up higher into her hair, cupping the back of her head. Her dark silken tresses caressed his hand, reminding him of previous encounters such as this. Reminding him of having found ecstasy in her arms before.

Her soft sighs drifted to his ears, while her rapid heartbeat reverberated in his chest, echoing his. His other hand now drifted lower, sliding over the curve of her back down to her shapely ass. As he palmed it and yanked her harder to him, she moaned into his mouth, before her tongue swiped against his fang.

Panting heavily, Cain ripped his lips from her. "Fuck!"

Licking a vampire's fangs was the most erotic thing a vampire could experience—short of having full-blown sex. And even though she'd licked his fangs before, the intense pleasure now coursing through his body almost undid him.

"I know you want it," she coaxed, looking at him seductively.

He ground out a curse, grabbed her and took a few steps toward the wall, where he pressed her against it, all patience gone, vanished into thin air. "Have it your way."

Then he captured her lips again. This would be a short interlude if she continued to use her wiles on him like this. But, damn it to hell, he didn't want to stop her. Instead, he attempted to open his pants with one hand, until he felt her hands on him, helping him. Clearly, she was as impatient as he.

Moments later, his tuxedo pants fell to the floor. He still wore his dress shoes, but didn't have the patience to take them or his socks off. Instead, his pants pooled around his ankles. They wouldn't hinder him in his movements—not the kind of movements he was about to engage in anyway.

Cain gripped her thighs and lifted her up, while pressing her back against the wall. He spread her legs wide open, exposing her drenched sex. He looked down, then drew his hips back and adjusted his angle. When his cockhead touched the outer lips of her sex, he inhaled sharply. He'd been right: this wouldn't take long at all.

"I need it," she encouraged him. "I need you."

Cain plunged into her without preamble, seating himself in her warm channel, his balls slapping against her flesh, burning from the impact. The first time was always like this, intense, urgent. Later tonight he'd take his time with her, but right now he needed to still his hunger for her.

Air rushed out of her lungs. "Cain! Yes!"

She was perfect, better than anything else in his life. As if she was the solution to all his problems, all his worries. As if she could make everything right again.

His eyes met hers and, slowly, Cain began to thrust. Her green eyes now glowed red, a sign that her vampire side was ruling her. A feeling of possessiveness came over him, and the thought that she could ever be in another man's arms again stirred the beast inside him. Anger churned up from his gut, and he growled like an animal.

"You're mine!"

Her eyes flashed brightly, before she tilted her head to the side, baring her pale neck. "Then make me yours."

Without thinking, he drove his fangs into her neck, piercing her hot skin. Rich blood touched his fangs and filled his mouth. While the blood ran down his throat, coating it, farther down, his own blood pounded in his veins, filling his cock even more. And with every draw from her vein and every thrust into her pussy, the wildness in him grew.

For an instant, he removed his fangs, wanting to tell her what she meant to him. He parted his lips, wanting to speak, but her name didn't roll over his lips. He tried again, but there was only emptiness. He stared into her eyes and saw confusion there.

"Who are you?" he whispered.

Disbelief colored her eyes, but before her lips gave him an answer, a sharp pain pierced his skull. Still inside her, he arrested his movements.

His vision darkened. Cain brought one hand to his face and felt the sticky, warm liquid that ran over his face. He smelled it, too. The metallic scent was unmistakable.

Blood. Blood coming from his skull. He brought his hand up and felt the hole there. Blood gushed from it.

"No!" she screamed. "No! Don't leave me!"

He couldn't see her face anymore, and suddenly his hands were gripping nothing, as if she had slipped from his grasp. He searched for her in the darkness, but all he felt was a void. Despair. Hopelessness.

Was he dead?

"Nooooooo!" Cain screamed.

But she didn't answer him. She was gone.

Suddenly his vision cleared and a light source drew his attention. Something blinked in red. He focused his eyes. Numbers appeared before them. 07:24. He stared at the apparition. It took a second to realize that he was looking at a digital clock.

Cain shot up to a seated position.

Gone was the room he'd been in, replaced by a bedroom with little personal effects. No opulence. No luxury. Just a simple bedroom with a large bed, a dresser, and a chair with casual clothes somebody had tossed onto it. No tuxedo in sight.

Cain ran a shaky hand through his ultra-short hair and realized he was bathed in sweat.

Regret filled him. It had been a dream, all of it: the woman, the room, the blood.

Nothing was real. Just like Cain himself. Because how could he be real when he didn't remember anything about his past?

For several months now he'd had these dreams. Different ones, but all involving the same woman, and all ending the same way: with blood gushing from his head. As if they were a warning somebody was trying to send him. Or a message from the past.

Cain swung his legs out of bed and shook his head. Wishful thinking! A little over a year ago he'd woken up one night without a memory. All he remembered was a male voice. *Your name is Cain,* the man had said. As much as he'd tried to find out about his past, he'd come up empty.

The dreams were haunting him, dangling pieces of information in front of him, yet never letting him get close enough to grab one and examine it. It had made him irritable and unpredictable. His colleagues at Scanguards, where he worked as a bodyguard, had started noticing and avoided him whenever he was in one of his dark moods.

And just now, one of those dark moods was washing over him, lashing despair and hopelessness at him like a torturer whipping him with a flogger. Pain crippled his body and made him want to inflict the same pain on others. But there was nobody on whom to let out his anger.

A ringing sound suddenly pierced the silence of his bedroom. He turned to the bedside table and reached for his cell phone.

"Yeah?"

"Where the fuck are you?" The deep, pissed-off voice belonged to Amaury, one of his superiors at Scanguards.

Rage boiled up in Cain. He didn't like Amaury's tone, nor did he like being questioned about his whereabouts. He hated being ordered around.

"What the fuck do you want?" Cain replied, raising his voice.

"You're supposed to be patrolling tonight!" Amaury growled. "And don't take that fucking attitude with me. I'm your boss!"

Cain jumped up and slammed his fist into the drywall, leaving a dent there. "I need no boss! I'm my own master!" The moment he said it, he knew it was true. He wasn't used to having anybody tell him what to do. He was used to giving the orders.

On the other end of the line, Amaury breathed heavily before giving his response. "Fine! You wanna have it out, once and for all? I'm sick of your attitude lately. I think it's time we had a chat so you understand who's in charge here."

The way he spoke made it clear to Cain that this would be a very physical kind of chat.

"My place. In ten minutes, or you're on your own."

"You got it!" Cain responded to the open challenge.

A fist fight with the linebacker-sized vampire was just what he needed right now. Maybe then he'd feel better.

2

The winter garden was as beautiful at night as it was deadly during the day. Encased in bulletproof glass on three sides, it provided no shelter from the sun.

Faye looked up at the starry sky above the glass roof. Was he watching her from somewhere up there? Or were vampires doomed to burn in hell when they met with the true death?

She couldn't remember how often she'd stared up at the night sky asking herself these questions ever since his death. Every time she did, she felt the same kind of longing, the same kind of emptiness. But life had to go on. She knew that. The time for mourning was almost at an end.

Footsteps made her aware that she wasn't alone anymore. Even before she turned, she knew who had entered the winter garden from the house. Well, it couldn't really be called a house. It was a palace.

Faye inclined her head slightly, before lifting her eyes to her visitor. "Your Majesty."

"Faye, Faye, how often have I told you that between us there's no formality. I'm still Abel to you. Always will be. Besides, I'm not king yet."

"Of course." She allowed her eyes to roam over him. There were days she could barely look at him, so much did he remind her of the man she'd lost. The man she'd loved.

Abel pointed to a bench, motioning her to sit there with him. She took a seat, and he joined her.

"I've come to talk to you."

Her stomach instantly clenched. She knew what this was about. She'd counted the days too, though for other reasons than he had.

"We all miss him," Abel started.

Faye pressed her lips together, suppressing the emotions that threatened to overwhelm her and rob her of the ability to think clearly. She had to remain strong.

"The time is nearly up."

She nodded. "One year, one month, and one day. I marked it on my calendar." Though she didn't have to. She would always remember the horrible day when she'd been robbed of the love of her life.

"Yes, in less than two weeks his official reign will end, and the new king will be crowned."

"I've never really understood why there is such a long period after the death of one king before his successor can take the throne," Faye said to fill the air between them with words.

Abel reached for her hand, clasping it. She shuddered internally, but let it happen. He would be her king soon, and her destiny lay in his hands. The privileges she'd enjoyed as the dead king's fiancée would expire at the new king's coronation. She would lose her home, her standing in their society, her influence. Though nothing mattered much to her anyway. Only love for the vampires who would have been her subjects, had her fiancé lived, had made her stay. Otherwise, she would have left the clan altogether.

"It's meant to give the people time to grieve without having to pledge their allegiance to the new king while they still mourn the old," Abel explained.

"It must be hard for the king-in-waiting, though."

"As regent, I already have many of the powers the king has. And it gives me a chance to get to know my subjects better and find out what they want from me." He raised her hand toward his face. "Or what I want from them."

Faye's breath hitched. "Yes, yes, of course." She rose, making him drop her hand, and walked to a raised flowerbed. She reached for shears and started to prune the plants.

Since that horrible day over a year ago, no man had touched her. And the thought of another man's hands or lips on her sent panic shooting down her spine. She knew she had to do something about that, but tonight wasn't the right time.

Behind her, Abel rose from the bench. She heard his footsteps as he approached her.

"Decisions have to be made. As you know, soon—"

"I know," she interrupted him. "I have been thinking about it. I'm preparing myself to leave." She would be without protection once again. The last time that had happened she'd fallen prey to the cruelest of vampires.

When Abel's hands clasped her shoulders from behind, she sucked in a breath, trying to calm herself.

"I didn't come to ask you to leave. I came to ask you to stay."

Faye turned her head halfway. "But clan law is clear on it."

"I don't give a damn about clan law. In two weeks, *my word* will be law."

Surprised at his sharp tone, her heart rate doubled instantly. She knew he would sense it. A vampire's hearing was sensitive enough for it. Besides, his hands still lay on her shoulders, and by touching her he would not only feel her heartbeat, but also perceive the blood that rushed through her veins like a runaway train.

"Forget what I said," Abel added quickly. "This isn't about the law. It's about you. You were meant to be queen. The members of our clan love you. Your dream doesn't have to end with my coronation."

The implication of his words sank in immediately. When he turned her to face him, she wanted to avoid his gaze, but out of respect for the position he held she didn't.

His dark eyes looked at her with an intensity she'd always loved about his brother. But in Abel, it scared her. Or was she simply scared because it meant she would finally have to admit to herself that it was time to move on and let go of the memories she treasured, the memories of true love?

"I need a queen. A woman like you, one who is loved by her subjects. I know I'm not like him. I could never be the just leader he was. But with you by my side, with you guiding me to show me what he would have done in my stead, I can be a good king. I need you."

Faye searched his eyes, trying to see past his words, past the face he showed her. Did he mean it? Did he really need her in order to be the kind of king their vast clan needed? And could she truly help him be that man? Was that her calling? To be queen, so he could be king?

Her chest lifted as she took a breath. "I don't know, Abel. I loved your brother."

Abel pressed a finger to her lips. "And he loved you. He would want this for you. He would want you to have what was meant to be yours. He would want you to move on and be happy again. To see you smile again. I remember that smile. But I haven't seen it for so long."

She lowered her lids and nodded. "It is hard to get over the death of someone so . . . " She couldn't even continue her thought, nor say his name, without risking dissolving into tears.

"Give me a chance," Abel said gently.

"This is all so unexpected. I need time to think about it," she answered quickly, desperate to buy herself some time and at the same time not offend him. This was a decision she couldn't make, not without thinking about the consequences. She didn't love Abel. He was in so many ways not like his brother. Where his brother had been kind and lenient, Abel was harsh and stern. Their personalities couldn't be more different from each other.

Faye wanted to scream, to lament that the wrong brother had died. If only that night she'd not let him out of her arms. Then he would still be alive. He would still be king, and she would be his blood-bonded mate and his queen.

"Do it for the clan, if not for me."

Faye looked past him, her eyes peering into the darkness beyond the palace she lived in. It was vast, a huge structure built like a fortress, impenetrable and awe-inspiring. A large palace for a large clan, one that encompassed all of Louisiana and spilled over its borders. A clan so secretive, yet influential way beyond its physical boundaries, that few vampires outside knew of its existence. All previous kings had wanted it that way, knowing that in anonymity lay safety.

The old ways were still strong within the clan. The laws they lived by had been passed down from their founders, though the living accommodations were modern and the castle—tucked away in a remote wooded area north of New Orleans—was equipped with state-of-the-art security. Just as it behooved a king. Guards and other key members of the clan lived in the palace, while in buildings surrounding the well-kept grounds, other vampires made their home.

Faye's eyes drifted back to Abel. "You deserve a mate who loves you."

He smiled. "I'll settle for one who may one day *learn* to love me."

She sighed. "I don't know."

"We could be crowned together in two weeks if you say yes."

She swallowed hard. "I'll give you my answer. Soon."

Then she turned quickly and rushed through the open door into the corridor beyond. She almost collided with somebody and looked up in shock.

"Apologies, Faye," he said. "I didn't mean to startle you."

"John, uh, you didn't," she lied, wanting to get away from him as quickly as possible.

John was tall and broad, a strong vampire with a fast hand and a quick mind. It was those qualities that had made him the leader of the king's elite guard, the small hand-selected group of vampires who guarded the king and queen.

But John had failed guarding his king. Under his watch, the king had been assassinated. When Faye had seen the telltale ash and the signet ring on the floor—the remains of her lover—she'd accused John of neglecting his duty. He'd hung his head, accepting her hateful words in stoic silence, never even attempting to offer an excuse or apology.

She'd never understood why Abel hadn't punished John. Had she been in the position to give orders, she would have demanded John's execution for his failure to keep the king safe.

For a moment, she paused. Maybe Abel had a kinder heart than she gave him credit for, and she was the one who was bad for wishing to punish the leader of the king's guard.

3

Amaury not only lived in one of the shabbiest neighborhoods of San Francisco, he owned an entire apartment building there, the penthouse of which he and his human mate, Nina, called home. When Cain had once asked his fellow vampire why he'd bought the property, Amaury had said that nobody else had wanted it and it had come cheap.

Cain now looked up at the six-story apartment building and noticed the light coming from the top floor. A broad shadow moved in front of one of the large windows, then a smaller one joined and the two melted into one figure. A second later they retreated from the window.

Cain didn't have to wait long. It appeared that Amaury was just as eager to get this over with as he was. The sound of an opening door drifted to his ears, and an instant later Amaury emerged.

The bodyguard with the shoulder-length dark hair was built like a tank. Technically Amaury wasn't a bodyguard anymore; he was a director of Scanguards but, despite his rank in the company, Amaury loved getting his hands dirty.

With a motion of his head, Amaury walked into the alley next to the building. Cain followed without a word, then stopped a few feet from where Amaury stood in front of a dumpster.

"What the fuck's wrong with you?" Amaury asked without a greeting.

Cain pulled his shoulders back and broadened his stance instinctively. He was ready for this fight. "I don't like your tone."

"Guess we've got that in common. 'Cause I don't like yours, either." Amaury glared at him. "What happened to you? When we took you on, I thought we'd struck gold! Of all the bodyguards I know, you've turned out to be the one with the best instincts. As if it had been bred into you! And look at you now!"

Cain took a step toward him, balling his hands into fists. "Nothing's changed!"

"The fuck it hasn't! Ever since Oliver's wedding three months ago, you've been slacking off! You don't show up for your shifts. And when you do, you're in a stinking mood!"

"My mood's my business, not yours!" Cain ground out between clenched teeth.

Amaury narrowed his eyes. "It is when you turn into an insubordinate prick!" He flashed his fangs. "There are rules if you want to continue working for Scanguards. And you'd better be following them, or—"

Cain's hand shot out by itself and slammed Amaury against the dumpster, as if somebody else had taken control over his body. "You think you can order me around?" Instinct told him that he wasn't used to following orders. He was meant to give them.

Amaury pushed back, using both hands to catapult Cain against the wall of the building. "You listen to me now, you little shit! Samson and I agree on this. Either you follow the fucking rules, or you're out. You understand me?"

So they'd all conspired behind his back. That was just perfect! Fucking perfect! "Fuck you, Amaury! Fuck all of you!" But just cursing Amaury wasn't enough. Hurling the words at him didn't give Cain the satisfaction he needed. Only one thing could do that now.

Cain brought his fist up and delivered an uppercut to Amaury's chin, making the hulky vampire tumble back. He caught himself just as quickly and lashed a furious glare at Cain.

"You wanna fight? Fine," Amaury bit out. "Let's fight."

Before the last word was even out, a fist slammed into Cain's face, whipping his head sideways. Pain radiated through his body and made him feel more alive than he'd felt for the entire last year. It was a thousand times better than the numbness and void he'd been feeling.

With a growl, Cain aimed his fists at Amaury and delivered blow after blow. But the huge vampire was no willing punching bag. He gave as good as he got, alternating between kicks and blows. Despite his size, his opponent was more agile on his feet than anybody would have guessed.

Cain let his instincts take over. He'd known himself to be a remarkable fighter, but in this fist fight with Amaury, Cain sensed that his skills were superior to those of his boss. One thing that Amaury had said rang true: fighting had been bred into him. He was no novice, and he was proving it now by pummeling Amaury with his fists, kicking him with skilled and lightning-fast moves, while Amaury was forced into defense.

Satisfaction surged inside Cain. This felt right. Making another vampire submit to him, beating him down and showing him who was stronger, triggered a spark in him. As if a tiny candle was illuminating something in his past. Something that lay just beyond his reach. So close, yet so far away.

Amaury's next punch hit him in the stomach, making him fold over for an instant. Another blow followed the first, confirming that Cain's moment of contemplation had cost him the upper hand.

"Fuck!" Cain growled and cleared his mind.

He avoided Amaury's next punch by swiveling on his heel and jumping behind his opponent. Cain kicked his leg out and hit Amaury in the back of his knees. The linebacker-sized vampire lost his balance and fell backward, landing hard on the concrete ground.

A whoosh of air expelled from Amaury's chest, but already he tried to jump up. Cain was faster. He landed on him, pinning him to the ground, when Amaury's eyes suddenly stared at him in shock.

It took a second for Cain to realize what Amaury was looking at.

In horror, Cain recoiled, scrambling backward to release him, while he looked at his own hand in disbelief. He was holding a stake. A ragged breath tore from Cain's chest. He hadn't even noticed pulling his stake from his jacket pocket.

"Shit!" he cursed and dropped it to the ground.

Amaury sat up. "I've never seen anybody as fast as you."

Cain rubbed a trembling hand over his face. "I didn't mean to—"

The simultaneous pinging of two cell phones saved him from completing his sentence. Automatically Cain pulled his phone from his pocket to look at it.

Trouble at the End Up. Vampire involvement suspected, the text message read. *Accept or reject*, it flashed an instant later.

The End Up was a popular nightclub in the South of Market area. He knew from experience that it could be a hotspot for trouble. Heck, most nightclubs in the city were.

"Crap!" Amaury cursed, clearly having received the same message.

Their gazes met.

"Are you with me?" Amaury asked.

It wasn't an order, but a request that he saw in his fellow vampire's eyes. It made all the difference.

"Let's go and kick some ass." Cain jumped to his feet and reached his hand out to Amaury.

Amaury flashed a grin. "They're not gonna know what hit them."

4

From the door of the End Up, which was guarded by a bouncer with way too many tattoos on his face, neck and arms, loud techno music emanated. A crowd of youngsters stood in line, waiting to be let in.

Without hesitation, Cain followed Amaury as he walked to the head of the line and stopped in front of the bouncer, ignoring the verbal protests of the waiting clubbers.

"Hey, there's a line!" one of them complained.

Cain turned, letting Amaury do his thing with the bouncer, while he glared at the kid who'd dared make a stink. "Official business. So butt out, little punk." Without waiting for a reply, he turned back just as the bouncer made a motion for him and Amaury to enter.

The *thing* Amaury had done was a little trick known as mind control. Every vampire possessed the skill, which had always been thought to work only on humans. However, only recently they'd found out the hard way that there were vampires who were capable of exerting mind control on other vampires. To Cain's knowledge, all vampires possessing that particular skill had been eradicated—all but one: Thomas, the chief of IT at Scanguards. And luckily Thomas was one of the gentlest creatures Cain had ever met and absolutely devoted to Scanguards. Almost as devoted as he was to his blood-bonded mate, Eddie.

Cain entered the club, his eyes instantly adjusting to the dim interior. A vampire's vision was superior to that of a human, and he could see everything as clearly as if the place were lit up like a Christmas tree. The noise was deafening, and unfortunately not something Cain could easily drown out.

It wasn't hard to see why Scanguards had gotten a call from one of their informants—trusted humans and civilian vampires who kept their ears to the ground to alert Scanguards to any problems that needed to be taken care of immediately.

While Scanguards was primarily a company supplying bodyguards and other security personnel to politicians, celebrities, foreign dignitaries, and other rich people, the mayor of San Francisco, a hybrid himself—half human, half vampire—had recently hired them as an underground security unit that not even his police force was aware of. As such, Scanguards was now in charge of rooting out problems that human police officers were ill equipped to deal with.

Amaury pointed to the far corner which lay in almost complete darkness.

"I see them," Cain replied.

Paving the way through the throng of dancers on the dance floor that occupied the middle of the club, Amaury charged ahead, Cain on his heels. He ignored the come-hither looks he received from some of the women he passed.

The three punks looked high, but the moment he laid eyes on them Cain knew it wasn't alcohol or drugs that had caused their inebriated state. After all, alcohol or drugs didn't have any effect on a vampire. Only blood—massive amounts of it—could make a vampire high. That, or tainted blood. The kind of blood that ran through the veins of Ursula, his colleague Oliver's mate. But to Cain's knowledge, all women with the special blood that could drug a vampire had been removed from San Francisco and given new identities.

It appeared that the three juveniles had indulged in too much of a good thing.

Cain exchanged a quick look with his colleague. "You've gotta be kidding me."

Amaury grunted. "Why is it that I always get the babysitting jobs? Do I look like a fucking kindergarten teacher?"

"Well, let's take 'em out back before they cause any more trouble."

The three vampires still hadn't spotted them, too busy with their prey: three scantily-clad women who couldn't be older than eighteen or nineteen. And who clearly didn't know what they were getting into.

They had no business being in this club. How they'd gotten past the bouncer who was supposed to check ID was anybody's guess.

Cain had to hand it to the three vampires. They were warning their potential victims. Their black T-shirts had it imprinted in bright red letters: *I'm a vampire. Come closer and I'll bite you.*

Clearly the three females hadn't heeded that warning.

"Sick fuckers," Cain cursed and grabbed one of the bloodsuckers, pulling him up so he had to release the woman he was about to dig his fangs into.

A startled outcry from the vampire was the response, while the girl dropped back onto the sectional, her glazed-over eyes testament to the fact that the vampire had used mind control to make her unaware of what was happening to her.

From the corner of his eye, Cain noticed that Amaury snatched the other two in a similar fashion, barely exerting any strength as the two vampires in his grip struggled.

"What the fuck?" the one Cain was restraining cursed.

"Yeah, I could say the same!" Cain snarled. "Retract your fucking fangs, jerk!"

When the guy didn't immediately comply, Cain kneed him in the back, forcing him toward the ground, while he bent his arms back so the idiot lost his balance and fell face forward onto the floor. Cain jammed his boot on his neck, pressing his cheek into the ground.

"Now let me translate that into a language you understand: retract your fucking fangs or I'll rip them from your mouth!"

"You can't do that," his captive ground out.

"Watch me!"

"Lay a hand on me and the mayor will have your hide!" the idiot claimed, glaring at him with red eyes.

Cain glanced at Amaury. "You know this punk? He claims the mayor will protect him."

Amaury shot him a quick look, while the two vampires in his grip still continued to struggle. "Will you fucking stop it?" he commanded them. "Ah, fuck it."

With amusement, Cain watched as Amaury simply knocked the two vampires' heads together, making their resistance crumble instantly.

"You should learn when to listen. Didn't your mother teach you anything?" Amaury asked, before he turned his head back to Cain. "Now what were you saying?"

But before Cain could respond, the vampire on the floor piped up. "My uncle will kick your ass if you hurt me."

Cain exchanged a look with Amaury. "Do you want to tell our out-of-town guest or shall I?"

Amaury feigned a bow. "Go ahead. I like watching."

Cain crouched down to the juvenile vampire. "Here's the deal, buddy. The mayor sent us to clean up, and guess what: you're the trash."

The vampire's eyes widened.

"I'm not done, so don't even think of interrupting me," Cain warned, though his voice wasn't as ice cold as it had been before. He had to admit he was having fun now. Working for Scanguards did have its perks, such as teaching some assholes a lesson. "You and your two useless friends here—" He jerked his head in the direction of the two vampires who now hung their heads like dogs with their tails between their legs. "—will be taken to a nice, cozy cell tonight, where you can sleep it off. And once you're sober, the mayor will pay you a visit and decide on your punishment." He pulled the jerk up by his shirt. "Because, believe it or not, wearing stupid T-shirts saying you're a vampire, and biting people in public isn't something we tolerate here in San Francisco. Maybe you can behave like that in the shithole you come from, but not on our turf."

"He'll never punish me!" the vampire said, full of defiance.

"Oh, I see, you're a betting man." Cain grinned at Amaury. "Wanna make an easy twenty bucks?"

Amaury chuckled. "It would be like taking milk from a baby. I have ethics."

Cain winked at him. "I keep forgetting." Then he wiped the smile off his face and glared at his captive. "Now move your fucking ass out of here before I get really pissed off."

The other two vampires seemed to shiver at his commanding voice, but the mayor's nephew clenched his jaw. His eyes darted past Cain, as if looking for an escape route.

"Don't even think about it."

When the idiot lunged for one of the girls, in a misguided attempt to use her as a shield or a hostage, Cain had had enough. He jumped and wrapped his arm around the kid's neck, taking him down in a chokehold. For a few moments, the mayor's nephew struggled, trying to use his hands to pry Cain's arm off him, but not even the claws digging into his forearm stopped Cain from choking the air out of the defiant vampire.

Only when the kid went slack in his arms, did Cain ease off the pressure. While vampires could lose consciousness when out of oxygen, they couldn't die from loss of air.

Amaury shrugged. "You put him out, you carry him."

Cain shook his head. "I have a better idea." He motioned to the two other vampires. "You two carry him."

"You heard him," Amaury concurred and pointed toward the back of the club. "Back exit. Now."

Cain had never seen two juvenile vampires follow a command so swiftly and without complaining. It only took moments until they reached the door that led to the back exit. Cain opened it, peered outside, and surveyed the area.

"The coast is clear."

As they reached the outside, Amaury pulled his cell from his pocket. "I'll get us a van."

Cain nodded and kept his eyes on the three delinquents. "You're a disgrace to our race."

"It was his idea," the shorter one said, motioning to his unconscious friend. "I swear."

Most likely it was true, giving that the one Cain had tackled was the one putting up most of the resistance. "That's not an excuse for bad behavior!"

The vampire dropped his head. "No, sir."

"Don't call me sir!" Cain growled.

"No, don't call him that. He deserves more than that," a voice from the other end of the alley said calmly.

Cain's head snapped in the direction of the newcomer. From his aura it was instantly evident that he was a vampire. And not just that. He looked like a warrior, one who'd seen countless battles and emerged as the victor. A force to be reckoned with.

"If you must address him, show him the respect he's due. Call him *Your Majesty*."

5

In shock, Cain stared at the stranger, not believing his own ears. In human years he looked to be no older than thirty-five, but there was no indication as to his true age. Although by the way he carried himself Cain suspected that he'd been a vampire for a long time. He wore loose-fitting cargo pants with plenty of pockets, which looked like they were filled with weapons. A black T-shirt stretching over his muscled torso and an open jacket made of the same material as his pants completed his outfit.

"Who are you?"

The vampire glanced at the two juveniles and the unconscious vampire they were still carrying. "If you remembered anything of your former life, you wouldn't want me to disclose that information in front of outsiders."

Next to Cain, Amaury grunted in displeasure. Cain put a hand on his forearm to stop him from whatever he was going to do. If this stranger had any knowledge about Cain's past, he needed to find out what it was.

Cain turned to his colleague. "I need to deal with this."

"Not alone, you won't," Amaury countered. "Scanguards looks out for their people."

For a moment, he wanted to object, but he knew Amaury well enough to know that the linebacker-sized vampire wouldn't take no for an answer. At the same time, Amaury's acknowledgment that Cain still belonged to Scanguards gave him peace of mind. "Fine." He motioned to the three juvenile vampires. "Let's send them on their way."

Amaury hesitated then grunted his approval a moment later.

Cain pointed to the three offenders. "Tonight's your lucky night. We're letting you go. But don't think you're off the hook. If we hear one word about you three behaving inappropriately again, we're on your ass like a fly on shit. Is that clear?"

The two nodded, seeming shell-shocked.

"Tell your friend, and make him understand that, if he doesn't comply, he'll regret the day he was turned."

The boys' eyes widened, but they nodded quickly. "Yes. We promise."

Amaury growled at them. "Now get the fuck out of here!"

The two rushed out of the alley, taking their unconscious friend with them. The moment they were out of earshot, Cain turned back to the mysterious vampire.

"Now talk!"

The stranger eyed Amaury. "What about him?"

"I have no secrets from Amaury."

"Very well." The man took a deep breath. "I'm John Grant, the leader of your personal guard."

Cain raised an eyebrow. "Personal guard?"

John inclined his head slightly. "The personal guard of the king of the vampires of Louisiana. You. Cain Montague."

Cain's breath caught in his throat when the outrageous claim reached his brain. "Fucking lunatic!" Anger churned up from his gut. Somehow this vampire had found out about Cain's amnesia and was now trying to make a fool of him. "I need nobody mocking me!"

"I would never dare mock you. You have my utmost respect," John declared.

Cain scoffed. "Who are you? I want the truth!"

The stranger remained surprisingly calm despite the accusing words Cain lashed at him. "I expected your reaction. If I were in your shoes, I would react the same way. But that doesn't change anything about the facts. You are the king."

"I say we take this joker to HQ and find out what he really wants," Amaury suggested, a sharp tone in his voice.

Not taking his eyes off John for even a second, Cain said, "I agree."

"You're making a mistake," John said. His hand came up, as if he wanted to reach for a weapon in his jacket.

Cain and Amaury pounced simultaneously, slamming John against the wall of the building and pinning him there. Air rushed from the vampire's lungs.

"I suggest you answer Cain's questions," Amaury said. "And make it quick, because my hand's twitching."

Surprisingly, there was no fear in John's eyes when he glared back at Amaury then shifted his gaze to Cain. "Is he your new guard? Well at least that means you still have your instincts and are protecting yourself."

"Amaury isn't my guard. I'm working with him. So cut the bullshit and talk!" Cain ordered.

He was at the end of his patience. Despite his instant suspicion of John, he'd gotten his hopes up of finally finding out who he was. Ever since he'd awoken one night over a year ago without a shred of memory of his former life, he'd longed to know his past. Even though he'd used Scanguards' resources and the help of their resident IT genius, Thomas, he'd come up empty. To be told by this stranger that he was a king was a cruel joke, one this vampire would be paying for.

"There was an assassination attempt. You were injured in the head. When you came to, you'd lost your memory. I had no choice but to make it look like the assassin succeeded and smuggle you out of the palace. It was for your own safety."

Cain shook his head in disbelief. The story was too fantastical to believe. And he would prove that the man was telling lies by taking his story apart. Scanguards had taught him well when it came to interrogation tactics. "Why?"

"Why somebody wanted to assassinate you? There could be many reasons somebody would want a king dead."

"No! Why smuggle me out?"

"Because you knew who was behind the assassination."

"What?"

John's lips set into a grim line. "You said so. But when you woke up, you couldn't remember anything. Not even who you were. But I figured that if you knew, then the person who was behind it might know, too. Keeping you in the palace without your memories would have put you in danger. A danger I couldn't protect you from."

"What exactly did I say?"

"*I know it was* . . . and then you passed out. You never got a chance to tell me."

"The story makes no sense." Cain glanced at Amaury, who nodded in agreement, before looking back at his captive. "And you know why?"

John narrowed his eyes, still showing no fear, only defiance. "Why?"

"Because if I learned anything from my time with Scanguards it is that a guard is never to leave his charge unprotected. You claim you were my personal guard, yet you abandoned me in a world where I knew nobody, not even myself. If I were really a king, you would have protected me. So where were you during the assassination attempt, and where were you during the last year?"

John's eyelids dropped in shame. "A ruse. Somebody set it up so that I would be led to a different part of the palace, away from you. I didn't recognize my error until it was almost too late. I failed you."

The sincere tone in John's words gave Cain pause. The vampire seemed genuinely saddened. Could there be a kernel of truth to his story after all? Cain pushed the thoughts away. No, he was just so desperate to find out about his past that he was trying to cling onto anything that might lead him to his old life. He couldn't allow this stranger to get to him and fill his head with nonsense like kings, assassinations, and palaces.

"Yes, you failed. In more ways than just one. Your reasoning doesn't square up. Even if you couldn't prevent the assassination, why send me away without protection?"

John glared at him. "Because I was being watched! I could sense it. Had I made any attempt to provide protection for you, whoever wanted to harm you would have found you and killed you. I couldn't risk it. It was safer this way. Everybody believes you're dead. I made sure of that. I took your ring and some of your personal effects and placed them with the ash of the dead assassin so everybody would think it was you."

"And now?" Cain asked. "Why come to me now?"

"Events have forced my hand."

"I don't believe you."

"Let's take him downtown and lock him up," Amaury suggested.

"Let's go," Cain agreed, tightening his hold on their captive and trying to pull him away from the wall.

John resisted and dropped his head, motioning to his jacket. "Please. I have proof. In my inside pocket."

Cain hesitated.

"Let me," Amaury interrupted and patted the area with his hand. "No weapons."

Cain gave a nod then reached inside the vampire's jacket. He felt a piece of smooth paper, gripped it and pulled it out.

A moment later, his heart stopped beating, and it felt as if the earth underneath his feet had stopped turning.

Cain stared at his own likeness. Though he'd never seen himself in a mirror since vampires didn't reflect in mirrors, when he'd gotten his ID at Scanguards, they'd taken a picture of him. The man in the picture he was holding in his hands now and the photo on his ID were identical. But this fact wasn't the reason his heart had stopped. It was the woman next to him.

She was the voluptuous beauty he'd made love to in his dreams. The woman whose name he couldn't remember.

"Who is she?" His voice was only a faint echo.

"Faye. The woman you were going to marry."

Cain stroked over the picture, wanting to touch her face. She was real. He hadn't invented her. He met John's eyes. "I have to see her."

John hesitated. "There's something you need to know."

A bolt of adrenaline shot through his insides. "Is she alive?"

"Yes, yes, of course. But . . ."

Cain gripped John by the collar. "Damn it! What is it then?"

"Your brother Abel has asked Faye to marry him when he ascends to the throne in less than two weeks."

Cain released John and jerked back. The news crashed over him like a tsunami, drowning him in a devastation he hadn't thought was possible.

"No!" The scream dislodged from Cain's throat without any conscious effort on his part. Only when he heard it echo in the night did he know that he'd screamed.

With it one thought settled in his mind: he would take his old life back.

6

Faye heard the angry voices before she reached the large room on the ground level of the palace where the king, or now the regent, conducted business. It was part office, part living area, with a comfortable seating arrangement in front of a roaring fireplace.

She remembered the many times she had sat there in Cain's arms after he'd dismissed everybody when his work for the night was done. She'd looked forward to those rare moments with him where Cain would talk to her about everything that concerned him. She'd become his sounding board.

Faye swept into the room, ignoring the two guards who stood at the open double doors. They'd once been Cain's guards and didn't stop her, still affording her the same courtesy as during Cain's reign.

She wasn't the only spectator to the scene that played out in Abel's presence. Other members of the royal household were present, too: advisors, guards, and other staff. All watched the vampire who stood before Abel, his head hung in defeat.

Faye recognized him instantly. "Robert!" She rushed toward him and Abel. "What's going on?"

Abel turned his gaze to her, but Robert, the man who was in charge of procuring human blood for the palace—both packaged as well as in the form of actual human donors—didn't turn his head.

"I'm afraid Robert has been caught with his hand in the cookie jar," Abel said, his voice even. Then he looked back to the man before him. "It's a grave offense. I'm sure you're aware of it."

"I didn't steal it. I—"

Abel lashed the back of his hand across the other vampire's cheek, slicing it open with the diamond ring he wore. The scent of blood instantly saturated the air.

Faye's fangs involuntarily itched in their sockets, despite the fact that the blood she smelled wasn't human. She knew it was a survival instinct, because whenever vampire blood was in the air all vampires close enough to smell it became more aggressive. They were like sharks in that respect.

"I won't take any excuses! Be a man! Stand by your crime!" Abel ground out. "You're the only one apart from myself who has a key to the supply room. Are you telling me *I* was the one who removed two gallons of blood from our cellars?" Abel flashed his fangs at Robert.

One word came over the lips of the accused. "No!"

"Who did you sell it to?"

Robert raised his head by an inch, lifting his lids to shoot a defiant look at Abel. "I didn't sell anything."

A violent slap across his other cheek produced another cut from which blood began to drip. Though it was healing just as quickly as the first side, the insult had to hurt a proud man like Robert.

"Won't you hear him out?" Faye interfered. "Maybe he didn't do it." She'd known Robert to be an honorable man, one who took his duties seriously. One who'd become a close friend over the last year.

Abel turned to look at her. "Very well. I'll let him talk."

Robert took a deep breath before he spoke. "I didn't take money for it."

"You gave it away?" Abel thundered. "To whom?"

"The unfortunates who ask for our help. We've always done it. We've always helped those of our kind who needed our help. A few pints of blood to those in need don't hurt us."

Abel took a step toward the vampire. "You are giving our supplies away without my consent?"

"They were in desperate need."

"I don't care! I'm not running a charity! If these losers can't go and hunt for human blood themselves then they don't deserve to be vampires. Do you get that? No more handouts!"

Faye winced. Robert wasn't the only one who gave handouts to vampires in need. She was just as guilty as Robert, though she'd not taken anything directly from the cellars, but rather taken some of her own supplies and shared them.

"And now that that's clear, lock him up downstairs," he instructed the guards. "I'll teach you to obey me."

"No!" Faye yelled out before she could stop herself. "Not the cellars." She knew what would happen to Robert there. "Don't torture him."

"You want to save this man? Why?" Abel asked, giving her a curious look. "Don't you see that he defied my orders? As king I can't allow such behavior. I have to be firm."

"I beg you, please show mercy." Faye wrung her hands, her heart beating rapidly and uncontrollably. She had grown to care for so many of the vampires in this clan since she'd been accepted into their midst.

She loved them like her own family and couldn't bear any of them being hurt.

Faye took a few steps closer, approaching Abel. His gaze traveled over her. "It's not easy to be a fair ruler and make the right decisions. You'll have to understand that." He paused. "But as my queen, you would have the power to sway me. The power to make me change my mind."

His eyes locked with hers. She looked deep into them, searching for an answer there.

"I'm not infallible. But if you help me, if you could be my conscience, then maybe I can be the kind of ruler this kingdom deserves."

His beseeching words sank deep into her. Could she make this sacrifice for the people of her clan? Could she truly help him be the ruler they needed?

"Marry me," Abel said softly. "I won't punish Robert if you don't wish it. Be my queen. The queen you were always meant to be." He motioned his arm toward the window. "They love you. They need you. *I* need you."

Faye glanced past him where Robert still stood, now a hopeful sheen on his eyes. There was so much goodness in him and in the other members of the clan. She wanted to preserve that, preserve what Cain had fostered during his reign. And she could only do it if she had power.

She would stop grieving and go on with her life, for her people, and for Cain.

Slowly Faye turned her face back to Abel and nodded. "Yes, I'll marry you."

Abel took her hands into his. "You've made me the happiest man on this earth!"

When he leaned in to kiss her, she turned instinctively, offering her cheek. "I'd better leave you to your business," she said quickly, not ready for anything more than a kiss on the cheek.

"Of course," Abel said and released her.

When she rushed outside, she tried to breathe, but her lungs didn't seem to be able to get any air. Had she made the right decision?

***

Abel motioned for the guards to clear the room. "Send all of them out, except Robert." When a moment later, the guards closed the door, he was alone with the accused vampire and his personal guard Baltimore.

"Thank you, Abel, for your generosity," Robert started.

Abel chuckled. "Oh, don't thank me yet." He exchanged a look with Baltimore, who had a smirk on his face.

Noticing Robert jolt, Abel continued, "Don't worry. I won't kill you. Nor will I torture you. You'll remain free and in your position. However, you're in my debt now."

Robert bowed. "Yes, Abel. I understand."

"I don't think you do." Abel moved closer and flashed his fangs at the other vampire. "You'll do what I say from now on. I'm your master, the only one whose orders you'll follow, no matter the law. I'm the law you'll follow now. Or Baltimore's stake will find its target."

The light from the lamps in the room reflected on the six-foot-five-inch tall vampire's bald head. He didn't have an attractive face. He was downright unappealing, but that suited Abel fine. People feared Baltimore because of the way he looked, when they should fear him for the things he did. Brutality was his way of life, sadism his favorite pastime. A criminal during his human life, Baltimore had perfected his profession after becoming a vampire.

Robert nodded, clearly frightened. Abel had always found that frightened subjects made obedient subjects.

"Good. Now go! I will call upon you when I need you."

With a quick bow Robert opened the door and disappeared outside. When the lock clicked shut again, Abel turned to his guard, concerned with another matter.

"Where the fuck is he? Have your men found him yet?"

Baltimore shook his head. "John is nowhere to be found."

Abel slammed his fist onto the desk. As much as he couldn't stand the guard who'd been so loyal to Cain, he needed him. John was the only one left now who could pass on information only the king and the leader of the king's guard were privy to. He needed John at least until the coronation, until he'd passed on that information to Abel as the new king. "I don't like it."

"I figured that. That's why I kept looking. It appears that John isn't quite as devoted to his duties as he used to be."

Abel whirled his head in Baltimore's direction. "What are you saying?"

"I found his Achilles Heel."

Abel let a genuine smile curve his lips as his guard's words sank in. He could always count on his loyal Baltimore to come up with something useful. "Perfect."

7

Cain stepped into the private jet and looked around. There was space for a dozen passengers. The leather seats looked roomy and comfortable, just like they should in this specially equipped Learjet that transported vampires associated with Scanguards around the country. This was more luxurious than flying first class on any commercial airline.

The door to the cockpit stood open, and he could see the pilot and co-pilot go through their pre-flight check. They were human and fully aware of the precious cargo they were transporting. And for their loyalty and secrecy they were compensated more than handsomely.

"That's very generous of your boss to let you borrow this plane," John said from behind him.

Cain nodded, turning.

"Though I guess he's not your boss anymore."

"It's to be seen if I'm king and your story checks out."

The other vampire inclined his head slightly. "I understand your caution."

"Good." Cain motioned to one of the comfortable leather seats. "Make yourself comfortable then while we wait for the others."

"The others?"

"You didn't think that I would go to New Orleans without protection, did you?"

John puffed up his chest. "But I'm your protection. I'm your personal guard."

"Yeah, so you say. Yet under your watch, I was nearly assassinated if I believe your own words. Don't mind if I stack my odds of survival with a few trusted friends, do you?"

He wanted to trust John. But everything he'd said was fantastical. Nobody at Scanguards had ever heard of the King of Louisiana, nor had the name John had given him—Cain Montague—yielded anything during a web search. During his time with Scanguards Cain had learned that it couldn't hurt to have backup. And judging by the sound of footsteps on the stairs, it seemed that his backup was arriving this instant.

Cain glanced at the open door and watched as Thomas, followed by his blood-bonded mate, Eddie, entered the fuselage. The two blonds wore their usual biker outfits, consisting of leather pants, jackets, and black T-shirts.

"John, meet Thomas and his mate Eddie. They'll be joining us on our trip."

John's eyebrows twitched for a short moment. Clearly, where John was from, gay vampires, and ones who were mated on top of it, seemed out of the ordinary.

Thomas appeared to notice John's hesitation and stiffened visibly. "Cain," he said with a nod. Then he waited.

"Nice to meet you, Thomas," John quickly said, extending his hand.

Thomas shook it briefly. "Likewise."

"Hey," Eddie said lightly and shook John's hand. Eddie had always been the more laid back of the pair. Maybe because he was a good hundred years younger than his partner and didn't carry the emotional baggage Thomas did.

"Eddie," was John's reply. "I assume you two are working for Scanguards?"

"Bodyguards, yeah." Eddie grinned. "I hear you're a guard, too."

"The king's personal guard," John corrected, pulling his shoulders back.

Cain heard the prideful tone in John's voice and couldn't help but feel that if John was indeed telling the truth, then Cain would be lucky to have such a loyal man in his service. But he was getting ahead of himself. First, he'd have to confirm John's story. The rest would follow.

"Is anybody else coming?" Cain asked. "Samson wasn't sure who else could be spared when I spoke to him."

Thomas squeezed his hand luggage into one of the compartments underneath the windows, before turning to him. "He's shifting assignments. Of course, not knowing how long we'll be gone means we can't take Amaury, Zane, or Oliver, since they're blood-bonded to humans and won't be able to go without their mate's blood for long. And Gabriel and Samson need to stay put."

Cain nodded. He was aware of that fact. "So who does that leave us with?"

"I'm afraid you're stuck with me," a gravelly voice came from the door.

"Maybe an ex-vampire hunter isn't too bad a choice." Cain grinned at Haven, as the witch-turned-vampire entered the cabin. He was bonded to Yvette, a vampire, and therefore able to consume any human's blood despite the bond. Haven's beefy frame filled the entire door. He'd been strong even as a human, fighting vampires most of this life after his mother, a witch, had been killed by one. Only after he'd fallen in love with Yvette and realized that not all vampires were bad, had he switched camps and sacrificed his human life to save the vampire world from certain destruction at the hands of an evil witch.

"You might change your mind once you hear who I brought," Haven answered and motioned to a spot behind him.

The moment he cleared the door, Cain saw what he meant.

"A human?" John asked, before Cain could say anything. "You're bringing a human?"

"Hey, guys!" Blake greeted everybody, a broad smile on his face. "This is great! How cool! I've never been to New Orleans. We're gonna have a blast." The dark-haired clothes horse, who generally meant well, was a dufus, but he was family.

"This is not a sightseeing trip," Cain admonished.

John tossed him an annoyed look. "He can't come with us."

Blake fisted his hands at his hips, puffing up his chest. "Why not? I'm a bodyguard, too."

John took a step toward Blake, who to his credit didn't flinch. "Because no humans other than blood donors are allowed in the palace or its grounds. So unless you want to turn into food, I'd suggest—"

"He's coming with us," Cain interrupted, though a moment earlier he himself had wanted to deny Blake a seat on this plane. However, he couldn't allow John to think that he could be easily influenced. It would undermine his authority. Even though he wasn't keen on having to keep an eye on Blake, he now had to take him to New Orleans just because John didn't want him there. "And nobody is going to turn him into food."

John's head whirled to him. "With all due respect, that's unwise. Your friends here at Scanguards may live side by side with humans, but I can promise you, your subjects won't like it."

At the word *subjects* Cain wanted to shake his head. Did he really have subjects?

"Blake isn't just any human. He's the grandson of a vampire."

John tossed him a quizzical look, then sniffed at Blake. "He's not a hybrid."

"No, he's not," Cain agreed. "But he descends from a vampire, who started the line when he was still human. But that's beside the point. We need a human with us to give us flexibility during daytime hours. My decision stands." Cain held John's gaze until the other vampire lowered his lids in acquiescence. "It's settled then. Blake, take a seat. We'll be leaving shortly."

Cain turned to the open cockpit door while the others took their seats and put on their seatbelts. "Are we ready to leave?"

The co-pilot looked over his shoulder. "Ready when you are."

"Good, then let's close the door and get this show on the road."

The co-pilot acknowledged his request with a nod. "Yes, Cain."

Cain walked to one of the empty seats and noticed how Thomas and Eddie had taken the two seats in the back of the plane. Thomas's hand lay on Eddie's thigh, and the two were talking quietly, their heads close together. They looked happy, and the fact that they were a blood-bonded couple could only help while checking out John's story: Thomas and Eddie could communicate telepathically via their bond, and it was possible that they would encounter situations in which such a skill could come in handy.

Cain sat down and fastened his seat belt when the co-pilot exited the cockpit and pulled on the door handle in order to lift the stairs and shut the door.

"Wait!"

The panicked request was echoing from the outside of the plane and the co-pilot cast a puzzled look over his shoulder.

Cain rolled his eyes and looked at Haven, who sat across the aisle from him. "Really?"

Haven shrugged and lifted his arms in surrender. "I didn't tell him."

"Wait!" the voice called out again, this time closer. A moment later, Wesley appeared on the stairs and stepped into the plane. He was out of breath and had clearly rushed to catch them. He was a little shorter than Blake, but a few years older, though not any wiser than his fellow Scanguards trainee.

He set a large bag on the floor.

"Phew! That was cutting it close!" he said.

Before Cain could show Haven's overeager brother the door, John leapt from his seat and pinned Wesley against the nearest wall.

"Fucking witch!" John snarled, flashing his fangs at him.

Cain reacted within a split second and was out of his seat in the same instant as Haven jumped up, too. They both reached John and Wesley at the same time.

Haven snatched John by his collar and pried him off his brother. "You harm a hair on his head and you're dust!"

"What the fuck?" John growled, glaring at them.

"He's my brother."

Disbelief spread over John's face. "A witch?" He turned his head to look back at Wesley, looking him up and down before turning to Cain. "You can't be serious! What is this? Scanguards employs humans and witches? What kind of vampires are you guys? How can you consort with witches? They're our enemies."

"They're not," Cain said. "Maybe where you come from, but we've found that witches can be our allies." He motioned to Wesley. "And Wes is family."

"And he isn't a real witch anyway. Half his spells don't even work," Blake piped up from his seat.

"Watch your mouth, Blake!" Wesley yelled back.

"Oh, yeah, or what?" Blake asked, leaping from his chair.

"I'm gonna turn you into a—"

"Nobody is gonna turn anybody into anything," Cain interrupted, glaring first at Wesley, then at Blake. "Sit down, Blake, or I'm gonna boot you off the plane."

Quickly, Blake took his seat again, keeping silent, though Cain could tell that he had a response already sitting on his tongue. Whenever Blake and Wesley were together, trouble wasn't far behind. The two Scanguards bodyguards-in-training couldn't help themselves; they always had to compete with each other. Inevitably, quarrels would ensue. There was no way in hell he'd take both of them on the same mission.

Cain lifted the bag Wesley had set on the floor and shoved it at Wesley. "Now take your stuff and leave."

Wes looked at him, genuine surprise in his eyes. "But I'm coming with you! You need me." Wes pointed at the human. "Why does he get to go? He's not a vampire! And he doesn't even have any special skills. I do."

"Yeah, turning dogs into pigs maybe," Blake taunted him.

"Shut it, Blake!" Cain snapped. "Or you're leaving too."

Huffing, Blake crossed his arms over his chest.

Cain turned to Wesley. "Thanks for the offer, but—"

The witch lifted his hand. "Hear me out first, please."

Cain sighed and exchanged a look with Haven, who grimaced.

"Leave me out of this," Haven said. "I don't want to be blamed later when he screws up."

Cain shook his head. "Make your case, Wes, and make it quick."

"So, I was thinking," Wes started.

Blake scoffed, earning a stern look from Wesley before he continued, "You're going into the lion's den."

"You mean a vampire's nest," Thomas corrected him from the back of the plane.

"Yeah, whatever. And you don't know who's friendly and who's not. You need all the protection you can get." He leaned in and lowered his voice as if the others in the plane wouldn't be able to hear him then. "I've been working on a protection spell."

"I hate spells," John grumbled.

Cain couldn't agree more. Vampires had no protection against spells. And he hated things he couldn't fight with a mortal weapon. However, Wesley saying he had been working on something didn't mean he actually knew what he was doing. "Last time you cast a spell, your spell tinted everything red."

"Which was the intention," Wesley claimed.

"Granted, at Oliver's wedding it was. But you turned the pigs red before that, and I doubt that was intended," Cain reminded him.

Wesley's lips curled up. "A little mishap. But I've got it all figured out now."

"You say that now, but when push comes to shove, we're gonna end up with some kind of disaster."

Wes pointed to Thomas. "I saved Thomas's life with one of my spells. When he was fighting against Keegan, my spell helped—"

"I didn't need your help!" Thomas ground out, his normally friendly attitude suddenly changed. Cain knew that he'd been utterly annoyed that Wes had interfered in the fight and not let Thomas prove that he could defeat his evil sire.

When Eddie squeezed Thomas's hand, Thomas turned and exchanged a look with his mate. Then he added, "However, Wes is correct. His spell worked when it counted."

Cain contemplated his next decision for a few seconds. Thomas was the most levelheaded of them, and Cain respected the other vampire's opinion.

"Fine. You may come. But you follow my orders. One instance of insubordination and you're on the next plane home. Don't make me regret this."

Wesley grinned triumphantly. "You won't. I promise."

Moments later, when everybody was strapped into their seats, Cain turned to John, who sat next to him. "Now tell me everything I need to know about my former life."

8

Abel walked through the busy streets. It was shortly after sunset, and the French Quarter was teeming with tourists and locals. He hated the putrid smell in this part of town; that's why he rarely ventured into this area. He preferred to go hunting in the Garden District or in some of the smaller towns around New Orleans when the urge took him and he needed to drive his fangs into a human rather than drink from the donated supply of blood in his cellars.

Once he was king, he would do away with pre-packaged blood and encourage his subjects to hunt for their food again. How it was always meant to be. Drinking packaged blood had turned them into cowards and weaklings. He would change that and turn his race back into a species to be feared.

No more mainstreaming. No more pandering to the sensibilities of humans. Soon all those things Cain had instituted would be gone, and a new reign would start. Things would be better then. Their clan would become strong again and not be vulnerable to an attack by their rivals any longer. His subjects would be safe again. They needed a strong king, and he would be that king.

"We're nearly there," Baltimore said beside him and pointed toward a small alley.

"You'd better be right about this." He didn't like to waste his time when there was so much to do before the coronation and the wedding. Abel smiled to himself. Faye would finally be his. Ever since she'd joined their clan, he'd wanted her, but she'd only had eyes for Cain, the hero, the king.

"Trust me." Baltimore lengthened his stride and turned into the cobblestone alley.

They'd reached the northeast end of the Quarter where few tourists ventured and few hotels were located. Little houses, split up into multiple apartments, lined the street. His faithful guard steered him to one of the houses then stopped in front of the entrance door.

"In there."

"How many?"

"She's alone."

Abel nodded. "What are we waiting for then?"

With one forceful move, Baltimore kicked the flimsy door in so that it splintered at the hinges. His guard had never understood the concept of subtlety.

From inside, Abel heard a surprised gasp coming from one of the rooms in the back. The smell of a human filled his nostrils, while his ears perceived her footsteps as she ran toward the back door in an attempt to flee. Her actions only fueled his hunting instinct.

Stupid human!

No wonder humans were inferior to vampires. They didn't know the first thing about survival. Though this specimen still had her instinct of fleeing rather than fighting him, she should know better and bow before him instead.

"Get her!" Abel ordered Baltimore with a motion of his head, while he glanced around the living room they'd entered. The little houses in the Quarter were all like this: the front door led directly into the living area without a foyer or hallway as a buffer. From there one room led into another without the benefit of a hallway.

The furniture in the small place was surprisingly new and luxurious, the decorations tasteful. Despite the fact that the windows sported shutters on the outside, the inside was hung with dark red velvet curtains, a sign that whoever spent time here didn't like sunlight to penetrate the interior.

Abel turned his head to the door which led to the back of the house when he heard Baltimore return with the struggling human. He ran his eyes over her.

Her skin was the color of milk chocolate, her eyes a mix of blue and grey, attesting to her mixed heritage. A Creole beauty for sure. And who wouldn't want this luscious woman in his bed, feel her plump lips around his cock, her elegant hands on his skin? Abel saw her appeal immediately. And even though there were no marks on her graceful neck or that beautiful cleavage her dress revealed, he instinctively knew she'd felt the fangs of a vampire in her flesh before. Many times in fact.

Abel inhaled. The scent of her blood sent a thrill through his body.

"A veritable love nest you and John have got yourselves here," he finally addressed her.

At the name of her lover, the woman flinched.

"Oh, you thought I wouldn't find out, did you?" He paused and narrowed his eyes. "Is that what John told you? That you'd be safe? That nobody would ever find out that he was keeping a human lover?" Abel chuckled. "How naive of him."

He motioned to Baltimore, who followed his unspoken command and tossed her on the leather couch. She scrambled quickly to sit upright, fear coloring her pretty eyes.

"What do you want?"

"Ah, the human speaks," Abel said. "Do you have a name?"

She swallowed. "Nicolette."

Abel stepped closer. With every step he made, Nicolette shrank farther back into the sofa cushions. He could firmly smell the fear that oozed from her pores. It made his fangs itch, and he saw no reason to prevent them from elongating. When he was less than a foot away from her, he stopped.

"Here's what you're going to do now, Nicolette. You'll answer the question I ask you without trying to lie to me. Because if you lie, I'll know, and then I won't have any choice but to have Baltimore punish you for it. Do you understand?"

Visibly intimidated, she nodded.

"Where is your lover? Where is John?"

"I don't know."

Abel pounced, gripping her shoulders with both hands and pressing her against the back of the sofa. "Try again," he gritted from between clenched teeth, drowning out her shriek with his booming words.

"I don't know. He didn't tell me."

Abel narrowed his eyes and peeled his lips back from his gums, revealing his long, sharp fangs, letting her guess what he was going to do to her if she didn't comply.

"Please! He didn't tell me." Tears formed in her eyes. "He said he had to leave for a few days."

"To do what?" he ground out.

A sob tore from her throat. "He didn't want to tell me. He said he couldn't."

Abel tilted his head to the side, eyeing her with suspicion. "Now, you wouldn't be lying to me, would you?"

"No! It's the truth. He said he'd be back soon."

He exchanged a look with Baltimore, pondering Nicolette's words. What was John up to? Clearly something he didn't want anybody to know about, something he couldn't even trust his lover with. As if he were afraid that somebody could torture the information out of her.

"Fine," he finally said. "I believe you."

A sigh of relief rolled over the human's lips.

Abel chuckled as he looked back at her. "But it changes nothing about your fate." He reveled in the panic that returned to Nicolette's eyes, the shudder that wracked her body, and the smell of fear that leaked from her pores. "Let's go on a little trip."

He released her and straightened, addressing Baltimore. "Take her and lock her up."

His guard nodded and approached amidst the woman's protests.

"No, please! No!"

Abel ignored her. Instead his eyes fell on a cell phone that lay on the coffee table. He snatched it. "And then let's find out how much John loves you."

And he hoped that John didn't simply see Nicolette as a momentary distraction, but actually had feelings for her. Feelings that would provide Abel with leverage.

9

"I want to see her first," Cain demanded, looking at John.

Cain, his friends from Scanguards, and John stood in an abandoned shack a few miles from the palace, which was located about a half hour north of New Orleans. John had brought them to this wooded area, avoiding any guard posts that may have alerted the palace security team to their approach.

"I have to caution you," John said. "If I bring you to her, you can't let her know that you remember nothing. You have to be careful what you admit to her."

Cain looked past him. "I know that. Nobody can know that I suffer from amnesia." It would undermine his position, should John's claim be substantiated. Nobody wanted a king who was clueless. "Not even Faye. But I need to talk to her in private before we go in."

"What do you mean to accomplish by that?" Haven asked, putting his hand on Cain's forearm. "What if she gives away that you're back and gives your enemies time to prepare? I'd rather we go in without them knowing in advance that we're coming. It gives us the element of surprise."

Cain stared at his colleague, appreciating his advice. But this was something he had to do. "Faye will be the most likely person in the entire palace to be able to corroborate John's story. No offense, John." Despite everything that John had told him, he needed proof of who he was before he marched back into his old life.

"None taken. You were always a cautious man. At least that hasn't changed."

"Besides, I need to know whether she's still . . . with me," he said, instead of saying what he really wanted to know: whether she still loved him or had turned her affections over to Abel.

"Very well," Haven conceded. "But how are you going to arrange a meeting with her without anybody knowing?"

"It won't be a problem," John claimed, before Cain could answer. "There are secret tunnels underneath the property."

Cain raised an eyebrow. "Tunnels?"

"It's an old plantation, and the owners had the slaves build tunnels underneath it. A precaution when the civil war broke out," John explained. "Once the tunnels were built, the master killed all the slaves involved in the construction, making sure there was nobody left who knew of their existence but him and his foreman."

"Who knows of the tunnels?" Cain wanted to know.

"Only a select few."

"Abel?"

John shook his head. "You and I. Though it's possible that you told Faye, but I can't know that for sure. You never said anything to me. But we have to assume since you were going to make her your queen, you would have told her about the tunnels."

"How come only you and I know about the tunnels? Why not Abel?"

"The first leader of the king's guard was a descendent of the plantation's foreman. He passed the knowledge on. And now it is passed on from the leader of the king's guard to whoever becomes king. And Abel isn't king yet."

"Does he suspect that there are tunnels?"

"No. Though he knows that the leader of the guard will pass all he knows to the new king after the coronation. He must assume that there are things only I know."

"Good, we'll take the tunnels. Thomas will come with us. The rest will stay here," Cain ordered.

"No!"

John's protest took him by surprise. Cain glared at him. "As your king—"

"As my king, you would never demand such a thing," John interrupted, his voice firm, his face unflinching. "You would never reveal the location of the tunnels to a stranger, let alone allow someone into them. If you insist on Thomas coming with us, I won't show you the entrance." John crossed his arms over his chest, waiting.

Cain didn't move. He simply stood there facing John in a silent battle. But it was clear instantly that John wouldn't budge. On one hand, Cain had to admire him for it. It showed loyalty and strength. On the other hand, it ticked him off to have to concede to this man who he still couldn't fully trust. But if he wanted to see Faye in private without anybody knowing, he had no choice.

"Just you and I then. But I'm warning you: I might not remember who I am, but I'm deadly with any weapon. You cross me, you're dust."

John acknowledged the threat with a curt nod. "Follow me." He turned and walked out of the shed.

Cain glanced at his friends, then addressed Thomas, "Any trouble, you text me immediately. My cell is on vibrate."

"Understood. Be careful. If you're not back within an hour, we'll head for the palace."

Without another word, Cain walked outside. The air was humid, so different from what he was used to in San Francisco, where even summer nights could be chilly and require a light jacket. Here, his cotton shirt already stuck to his sweaty body. To his surprise, he didn't mind the heat, almost as if he were used to it.

In silence Cain walked alongside the other vampire, his eyes watchful, his body ready to attack should anybody approach them. Scanguards had taught him well. He wasn't afraid of any enemy he would encounter, but that fact didn't alleviate the knot in his gut. He was uneasy about seeing Faye, seeing the woman he'd made love to in his dreams, the woman who in his former life had belonged to him. Did she now belong to Abel, the man John claimed was his brother?

"We're here," John announced and stopped.

Cain looked at the spot John pointed to, which didn't look any different from the terrain they'd crossed during their short walk. There were moss-covered trees, bushes, and dirt. They hadn't walked on any sort of recognizable path, but had gone clear through a wooded patch.

"I don't see anything."

"It's well disguised."

John walked toward two trees which stood at a slight incline. Behind them, moss covered a boulder. Instead of walking to the boulder, John veered left to another copse of trees where broken branches had accumulated and were rotting. He gripped one of the protruding sticks and pulled on it. The entire hovel of branches moved, and only then did Cain notice that they were all interconnected in such a random but ingenious way that to a casual observer it didn't look like anything else but a heap of rotting branches, while in fact it was a door.

When John held it open for him, Cain suppressed his surprise. "Lead the way."

Cain walked into the tunnel behind John, immediately inhaling the scents around him. The air was stale. When John closed the door behind them, the earthen tunnel was robbed of the moonlight that had guided their way earlier. Cain's eyes immediately adjusted to the darkness, his vampire vision compensating for the lack of light.

"What keeps the tunnel stable?" he asked quietly, knowing his voice would travel far in this confined space.

John pointed to the ceiling. "Every few feet there's wooden reinforcements, but it's old construction and nobody has done any repairs here in decades. There's more and more moisture penetrating and weakening the structure. We're close to the bayous. Katrina did some damage here. One day, the tunnels will collapse."

"Then let's hope this is not the day," Cain remarked dryly.

John turned and walked down the long tunnel. Cain followed, taking in his surroundings.

"How long is the tunnel?"

"It's actually a tunnel system with many branches. It stretches over several miles, but the branch we're going down is only about a mile long. We'll be there shortly," John assured him.

"Where do all the different branches lead to?"

"Other exits around the property, as well as entry points into the palace."

"Where in the palace?"

"One directly into the king's suite, another into the cells, and a third one underneath the fireplace in your office."

"Underneath the fireplace? Sounds kind of hard to get to."

John gave him a sideways glance. "There's a mechanism to shift the fireplace to the side. Of course, it's best not to do that when there's an actual fire burning in the hearth."

Cain made mental notes of the entry and exit points and the branches that led away from the tunnel they were in, committing as much of the path to memory as he could. If John led him into a trap, he had to be able to find his own way out. However, Cain had to admit that had John wanted to kill him for whatever reason, he would have had ample opportunity earlier.

Still, trusting somebody didn't come easy. Even when he'd joined Scanguards a year ago, it had taken some time to trust his colleagues. Now, of course, he knew they had his back and he trusted them with his life. Just like they trusted him. They'd become more than just colleagues to him. They'd become his friends. His family.

But now this stranger was upsetting the tentative peace he'd found with his new family by making him want something that lay beyond his reach. He wanted his old life back, if only for one reason: to know what it felt like to be loved by the woman from his dreams.

"I carried you out through this tunnel when you were injured. You don't remember. You drifted in and out of consciousness. I couldn't risk anybody finding out that you were alive but without a memory. At first I thought it would come back, but when you woke, it was clear that the memory loss was permanent. For your own safety I had to get you as far away as possible."

"I don't remember waking up and seeing you."

"Because you didn't see me. The blow to your head injured your optic nerve."

Was that what the dream had wanted to show him when everything had gone red in front of his eyes?

"It was healing only slowly, as was the rest of your body."

"Yet you abandoned me while I was still in recovery," Cain interrupted him harshly. "So much for your concern for me."

"I couldn't stay with you. I only had enough time to make arrangements to get you as far away from here as possible, before my absence would have been noticed. I had to make sure whoever wanted you dead thought he'd succeeded. Only that way could you be safe."

"Any thoughts on who wanted me dead?"

John hesitated, breathing audibly.

"Spit it out!" Cain ordered.

"I have a suspicion, but no proof. And if you remembered me at all, you'd know that I don't like to accuse anybody without being able to back up my claim."

"Well, that's the crux of the problem, isn't it? I don't remember you."

"You trusted me once."

Cain locked his jaw, trying to appear unaffected by the other vampire's words, when in reality he sensed John's need to gain his approval for the decisions he'd made when Cain had been incapacitated.

"Trust isn't something I give freely."

John gave a slight nod. "You didn't back then either. But we were more than just a king and his guard. We were friends. And I mourned the loss of that friendship more than the loss of my king."

"Was I not a good king then?" Cain deflected, not wanting to respond to his guard's claim.

"That's not for me to judge."

John's words were too evasive for Cain not to react to them. "Are you trying to say I was a bad ruler, and that's what prompted the assassination?"

"As I said, that's not—"

"—for you to judge, I get it," Cain finished the sentence.

Suddenly John slowed and turned to him, placing a finger on his lips thus ending their conversation. He pointed to another tunnel. From where Cain stood, he could see that it was short, only a few yards. At the end of it, he could make out the outlines of a door.

John bent to his ear, whispering now, "It leads to the secret corridor that connects the king's chambers with those of the queen. The king's are to the right, the queen's to the left. You will find Faye in the queen's suite. When you get to her door, move the lever on its left. It'll open a tiny spy hole to look into her room, so you can assure yourself that she's alone before you enter. Don't worry, the door is disguised with an elaborate piece of art on the other side, so that nobody will notice the spy hole or the door itself."

Cain nodded, his heart suddenly thundering.

"I'll wait for you here. If you're not back within fifteen minutes, I'll come for you."

Wordlessly, Cain conveyed his agreement. Taking a deep breath, he marched toward the door and walked up the few steps that led to it. He eased it open, making as little noise as possible as he stepped inside the corridor and pulled the door shut behind him.

The hallway he found himself in was made of stone, and the air inside was cleaner and less damp than what he'd encountered in the tunnel.

His eyes darted to the right. He felt physically drawn in that direction, as if the answers to his questions lay there. But he forced himself to go left, knowing there wasn't enough time to both investigate the king's rooms and talk to Faye. His friends from Scanguards wouldn't hesitate to make good on their promise to search for him should he not return in time, and he had no intention of putting them in undue danger. There would be plenty of time later to find out more about his old life.

If this was indeed his old life.

Careful not to make any sound with his shoes, he walked to the door John had indicated and perused it. The lever next to it was shaped like a stake. Cain shook his head. Somebody around here had strange tastes, and he sure hoped that he wasn't the one to blame for this odd choice of handle.

Cain twisted the lever and immediately saw a tiny beam of light shine through the hidden door. He moved to bring his eye in line with it and peered through the small hole.

His heart stopped.

There was no mistaking her. Faye looked exactly like she'd appeared in his dreams, though she was dressed in casual clothes, a pair of tight jeans and a loose-fitting sweater. It had slid to one side, exposing one creamy shoulder. Her hair cascaded over her shoulders and back, and her eyes were as green as a meadow in the spring.

The room looked eerily similar to the one in his last dream. He'd been here before. He'd made love to her in this room. Yet as much as he wanted to open the door and walk to her, he couldn't.

Faye wasn't alone.

The vampire who was with her stood with his back to Cain, preventing him from seeing his face. The stranger now extinguished the distance between him and Faye, his hand already clasping her bare shoulder, the other one sliding around her waist to pull her to him.

The moment the vampire kissed her, Cain closed his eyes.

The man whose face he couldn't see had to be Abel. Faye had gotten over his death and maybe even forgotten him. She was in love with somebody else.

Cain released the lever. He'd come too late.

His entire body numb, he walked back to the door that led to the tunnel. When he reached it, he rested his forehead against it, feeling the cool surface against his skin. Could he really blame her? She'd thought him dead for a year. She had to get on with her life.

Yet that thought was no comfort to him. Although Cain had no memory of her or the love they'd shared, he knew instinctively that had Faye died instead of him, he would have grieved the rest of eternity for her. Yet she had given herself to another man a mere year after his death.

However, nothing of this would change anything now. He'd come so far and wouldn't turn back. This was his old life, and he would reclaim it. And he'd be damned if he wouldn't mount a fight to win Faye's love back, because one thing was clear: in his dream he'd loved her. Having seen her in the arms of his brother only moments earlier made his heart clench in pain, a pain he had no trouble identifying: he was jealous.

With purpose in his mind, Cain lifted his head and opened the door to the tunnel, leaving the corridor behind him.

He let his gaze roam, but only emptiness greeted him.

"John?" he whispered.

But John was gone.

10

Faye felt Abel's lips on hers and tried to let herself go. But no matter how hard she tried she couldn't do this. Kissing Abel was nothing like kissing Cain.

She pressed her hands against Abel's shoulders and pushed him back, not forcefully, yet determined. She wasn't ready for intimacy with him. Would she ever be ready?

Abel's eyes blazed at her with unchecked lust, his fangs already extended. Had she never met his brother, she would have found him attractive, handsome even. And maybe she would be able to fall in love with him. But the moment she'd laid eyes on Cain, her heart had spoken, and she'd known even then that she could never love another.

Faye averted her eyes and stepped back. A low growl came from him, confirming that his vampire side was ruling him in this moment. She sensed his displeasure physically, felt the waves of annoyance rolling off him. Could she blame him? No. After all, she'd accepted his proposal, and they didn't live in the Middle Ages where intimacy before the wedding night was unacceptable. This was the twenty-first century, and sex was expected, particularly by a virile vampire like Abel.

"I'm sorry," she murmured. "I can't. Not yet. It's all happening too quickly."

Abel sucked in a breath. "I understand," he pressed out from between clenched teeth.

"I didn't mean to lead you on," she said quickly. "Just give me a little more time. Until the wedding."

Abel wasn't a man to be denied what he wanted. He didn't speak for seconds that seemed to stretch to minutes. She heard her own heart pound in her chest.

"Very well. Until the wedding then."

He turned abruptly and left her room, shutting the door behind him with a loud bang.

She'd bought herself a few more days until she would have to give into his sexual demands. A few more days during which she could remain faithful to Cain. Faithful to his memory.

If only that night she hadn't let him go, if only she'd bonded with him then, maybe he would still be alive.

One year earlier

A hot breath blew against her nape, causing a pleasant shiver to run down her spine. Faye turned in the silk sheets, her naked body sliding against hard muscle and soft skin.

She ran her eyes over her lover. Cain's skin was bronzed and flawless, his chest nearly hairless, his hair cropped short. He sported a permanent stubble, one that he shaved occasionally, but which returned after each restorative sleep cycle. His eyes were a golden brown, but often when they were together his eye color would change to a glowing red, a sign of the passion that raged between them.

Faye put her hand on his chest, tracing the ridges of his pectorals with her fingernails, before sliding down to his abdomen.

He hissed in a breath, but didn't stop her descent.

"You're quite insatiable today," Cain said.

She met his gaze and saw the color of his eyes change, evidence enough that he wasn't going to deny her.

"I'm only adapting to your appetite," she responded and wrapped her hand around his erection.

She'd already felt his cock inside her several times during the past hours. They'd barely slept since they'd gone to bed just before sunrise. It was almost sunset again, and soon they would have to leave the privacy of his suite and deal with clan matters. But before he'd be all business again, she wanted to feel him once more.

Faye brought her lips to his mouth. "Make love to me."

"Again?" he murmured back.

"Are you getting tired of it?"

Cain threw his head back and laughed. Two rows of brilliantly white teeth flashed. "Tired?" His eyes sparkled when he looked at her. "My love, I'll never get tired of making love to you. That's why I want you as my blood-bonded mate."

He pressed her back in the soft mattress, making her lose her grip on his cock. His knee pushed her legs apart, making room for him. He slid into the space, bringing himself above her. Before she could take another breath, his cock thrust into her, until he was seated to the hilt.

His hand pushed a strand of her long hair to the side, exposing her neck.

"Why don't you bond with me now?" Cain asked.

Her heart stopped, but she knew she couldn't accept the offer. "Because you need to be sure that you love me." There were moments when she knew he hesitated between her and his kingdom. Whenever she saw him torn between love and duty, she knew he wasn't ready. But she would patiently wait until he was. It was also the reason why she hadn't let him pin her down on a wedding date even though she'd accepted his proposal.

"But I am," he insisted, caressing her neck and making her tremble in the process.

She smiled at him and shook her head. "I've loved you from afar for so long, ever since you saved me. But you never even noticed me until two months ago. You—"

He put a finger on her lips, stopping her. "I noticed you. But I had no right to make you mine. You'd gone through so much. You were vulnerable and trusted nobody. Had I shown my love for you then, you would not only have been scared but also become the object of everybody's dislike. Nobody would have accepted you as the king's mate. That's why I had to wait. To give you a chance to heal the wounds of your past and make my subjects love you for yourself. And they do love you."

Her heart melted at his confession. "Why didn't you tell me?"

His fingers traced the vein along her neck, and farther below, his cock pulled out, only to slowly slide back into her.

She sighed contentedly.

"Tell you that I loved you?" Cain smiled. "It was enough that I suffered every day that I had to spend alone in my bed. Besides, I didn't know you felt anything for me. You weren't exactly very demonstrative with your feelings toward me. In fact, there were moments when I thought you disliked me profusely."

She closed her eyes, ashamed at how she'd treated him in the past. But it had been so hard to trust anybody, even Cain. "I had to protect myself. And it was painful to be around you, thinking I meant nothing to you."

Cain pressed small kisses on her face. "So that's why you were so cold to me?"

"I wasn't cold," Faye protested.

"You were. I think I'm going to have to punish you for it. After all, nobody treats the king badly and gets away with it."

"How?" She nearly swallowed the word, when Cain's hips drew back and his cock plunged deep into her, repeating the same motion again and again.

"That's the punishment," he announced, his breath bouncing against her lips.

"If that's punishment, then you're not doing it right."

"Wrong answer, my love," he replied before he captured her lips and drowned her in a passionate kiss that robbed her not only of her breath but also of the ability to think.

All she could do was respond to him the way her body dictated. Her hands slid to his firm ass, where her fingernails dug into his flesh to force him deeper into her, while her legs wrapped around his upper thighs. Cain moaned and released her mouth only to bring his lips to her neck to kiss her where her pulse beat like a violent drum.

A fang scraped against her skin, and she shivered involuntarily.

"Oh God, Faye, I need you." His words vibrated against her heated flesh.

His mouth opened wider, and she knew what he wanted. Her blood. Despite the fact that the blood of a vampire provided no nourishment; only human blood did. But the bite would heighten their pleasure, his as well as hers. She knew that, though she'd never experienced it. Cain had always held back until now, but today he was different. As if having confessed that he'd loved her all this time had brought them closer.

"Bite me," she whispered her consent. "Drink my blood."

A deep growl came from his chest, a sound more like that of a beast than that of a man. His vampire side was breaking through now. For a moment, he lifted his head and stared at her. His eyes glowed red and his fangs were fully extended. Long and sharp. Deadly. He'd never looked more regal than now.

A thrill shot through her body. The most powerful vampire near and far loved her and wanted to make her his.

"You're everything to me," Cain said and lowered his lips to her pulse.

His fangs pierced her skin, sending a bolt of adrenaline through her body. As he lodged them deep in her neck and drew on the vein, she shuddered, unprepared for the sensations that overtook her body.

Cain's hips moved relentlessly, his cock filling her tight channel and stretching her, his pelvis rubbing against her clit with each thrust. Those actions alone would bring her to a monumental climax, but feeling his fangs in her neck made everything even more electrifying. Her entire body seemed to burn, the flames inside her threatening to incinerate her, yet she couldn't stop, didn't have the will to douse the fire inside her.

She felt Cain's power in her. She sensed him wanting to share himself with her, to prove his love to her. They moved in synch as if they'd made love for centuries when they'd only been lovers for a few short weeks. Everything was new, yet familiar. The scent of Cain's clean sweat filled her nostrils and made her womb clench. She'd never wanted a man as much as she wanted Cain. Never dared hope that she would find such happiness after all she'd endured.

"I love you," she murmured.

The words seemed to spur him on, because his movements became more frantic, faster and harder, as he pounded into her with such force that had she still been human, he would have killed her. But her vampire body greeted his ferocity with a wildness of its own.

Her fingers turned to claws, drawing blood where they were digging into his flesh. The scent filled the room and combined with the smell of her own blood. Mingling with the perfume of their lovemaking, it was a powerful aphrodisiac that she couldn't fight against any longer. Her body exploded, waves of pleasure rolling over her, when she felt Cain's cock spasm inside her.

He pulled his fangs from her neck and groaned as he came, shooting his seed into her. "Fuck!"

Again and again, he drove his steel-hard cock into her, until he finally stilled and brought his lips back to her neck. She felt his tongue lick over the spot where he'd drawn blood. The tenderness with which he kissed her skin now seemed to be contrary to the wild man who'd made love to her only moments earlier.

Cain lifted his head and looked into her eyes. The golden brown color was back in his irises. "I love you, Faye. Don't make me wait much longer."

Tears shot into her eyes. She didn't want to wait any longer either. She knew now that they were both ready, ready to blood-bond with each other. She was ready to bind herself to the only man who could ever make her happy and wipe away the painful memories of her past. The only vampire she could ever entrust her heart to.

Faye parted her lips, ready to give him her decision, when a ping from the bedside table interrupted her.

Cain turned his head and glanced at his cell phone. A scowl crossed his handsome face almost instantly, before he pulled out of her and sat up. He grabbed the cell phone and swiped his finger over it.

"Fuck!" he hissed a moment later.

On alert, she rose. "What's wrong?"

He cast her a sideways glance. "I have to deal with this." He jumped up and reached for his clothes, all business now. The passionate lover from moments earlier was gone, replaced by the man who was married to duty.

Her heart pounding now, Faye watched him get dressed in a hurry. "Tell me what's wrong."

When he looked at her, she flinched at the savage look in his eyes. "Someone's gonna lose his head tonight."

Cain stormed to the door.

"Wait! Cain!"

But he charged outside, slamming the door behind him. The echoing sound reverberated in her body, making her shudder, while the cell phone he'd hastily placed on the edge of the nightstand fell onto the floor.

Something was wrong.

11

Cain closed the door to the shed behind him and looked at his colleagues. They were all still there: Thomas, Eddie, Haven, Blake, and Wesley.

"Where's John?" Thomas asked immediately, glancing behind Cain.

Cain ran a hand through his short hair. Had John betrayed him? "I don't know. I was hoping he was here with you."

"But he left with you," Haven interjected.

"When I entered the palace through the tunnels, he was supposed to wait for me there, but when I came out, he was gone."

"Shit!" Thomas cursed. "Have you tried his cell?"

"It's going straight to voicemail."

"Do you think he warned the palace of your coming?"

"We have to assume that," Cain admitted.

"It doesn't make sense," Eddie chimed in. "Why show you the tunnels so you can enter the palace, bypassing whatever security they have, and then alert them to your presence?"

"What are you suggesting?" Cain asked, staring at the blond biker.

"What if somebody snatched him?"

Cain shook his head. "The only people who know about the tunnels are he and I. Nobody would have been able to find him there."

"You can't know that," Eddie insisted. "All you have is his word that you and he are the only ones aware of the tunnels. We must assume he lied."

"I agree," Haven spoke up. "In either case, whether John betrayed you or whether he was overpowered by somebody, the palace might already know that you're here. Which doesn't give us much time. If whoever planned your assassination is still in the palace, he'll prepare to fight you when you come back. Let's not give them time to mount an attack. We've gotta go in now while we still have the element of surprise. Did you speak to Faye?"

Cain shook his head. "She wasn't alone. I couldn't risk it. Nevertheless, I'm certain now that I am the king. I recognized my surroundings from the dreams."

Haven nodded.

When making his case to Samson about needing men to check out John's story, Cain had informed his boss about the dreams he'd been having. No details of course, but only what Samson needed to know: that the woman in the picture John had presented was the same woman as the one in his dreams.

"You're right," Cain now said to Haven. "We can't allow them to mount an offensive. We have to go in now. But we'll split up."

"No!" Thomas protested. "We'll go in with full force. You'll need as much protection as possible. We have no idea how many vampires we're dealing with, and how hostile they are."

"It's not wise. Two of us will stay back," Cain ordered, firm in his decision. "Eddie and Blake won't enter the palace grounds."

Thomas glanced at his mate, then clenched his teeth. "Why them?"

"Because Eddie is your mate. If anything happens in there and we're unable to use cell phones to communicate, you'll still be able to convey that we need help via your telepathic bond. And nobody in the palace will even realize it."

Slowly Thomas nodded his agreement. "Fine."

"Yeah, but that doesn't mean that *I* have to stay back. I want to come," Blake complained and pointed to Wesley. "Why does he get to go?"

Cain put a calming hand on his shoulder, knowing he had to placate Blake with something so that he didn't feel left out. "I need you out here with Eddie. The two of you will search for John. Should we find him in the palace, Thomas will send a message to Eddie, but if he's not in the palace, we need to find out what happened to him. I rely on you for that. You're human. You'll be able to go places that Eddie can't."

Blake's chest swelled, and a proud smile formed on his lips. "You can count on me."

How easy it was to manipulate the young human. Cain almost felt a little guilty, though he knew it was for the best. He had no idea how the presence of a human would be taken by this clan. Would they attack him because they saw him as the enemy? In any case, Cain didn't need the added hassle of having to protect a human whose fighting skills were inferior to those of a vampire. Wesley would have a better chance at holding off any hostile vampire: they would smell that he was a witch and would be cautious about approaching him, fearing he could cast a spell against which not even a vampire had protection. They had no way of guessing that Wesley's magic was weak. Perception was everything, which brought up another point: Cain's memory loss.

"Another thing," Cain now cautioned his colleagues. "The only way for the guards on the outside to even let us into the palace, is to make sure they know who I am. There can be no doubt in their minds when I approach them. When we are around them, you'll need to address me as *Your Majesty*. I reckon they'll recognize me, but we have to make sure that nobody suspects that I have amnesia. If they do, it weakens my position and may play into the hands of the assassin."

"That's understood," Haven said, then scratched his head. "But how are you gonna explain why you were gone for a year? They must wonder what happened."

Cain had already thought of that on his way back from the tunnels. "Don't worry. I have a story for that too. I'll fill you in on the way, so you'll know what to say." He motioned to the door behind him. "Let's go. It's about a half hour march to the palace."

As he turned to the door, he noticed Thomas pulling Eddie into a hug and kissing him.

"Be careful," Eddie said and ran his hand through Thomas's hair.

Thomas winked. "You know me."

Eddie rolled his eyes. "That's exactly why I'm saying it."

Cain opened the door and stepped outside, inhaling the humid night air. No foreign smells drifted to him, indicating that no other vampires were in the vicinity. John hadn't returned in the meantime.

As Cain marched ahead, his colleagues following him through the wooded terrain, he hoped that he hadn't misread the vampire who claimed to have been his loyal guard. He'd sounded so sincere when he'd spoken about Cain's past, and so full of regret about having failed him. Had John failed him again?

Mentally Cain prepared himself for taking his old life back. His heart pounded in his chest, and for the first time in his life he felt nervous.

"What are you thinking?"

Cain turned his head to Thomas, who'd sidled up to him, while the two brothers walked behind them. "Just hoping that John didn't betray us. For all our sakes."

Thomas nodded gravely. "Everything still seems very unreal. As you know, I checked out all the information you gave me when you joined Scanguards, but I couldn't find anything about you. Nor has anybody at Scanguards ever heard of this clan and a king. I'm afraid we have no idea what we're walking into."

"I'm aware of that. Nevertheless, I know I'm the king. I can't ignore that feeling." Nor the fact that he recognized Faye from his dreams and that seeing her in Abel's arms had produced a bolt of intense jealousy. "The woman he claims was my fiancée . . ." He hesitated.

"You don't have to say it. You recognized her. She's the only reason Samson authorized this excursion. He spoke to Dr. Drake."

Cain raised an eyebrow. "What's that shrink got to do with it?"

"Drake believes that your dreaming about her is a sign that your memory is coming back."

Cain shrugged. He had thought the same thing, but tried not to get his hopes up for fear they may be dashed again. "And that's why Samson agreed to give me a few men to check things out?"

Thomas chuckled. "That and the fact that Samson is a big softy at heart and wants to give you a chance to reclaim the woman you love, if indeed you are the king and she your fiancée."

Cain didn't know how to answer. He wasn't somebody to share what lay in his heart. One question taunted him: could a man without a memory love a woman from a past he didn't remember?

"I'm grateful to Samson," he finally said. "And to all of you for supporting me. I hope you won't regret it."

"I hope so, too."

The rest of the way, Cain conveyed his plan of what to tell Abel and the rest of the palace about why he'd been away. Once he was satisfied that everybody knew what to say, they continued to walk in silence, mentally preparing themselves.

Cain's thoughts wandered back to Faye. Disappointment swept through him. She hadn't waited for him. Instead, she'd taken another lover—Abel, the man who would soon be king.

John had explained that the coronation would take place very soon, and Cain had found it odd that such a long time lay between the death of one king and the coronation of another. But this fact was to his advantage now. It meant that Abel wasn't king yet and Cain would be able to take back his throne by returning to the clan before the coronation of the new king. It was as simple as that.

Winning back his fiancée could prove to be harder.

"Ambush!" Haven suddenly shouted from behind him.

No sooner had Haven sounded the alarm, several men were coming out of the thicket and charged them. There was no mistaking what they were: vampires who were protecting the palace's perimeter which Cain and his companions must have breached.

One attacker had already jumped Wesley, and Haven was fighting him off his brother, slamming a fist into the attacking vampire's face. Two other hostile vampires came from the other side and engaged in a fight with Thomas, who did his best to fight back the blows and kicks. Cain pulled his silver knife from its sheath and charged into the fray when a sound behind him made him swivel.

Two massively built vampires barreled toward him, their eyes glowing red, their fangs extended. Not waiting for them to strike the first blow, Cain brandished his knife and went on the offensive, attacking the two vampires. Cain felt his body harden as he kicked one of them into the stomach, then managed to slash the other's arm. But the injury he'd inflicted made his attacker even more ferocious. A violent growl came from the other's lips, his fangs gleaming in the moonlight.

"We're not your enemies, we're—"

But Cain's words were cut off by the second vampire who was now slamming his fist into Cain's chin, whipping his head to the side. Cain tasted his own blood in his mouth and spit it out, while his hand holding the knife jerked upward in an attempt to drive it into his attacker's chest. But the vampire's arm blocked him in the last split second, making Cain lose his footing on the uneven ground. He swayed but caught himself, using a low tree branch to catapult himself back at the two hostiles.

Grunts and shouts came from his colleagues as the unequal battle continued.

"No!" Haven shouted suddenly.

Cain whirled his head in his friend's direction and saw him now fighting two other vampires. One of them had Wesley in a chokehold, and the witch's face was red, his hands trying to pry his attacker's arm off him, while gasping for air.

"Release him!" Cain cried out instinctively. "I command you as your king!"

The vampire's head snapped up, his eyes now pinning Cain, disbelief spreading in them like wildfire. His lips moved, issuing a soundless *Oh my God!* when Cain felt a blow to his head that knocked him against a tree. In the next instant, muscled arms pinned him there and a hand wielding a stake came toward him.

Shit!

"Cease!" a commanding voice echoed through the dark, making his attacker stop in mid-movement, just as Cain's arm came up to block the hit.

From the corner of his eye, Cain saw that the vampire who'd had Wesley in a chokehold had released him and was now rushing toward Cain in vampire speed.

The vampire, who was clearly the leader, pulled Cain's attacker away from Cain and fell on his knees, bowing. "Your Majesty. We thought you were dead."

Cain inhaled a relieved breath. "So did I."

His gaze wandered to his friends. They were unharmed. The vampires who'd attacked them were now bowing toward Cain.

Thomas cast a glance in Cain's direction, one side of his mouth curving upward. "I guess it's good to be king, huh?"

Cain pushed away from the tree. The certainty of who he was filled him with a sense of power and pride. He was Cain Montague, King of the vampires of Louisiana.

"Escort us to the palace!"

The vampire looked up at him, then cast a sideways glance at Wesley, his mouth twisting with displeasure. "The witch, too?"

Cain glared down at him. "Nobody harms a hair on his head or I'll strike him down in a heartbeat."

12

Walking behind the vampire who'd recognized him just in time, Cain approached the sprawling estate located in a large meadow and surrounded by a forest. Cain hadn't asked the man his name, not wanting to alert him to his memory loss. The other guards as well as Cain's friends from Scanguards marched behind them, though the king's guards made a point of staying as far away from Wesley as they could. They clearly didn't trust a witch.

Cain perused his surroundings. A broad road flanked by large oak trees covered in Spanish moss led up to a majestic mansion with white columns, a wrap-around porch, and balconies on the two upper floors. Without a doubt, this had once been a plantation, and the cottages dotting the property had housed slaves many years ago. During the flight to New Orleans, John had given him a cursory rundown on what the estate and the house looked like, though Cain had not expected it to be so grand.

Pride swelled in his chest. Though no memory emerged as he looked around, something inside him changed. A feeling of belonging spread within him, the same kind of emotion he'd started to feel as he'd grown closer to his brethren at Scanguards; however, now the sensation was more intense. This was his home.

The two vampire guards stationed outside the main entrance to the palace stared at Cain, their mouths gaping open.

Cain's guide ordered, "What are you standing here for like fools? Open the door for the king!"

"Yes, Marcus, of course!" one of them answered.

Cain made a mental note of the name.

The two vampires hastened to follow the command, and one of them reached for the door to open it, while the other moved out of the way to let them pass.

Cain stepped inside ahead of Marcus, while he clandestinely familiarized himself with his surroundings. He found himself in a large entry hall with a sweeping staircase leading to the upper floors, doors to rooms on the left and right, and walkways to either side of the staircase leading to the back of the house.

"Witch!" somebody screamed all of a sudden.

Cain cursed in frustration and whirled around. He saw how one of the two house guards leapt at Wesley, while Marcus tried to block him. All three tumbled to the ground.

In vampire speed Cain crossed the distance and pulled the attacker from the heap, gripping him by his shirt's collar, then slammed him against the door frame, flashing his fangs at him.

"The witch is with me! You harm him, you'll be dust." Then he turned to the other house guard. "That goes for you, too."

The vampire dropped his head obediently. Cain released the guard and set him back on his feet.

Meanwhile, Marcus had helped Wesley up. Wesley now dusted off his pants and readjusted his T-shirt. He took a step closer to the vampire who had attacked him.

"Jerk!" Wes ground out.

The vampire snarled.

"Shut it, Wes!" Cain ordered.

But before Cain could say anything else to reprimand the witch not to get too cocky, he heard footsteps of several people behind him.

The commotion at the door had obviously attracted the attention of the palace's residents.

"What the fuck is going on here?" an authoritative voice demanded.

Slowly Cain turned and faced the man who'd spoken. The vampire was dressed in expensive designer clothes that gave him a sophisticated look. His hair was dark, his brown eyes piercing, his body muscular yet not beefy. Cain saw the resemblance immediately. He had no doubt: this was Abel, his brother.

Abel froze, his gaze locked on Cain. His chin dropped, his chest heaved, and for a moment nobody spoke.

"Cain." The greeting was issued on a shaky breath and wrapped in disbelief. Abel took one hesitant step toward him. "But . . . we believed you were dead." He blinked, seemingly composing himself. "Brother!"

Abel closed the distance between them. Instantly Thomas and Haven were by Cain's side, ready to interfere if need be. Cain motioned them to stand down.

Abel glanced at the two then looked back at Cain. "Oh God, we missed you!" He opened his arms and pulled Cain into a hug.

Cain remained stiff until Abel finally stepped back and released him. "Abel," he greeted him coolly.

"What happened to you?" Abel asked. "We all thought you'd been killed. Heck, there was evidence!"

Cain nodded. "I know. I killed one of the assassins, but the others took me prisoner and made it look like I was dead."

His brother's eyes widened. "Prisoner? Who took you? What did they do to you?" He eyed Haven and Thomas suspiciously, before his gaze fell onto Wesley. Abel inhaled visibly. "What the—"

Cain raised his hand. This was getting old pretty quickly. "They're all with me." He pointed to his friends, introducing them. "These are Thomas, Haven, and Wesley. All three were instrumental in my escape from that hole where they kept me and tortured me. Without Wesley's magic I would have never survived. Nobody harms the witch."

The lies rolled off his lips like water down a fast flowing stream. Emphasizing Wesley's witchcraft and making him seem more powerful than he was had been Haven's idea. It would make sure the vampires wouldn't want to cross him and draw the witch's wrath on them.

Abel inclined his head toward the men from Scanguards. "I'm grateful to you for bringing my brother home. Consider yourselves our guests."

"They're not guests, they're my guards," Cain corrected his brother with a firm voice. To reestablish his rule, he had to make sure Abel knew who wielded the power. He couldn't show any weakness, not even for a second.

A perplexed expression spread on Abel's face. "But you have your guards here." He pointed to the men who'd brought him to the palace. "Surely you can't possibly want to have strangers guard you."

Cain narrowed his eyes. "The king's guards guarded me before, and look what happened: I was kidnapped under their watch. I hope you don't mind, my dear brother, that I've picked new guards to protect me." He stared his brother down, leaving him with no doubt that his words weren't meant to ask for permission, but to issue an order he expected to be followed without questioning.

"As you wish," Abel finally said.

"Good, then . . ." Cain stopped himself.

A scent suddenly drifted to him. It was subtle, but nevertheless caused his heart to beat erratically. His entire body reacted to it because, unlike his mind, his body recognized the scent. He felt it in every cell of his being.

Slowly Cain lifted his eyes to the top of the stairs, drawn to where she stood. Faye wore a colorful cotton dress with a pattern consisting of tropical flowers in various green, blue, and pink tones. The fabric hugged her generous bust and widened past her wasp-like waist to make room for her hips and the bare long legs that became visible just below her knees. Her toes peeked out from her high-heeled sandals. He couldn't tell whether she wore a bra or whether her breasts were naturally firm to give them such an appealing shape. Though if he could trust his dreams, he had his answer: in his hands her breasts had had the perfect combination of softness and firmness.

Swallowing away the lust that instantly surfaced, Cain forced himself to remain standing where he was. Instead, he brought his gaze back to her face, where her eyes stared at him as if he were a ghost. Her lips parted, and even from where he stood he could see how her chest rose to take in a breath.

Faye was even more breathtakingly beautiful than she'd been in his dreams. Combined with her scent that now wrapped around him like a cocoon, he didn't know how any man, vampire or not, would have any chance resisting her. Just looking at her he was lost. If he walked to her now, his lips would utter a confession he couldn't dare make. Nobody was allowed to find out that he suffered from amnesia. Not even Faye.

So he suppressed the urge to run up the stairs and sweep her into his arms. He couldn't allow himself to do that. Certainly not in front of Abel. She was engaged to Abel now, and until he had a chance to speak to Faye in private to get a sense for her feelings for his brother he couldn't show any of the palace's residents what he felt. He had to continue the charade and play the strong king who wouldn't lose his composure. John had told him on the plane ride here that he'd never been one to show his emotions in public. If he did so now, the vampires watching him would find it odd and become suspicious. And he couldn't give them or Abel any reason to believe that he'd changed or that he wasn't who he was pretending to be.

He ran one last look over Faye, before he nodded to her stiffly. "Faye. It's good to see you."

The casual words made his heart clench. Would she understand that for so many reasons he couldn't be more affectionate at this moment?

He'd loved this woman once. Not only had John told him so, but Cain had felt it in his dreams. Did she still love him? Or had the year that they'd been apart widened the gap between them too far to bring them back together? Looking at her now, knowing that she wasn't merely a figment of his imagination, he had no doubt that he could fall in love with her all over again.

13

"Cain," Faye murmured so quietly that he probably didn't even hear her.

Like a mirage he stood there in the entrance hall, several of the guards around him, three strangers by his side. But she had no eyes for anybody but Cain.

He was alive.

She couldn't believe her eyes and blinked, but when she opened them again, he was still there, still standing in the entrance hall of the palace as if he'd never left. His scent drifted to her, confirming that he wasn't simply a lookalike, but the real thing: Cain, her king and her lover.

His greeting echoed in her mind again. *Faye, it's good to see you.*

The words seemed so distant, so unreal. As if they weren't his. As if he were greeting a stranger and not the woman he loved.

What had happened to him?

So many questions invaded her mind, making her dizzy. She didn't know what to do first, what to ask first, what to say, how to react. All she wanted was to throw herself into his arms and feel his heart beat against hers. Feel his lips kissing her and assuring her that everything would be all right now.

Her feet carried her down the stairs, bringing her closer to the man she'd grieved for and shed tears for every day since he'd gone. A few more steps and she'd be with him again.

"Isn't it wonderful, Faye? My brother is alive!" Abel's voice suddenly penetrated her haze.

Faye froze, her feet refusing to take another step.

Oh God! She'd accepted Abel's proposal not twenty-four hours earlier. Despair slammed into her. Why hadn't she waited just another day? What would she do now? Her eyes drifted from Cain to Abel. Had

Abel already told his brother that his fiancée was now promised to him? Was this why Cain was making no attempt to take her into his arms and kiss her?

Her heart raced, her pulse beating into her throat, robbing her of the ability to speak. She wanted to turn back time, to make everything that had happened in the last twenty-four hours undone. Tears welled up in her eyes. They should be tears of joy, but instead they were tears of regret. Regret of having given up hope too soon. How could she ever forgive herself for that?

"Cain," Faye whispered again.

She was certain he'd heard her now. His eyes met hers, but she couldn't read them, couldn't see the love he'd professed so long ago. Had he stopped loving her?

"What happened?" she heard herself ask.

"I was kidnapped and held captive," Cain responded, having misunderstood the true meaning of her question.

She didn't correct him, knowing that this was not the time or place to talk to him about their relationship. Not in front of Abel who was watching them like a hawk.

"We thought you were dead," she said instead. "We grieved for you." She purposefully didn't say *I*. She couldn't, knowing she would break down if she revealed the depth of her despair.

"I'm back now." He motioned to the three strangers. "These three men helped me escape. Meet Thomas, Haven, and Wesley." His words were as businesslike as if he were talking to a stranger.

Only now did she take in the strange scent emanating from the man he'd introduced as Wesley. She leaned closer. He looked entirely human, but she knew he wasn't. He was a preternatural creature.

"Wesley is a witch, but he's not our enemy," Cain said, having anticipated her question.

She accepted his words silently and nodded.

Cain turned away from her and addressed Abel instead. "My men and I would like to get situated. I need accommodations for them."

"Of course," Abel agreed readily. "I suggest the guest suites up on the third floor. They are—"

"Not the guest suites," Cain interrupted, his voice icy. "The rooms of the king's personal guards next to my suite."

"But they're occupied by your guards," Abel protested.

Cain pointed to Haven, Thomas, and Wesley. "These are my personal guards now. They'll be by my side, protecting me."

Faye noticed how Abel's mouth set into a thin line, displeased that Cain wasn't agreeing with his suggestion. "As you wish. I'll make sure the guards vacate the rooms immediately."

"Good. Then send John to me. I'd like to speak to him."

Abel rubbed the back of his neck. "I'm afraid I haven't seen John."

Cain raised an eyebrow. "John isn't the leader of the king's guard anymore?"

"No, no, he is," his brother hastened to assure him. "But he disappeared a few days ago. Nobody knows where he is."

"Find him!" Cain ordered. "Now escort us to my quarters so we may talk in private. We've had a long journey and are anxious to get settled in before we begin our investigation."

"Investigation?" Faye asked in surprise.

Cain turned his head to look at her. "Yes, about which member of this clan ordered my abduction."

Faye pressed her hand against her chest. "But you must know who kidnapped you. You're back. You escaped them. You must have some idea."

"It's not as simple as that. The people who held me captive were hired by somebody. When I was able to overpower them with the help of my friends here, none of them survived, so I couldn't question them further."

Faye shivered involuntarily at the thought of how much danger Cain had been in all this time while she'd lived a life of luxury. "They deserved to die for what they did to you," she pressed out.

Cain gave a tight nod. "Just as the person behind it deserves the same."

Without waiting for her reaction, he turned and crossed the entrance hall.

"Are you coming, Abel?" he called over his shoulder.

Abel tossed her an odd look, then swiveled and followed his brother and the three strangers flanking him.

14

Cain marched toward the stairs that led into the underground part of the palace, recalling the drawing John had made for him on the plane so he would be able to find his way around without looking like he didn't belong here.

Still feeling shaken by the awkward exchange with Faye, Cain pushed away the thoughts of her for the moment. First, he had to concentrate on other things, the most important one being to make it clear to his brother that he would resume his reign with immediate effect.

Subdued light illuminated the corridors in the basement of the building, making it look like he'd stepped into a modern five-star hotel. When the corridor parted in two, one path leading to the left, one to the right, Cain hesitated, trying to find his bearings.

"Something wrong?" Abel asked.

"It feels unreal to be home again," Cain deflected. "Why don't you lead my friends to their new accommodations while I take a moment?"

His brother cast him a strange look, but nodded and motioned his friends from Scanguards to follow him down the corridor to the left. Cain let a few seconds pass before he followed them. He knew there would be many moments like these where he'd have to employ a ruse to cover up his amnesia.

When he reached the solid double doors that Abel had opened, Cain peered inside the massive foyer, which looked like the VIP reception area of an exclusive resort. The walls were painted red and adorned with priceless paintings. He recognized a Matisse and a Monet and had no doubt that they were genuine. A flower arrangement dominated the massive table in the middle of the room.

There were three doors.

He watched as Abel pointed to the one on the left and addressed Thomas. "The leader of the king's guards occupies this room, the second in command the room to the right."

"And the middle door?" Thomas asked.

Abel's gaze wandered to where Cain stood. "The king's suite. But I should let my brother show you around. After all, this is his domain."

Cain entered. "Later. First, we need to talk about the throne."

Abel took a step toward the door of the king's suite, making a motion to open it. Cain stopped him. "With my guards present."

Abel turned. "Surely, you don't want to discuss confidential matters in front of your guards."

"I have no secrets from them. As a matter of fact, I believe that too many secrets may have contributed to my abduction. And I have no intention of letting the same thing happen twice."

"What are you saying, brother?"

"I'm saying I want things out in the open. I understand that you would have been crowned king in a week, had I not returned. You must be disappointed."

Abel shook his head, letting out a breath. "Disappointed? Cain, as you remember well, I was disappointed when the clan chose you as the new king instead of me, though we'd planned it otherwise, hadn't we? Nevertheless, I stood by you and took the role you wanted me to take. Have I not served you well?"

Cain inclined his head, remaining impassive, not wanting to let on that he had no idea what plan Abel was talking about. What *had* they planned?

"No matter what my hopes were, I'm overjoyed to find you alive and well. The crown is yours. It's always been. As for Faye . . ."

Keeping his stoic face, Cain didn't show that he already guessed what Abel wanted to say. "What about Faye?"

Abel glanced at Thomas, Haven, and Wesley who stood watching the exchange silently. "Are you sure you want me to talk about personal matters in front of your men?"

"Talk."

Abel shifted his weight from one foot to the other. "Well, you might as well hear it from me, before the rumor mill spreads it. Faye and I are engaged."

His brother paused, clearly to wait for Cain's reaction. Cain complied, feigning shock.

Abel lifted his hand. "You must understand. She grieved for you; we all did. We had no idea you were alive all this time. She was lonely and sought comfort. And you know of course that the position she was in was a temporary one. She knew she would lose her home, her privileges, everything, once I would be crowned king. You can't really blame her." He shoved a hand through his hair.

"Blame her for what?" Cain ground out, not liking the direction the conversation was taking. What was Abel trying to tell him?

"Listen, Cain, I shouldn't really be the one to tell you this. Let her explain things to you."

Cain made a few steps toward his brother, grinding his teeth. "Blame her for what?" he repeated.

"Damn it, Cain, don't make me say it. I'm sure, deep down she's a good woman, but—"

Cain gripped his brother by the shirt. "But what?"

"I'm just a man. I have no defenses against a woman like her. You know she can seduce anybody she wants." Abel's eyes bored into him. "Damn it, do I have to spell it out? She threw herself at me once it was clear that I would be the next king. She wants to be queen, no matter what. And fool that I am, I couldn't resist her. To make love to a woman like her . . ." He let the sentence hang in the room.

Cain's hands curled into fists. His brother had made love to the woman who was meant to be Cain's. Jealousy reared its ugly head once again, launching a spear into his heart to make it bleed. Faye had been the one who'd made a play for Abel so she could be queen after all. Did this mean that the reason she'd wanted to marry him, Cain, was not because she'd loved him, but because she wanted to be sitting on the throne beside him? How could he ever trust a woman like her?

With a curse, he let go of Abel and turned away from him. "It's late. The sun will rise in an hour. We'll discuss court business tonight. Leave us now."

Only when he heard the double doors close behind his brother and his footsteps grow distant did Cain turn to his friends.

"You should listen to her side first, before you make any rash decisions," Thomas cautioned. "Your brother has reason enough to make you doubt her. Not only are you back to take away the throne that was within his reach, but you're also taking the woman back that he is most likely in love with. Wouldn't you too turn to dirty tricks to at least keep one of those things for yourself?"

Thomas had a point. And if Cain were ruled by logic right now, he would admit it. But even if Thomas was right, it still didn't change one thing. "My brother slept with my fiancée."

Haven took a step closer. "Hey, don't do that. You slept with plenty of women during the last year! So don't judge her."

Cain glared at him. "I had amnesia! What's her excuse?"

Haven went toe to toe with him. "She thought you were dead. That's her excuse! So get over it and leave your fucking male ego at the door. Think for a moment! Did you not see how she looked at you when she saw you?"

Cain looked away, avoiding Haven's gaze. "How did she look at me?" To Cain she'd looked uncertain, as if she didn't know what to feel. As if she wasn't sure whether to be happy to see him or not.

Thomas suddenly slapped him on the shoulder. "I didn't realize that becoming king causes blindness."

Cain whirled his head to him. "You're joking about this? Have you gone out of your mind?"

"I haven't, but I think you have. Be rational for a moment. You can't believe anything anybody around here tells you. Accept that as a fact. It will take some time to figure out who you can trust."

Cain forced his breathing to slow and his heartbeat to settle. "I know. We'll proceed as discussed: tomorrow we'll start interrogating the members of the king's guard. Each of them separately. We have to figure out who's loyal to me."

"You know, about Faye . . ." Wesley interjected.

Cain glanced at the witch. "I don't want to talk about her now."

"I was just thinking, maybe I could try to brew a truth potion or something," Wes suggested.

Haven slapped his brother over the back of his head.

"What?" Wes complained, rubbing his head.

"You're not gonna start brewing some stupid potion that's probably not even gonna work and will most likely end up blowing something up."

"Pessimist!"

"I'd rather be a living pessimist than a dead optimist!" Haven replied.

Cain turned back to Thomas, ignoring Wesley's scowl. "Get in contact with Eddie and Blake and see if they have any leads on John. Since he's not shown up here at the palace, at least we can assume he didn't come back here to warn anybody of our arrival or the fact that I have amnesia. We have to find him."

"I'll talk to Eddie shortly."

"Good. Get some shuteye. All of you. We've got a long night ahead of us."

"Don't you want one of us to stand guard?" Thomas asked.

"That won't be necessary. I'll sleep with a stake under my pillow."

Cain turned to the middle door and opened it. Instinctively he reached for the light switch next to the door and flipped it. Then he closed the massive door behind him, shutting out all sounds from the foyer. He could barely hear the opening and closing of the doors to the other two rooms, so well insulated was the suite.

Cain looked around. This was the room from his dreams. He'd made love to Faye here. He'd experienced ecstasy here. In the elegant bed truly befitting a king, he'd slept with Faye in his arms. He recalled the many dreams now that he'd had over the last few months. Many had taken place in this room. And she'd been in every single one of them, always taking center stage, always in his arms.

But tonight, he'd be alone. Because Faye had given herself to another man, and right now Cain couldn't help but feel enraged about it. If he went to her now to question her, there was no telling what he would do. It was best to leave this task to a later time, when he'd sufficiently calmed down and was able to let logic rule instead of jealousy.

15

Cain knew he'd only slept an hour or two before a sound woke him. Silently he slipped his hand underneath his pillow and palmed the wooden stake, while he continued to lay on his side, facing the door. He hadn't really expected that the assassin would make an attempt so soon after Cain's return, but was glad he'd prepared himself nevertheless.

He focused his eyes, adjusting them to the darkness in the room. But even though his vampire vision worked perfectly, he saw nobody coming from the door. Continuing to breathe evenly so he wouldn't alert the would-be attacker to the fact that he was awake, he waited. The sound of footsteps coming from behind him where the entrance to the passage into the tunnels lay hidden was faint as if the intruder walked barefoot.

He would have to allow him to come closer, before he could jump up from the bed and tackle the person who meant to harm him. Tense seconds passed when a scent drifted into his nostrils. His heart stopped and in the next split second he rolled to the other side, reached his arm out and grabbed hold of the intruder, while his other hand pressed the stake against a heaving chest.

"Cain!"

He'd recognized her even before she'd spoken, but that hadn't stopped him from wrestling her down onto the bed and immobilizing her by pinning her with his body. Only now that he was sure that Faye was unarmed did he remove the stake from her chest and reach for the bedside lamp. When its light bathed the room in a soft glow, he looked back down at her.

"Why are you attacking me?" she asked, a twinge of panic in her voice, while her eyes stared at the stake he was still holding.

Instead of an answer, he asked, "How did you get in?"

She gave him a bewildered look. "Through the secret passageway."

So she knew about the tunnels. Had he himself told her or had she found out some other way? Had he once trusted her so much to confide this secret in her?

"Why are you here?"

From the way she was dressed, he already knew the answer. Only a thin silk negligee covered her enticing body. He felt it rub against his naked torso. Lower down, his bare legs slid against hers, and the skin-to-skin contact heated his body. In a few seconds, his cock would be as hard as an iron rod if he didn't separate himself from her this instant. Unfortunately, he couldn't command his body to release her. Instead, he kept pinning her down onto the mattress, one hand encircling her wrist, the other braced next to her head, still holding the stake.

"I need to talk to you," she pressed out.

"Talk, huh?" He gave a quick shake of his head. "It doesn't look to me like you're here to talk." He gave her outfit a meaningful look. If she wanted to talk, she was wearing the wrong clothes. No man with a pulse would be able to listen to anything she had to say, while his eyes were busy devouring the tempting curves beneath the flimsy fabric.

"Why are you treating me like this?"

"How am I treating you?"

Faye turned her head to the side as if she couldn't bear to look at him. "You know then. He told you." An audible breath left her chest. "I wanted to be the one to explain it to you before you heard it from somebody else. That's why I'm here."

"Then explain." Cain released the stake to shelve her chin and turn her face to him. God, she was beautiful, her face as flawless as a precious doll. "And look at me when you do."

"My entire world shattered when you died. Every day I prayed for a miracle, I prayed to wake up from this nightmare. But you were gone."

A wet sheen formed on her eyes, and Cain had to refrain from comforting her and kissing her to wipe away her sadness.

"My love for you never died." Her hand came up, but before she could stroke his cheek, he'd grabbed her wrist and pinned her arm down.

"Yet you gave yourself to my brother! So you could be queen!" Cain ground out. "Your time of mourning wasn't even over yet, and already you were with him! As if I'd never existed! How do you think that makes me feel, Faye?"

White hot jealousy radiated through his entire body. His fangs itched for a bite, and he didn't stop them from descending.

Faye flinched. "I don't love him. I could never love another man but you."

He wished he could believe her words. But he didn't know Faye, had no idea what she was capable of, how far she would go to get what she wanted.

"God damn it, Faye! So if you don't love him, then why would you want to marry him?" He dropped his lids, disappointed. Some of the anger left his voice. He wanted to understand her, to find out why she'd chosen Abel. "Just so you could be queen?" He shook his head, his heart aching now, his voice cracking. "Is that all you want? Is that why you're here now? Because you know that Abel won't be king now? Because I'm king? Is that why you want me back?"

A single pink tear ran down her cheek, while she pressed her lips together. On her next breath, a sob tore from her chest. "You've stopped loving me."

He couldn't bear seeing her like this. Her tears broke his heart in two. "God damn it!" he cursed and sank his lips onto hers before he could stop himself.

Cain swallowed her surprised gasp and dove between her parted lips. Faye tasted as sinful as she looked. He knew instantly that she was everything he'd ever dreamt of. Her lips were soft and yielding to his demands, her body beneath him pressing against him with a voiceless plea. So much hunger and need emanated from her. The thought of her desires being directed at him made the vampire in him want to roar and beat his chest like an ape displaying his superiority.

With a growl, he deepened his kiss, lashing his tongue against her in a show of dominance, while his hands released her wrists to explore her body. His fingers trailed up to her shoulders, then swept down to her chest, lightly caressing her sides, not daring to touch her breasts yet, for fear he'd start something he couldn't pull himself back from. But her soft moans tempted him to throw caution to the wind, to take what she was so clearly offering.

As if to underscore her willingness to submit to him, Faye's legs spread wider, and he suddenly found himself sliding into the space between them. The hard outline of his cock rubbed against her center with only his boxer briefs and her thin negligee providing a barrier. A barrier that didn't prevent him from feeling her heat and the wetness that covered her sex.

Instinctively he thrust against her center of pleasure, rubbing his erection over it with unerring precision.

A gasp issued from her mouth as her hips arched in an effort to increase the friction he was providing. What he was doing was crazy, but he couldn't stop. The thought of driving her to ecstasy was too tempting to resist, the need to make her submit to him in every way too urgent. The desire to make the woman in his arms shudder with pleasure guided his next action.

His tongue swiped over her teeth, licking them. Faye's response was immediate. Her fangs elongated, extending to their full length, and her fingernails dug into his back, pulling him closer, while her legs wrapped around him, her ankles crossing behind his back.

Cain accompanied his next thrust against her clit with a swipe of his tongue over one fang. Faye trembled beneath him, her heart frantically beating against his chest, her breaths rushing from her lungs, while her pelvis ground against him more urgently now.

He could feel how close she was, just as close as he. Already now, pre-cum was oozing from his cockhead, and in a few seconds, he would spill.

Cain ripped his lips from her and lowered his head to her neck. Inhaling sharply, he could already smell her blood. He put his lips to her pulse, shivering at the gentle vibrations the blood rushing through her vein caused.

"Tell me you still love me, Cain!" she suddenly begged.

As if doused with cold water, he jolted back, releasing her. He couldn't make such a confession, couldn't tell her he loved her. He'd met her only hours earlier, knew nothing about her other than that she made his cock harder than it had ever been. She made him want to take her and ride her until they were both boneless. But he was wise enough to know that it wasn't love that caused his reactions, but lust.

He didn't know whether he loved her, whether he'd ever loved her. And he couldn't lie to her about it.

Cain disentangled himself from her and sat back on his haunches.

Faye's eyes widened as she reared up. "What's wrong?"

He turned his head away from her, away from the temptation she still presented, and swung his legs out of the bed.

"You have to go. I'm tired from my journey."

It was an excuse, and they both knew it. But what he couldn't tell her was that as much as he wanted to make love to her now, he couldn't. She'd accepted Abel's proposal. She was still Abel's woman. He couldn't trust her affections or her motives. And he didn't want to be loved by her only because he was king.

Faye scrambled to get off the bed. When he glanced at her, he noticed how her lips were pressed together tightly. She avoided looking at him.

Without a word she turned to the intricate work of art that adorned the wall and pressed the fingers of both hands into different indentations, before stepping back. The wall opened, revealing the passageway behind.

"We'll talk tonight," he called after her, but she didn't reply.

A moment later, the opening was once more hidden by the sculpture and Cain was alone.

16

Abel hated to venture out during daytime, but today he didn't have a choice. He gunned the engine of his red special edition Ferrari. It was equipped with a UV-impenetrable windshield and windows, thus allowing him to drive during the day when otherwise the sun would have burned him to a crisp.

When he turned off the main road leading south, he slowed the car and adjusted to the bumpy dirt road leading deeper into one of the bayous Louisiana was famous for. He didn't come here often, but he knew the way nevertheless. Few others did. And he preferred it that way.

Outside a rickety shack deep in the bushes, he parked the car as close as possible to the front entrance. He killed the engine and slipped on his gloves before pulling the hood of his dark sweatshirt over his head and donning a pair of big sunglasses that made him look like one of the Blues Brothers.

Abel opened the door and got out, slamming it behind him while already dashing to the door of the hut. He jerked it open and barreled inside, closing it behind him.

Inside the shack, one light bulb hanging from the ceiling illuminated the small structure which contained only two small rooms: the living and sleeping area with a tiny sink and refrigerator and a small bathroom in the back. The two windows were covered with plywood to prevent any sunlight from penetrating.

Abel looked around, finding the shack to be rather crowded. On the large bed, John's lover Nicolette was handcuffed to the metal headboard, and at its foot, John sat, his hands tied over his head by a silver chain hanging from a hook in the ceiling, his head dropped to his chest. Residue of blood dirtied his shirt.

Baltimore sat at the wooden table, repeatedly stabbing his knife into the surface, obviously bored with his duty as a prison guard. He acknowledged Abel with a nod.

"Well, well, well," Abel drawled, and took two steps toward the bed.

John's head shot up and the woman's eyes widened. But she didn't speak, the gag in her mouth preventing her from uttering a word. Abel looked over his shoulder.

"A gag, really?"

"The bitch wouldn't shut up," Baltimore complained and drove his knife deeper into the table's surface than before.

"What the fuck is this about?" John ground out, a murderous look in his eyes.

"That's what I was going to ask you."

John jerked on his chain, grimacing from the pain caused by the silver rubbing against his wrists. The scent of burnt skin and hair filled the air.

John narrowed his eyes at him. "This is no way to treat the leader of the king's guard."

Abel chuckled. "I don't think you're in a position to complain right now." He glanced at the woman who watched them fearfully. "She's pretty, I give you that. But to find you maintaining a human mistress came as an utter surprise to me. Tss, tss."

John growled low and dark.

Abel walked to Nicolette and took her chin, lifting her head so she had to look straight at him. "It would be a shame to destroy such a pretty face."

"Take your hands off her!"

Abel whirled his head to John and flashed his fangs. "Don't order me around!" Then he released the woman and jumped toward the leader of the king's guard. "Now let's talk! Where the fuck were you?" He lashed the back of his hand across John's cheek, whipping his head to the side. "And don't even think about lying to me."

John turned his head back to him. "I was following a lead."

Abel narrowed his eyes. "What kind of lead?"

"An informant told me that a man matching your deceased brother's description was spotted in the Pacific Northwest. I had to check it out. With your coronation next week I needed to make sure that nothing got in the way."

"And you couldn't tell me that in advance?"

"There was no time."

"Oh, I bet." He didn't believe a single word John was saying. After all, he'd been one of Cain's most loyal followers. "Did you find the person you were looking for?"

John dropped his head, seemingly defeated. "No. I lost his trail."

"Brilliant king's guard you are! He showed up here yesterday."

John lifted his head. "An imposter?"

"Cain in the flesh! Risen from the ashes like a phoenix!" Angry, Abel curled his hand into a fist and slammed it into John's face. Blood dripped from his nose. "You told me he was dead!"

"He's alive?"

Abel landed another blow in John's face, hearing his jaw break. "You fucking jerk! You never liked me. It wouldn't surprise me to find out that you had something to do with his reappearance. You never wanted me to be king."

Defiantly, John looked at him, blood dripping from his nose and mouth. "Just like you resent the fact that I'm the leader of the king's guard."

Abel bent closer. "Oh, that's something I'm going to change when I'm king." He motioned to the vampire behind him. "Baltimore will become the leader of my guard just as soon as you've passed your secrets on to me at my coronation."

"There won't be a coronation now that Cain is back," John ground out.

"That's where you're wrong. Nothing will stand in the way of my coronation, not even Cain. And you, my dear John, will make sure of that."

"Roast in hell!"

Abel tossed a look at the tied-up human. He'd expected John's reaction, but he knew how to make the stubborn guard change his mind. "Or your lover will pay for your defiance. Slowly and painfully."

John's gaze shot to Nicolette, who now pulled on the handcuffs. "I won't let him hurt you," he assured her now.

Abel grinned. "So, we're in agreement then?"

John pinned him with a furious glare, but Abel knew he'd won.

"Good. Make it look like a rival clan is responsible for it. It will appear that we're under attack." He grinned to himself. He would kill two birds with one stone: Cain would be dead, and because the kingdom would be believed to be under attack, Abel would ascend to the throne instantly. The waiting period which would start rolling from Cain's actual death once again—one year, one month, and one day—would be waived in a time of war.

Without taking his eyes off John, Abel instructed his guard, "Baltimore, make sure he's healed completely before you release him so Cain won't become suspicious. Then get two of your trusted men to watch the woman and return to the palace. I don't want your absence to be noted."

"Yes, Abel."

"Good, then my work here is done." He turned to the door, then looked back over his shoulder. "And just so you know how generous I am to those who serve me well, I'll grant you and your woman safe passage after the coronation. Releasing you from your position as leader of the king's guard is the only way for you to keep her, as you're well aware. I'm doing you a favor. Don't forget that."

Without waiting for John's response, Abel opened the door and left.

17

Cain noticed that the door to Thomas's room stood open and announced his presence with a knock before opening the door wider and entering.

Thomas, cell phone pressed to his ear, wasn't alone. Haven leaned against a desk, while Wesley slouched on an armchair, his legs hanging over the armrest. All three turned their heads to Cain, acknowledging him.

Haven pointed to the phone and said quietly, "Eddie."

"Keep monitoring that," Thomas now said into the phone. "Cain just got up. Yeah, I'll fill him in." Then he turned his face away and lowered his voice. "I miss you, too."

Tucking the phone back into his pants pocket, Thomas turned back to them.

"Have they found John?" Cain asked.

"I'm afraid not. They're in New Orleans right now, keeping their ears to the ground, watching for any vampire-related activities, anything that could lead them to John. But so far nothing."

"Crap!"

"Don't despair yet." Thomas lifted his hand. "I've messaged HQ to have them run a trace on John's cell phone. I don't have the right equipment to do anything from here, but I'm sure they'll be able to help us pin down his location if he's used his phone since he disappeared."

Cain nodded. "Good. In the meantime, let's get to work. We'll start with the king's guards. I want a full accounting of where everybody was and what they were doing the night I was attacked. Any inconsistencies and we'll spot them. If John told us the truth that he was indeed lured away from his post, then we're going to have to find out who might have done so."

"It's going to be hard to get an accurate account of what happened that night," Wesley threw in. "It's been over a year. They won't all remember exactly what happened and in what order. Hell, most people can barely remember what happened a month ago."

"This is different," Cain cut him off. "People have a much better memory when it comes to significant events. Just like we all remember where we were when 9/11 happened. Well, all except myself. But that's beside the point. The guards will remember where they were or what they did the night of the assassination, because their king being killed would have been a significant event."

"Point taken," Wesley admitted. "But that still doesn't mean they're gonna tell you the truth."

"That's what I've got Thomas for, right Thomas?"

Wesley stared at the IT geek. "You gonna put them on a lie detector?"

Thomas smiled and shook his head. "Of course not. I'm simply gonna watch their reactions, how their eyes move when they talk, how they breathe."

Wes sat up. "Oh, I know. I saw that show. What's it called again?"

"*Lie to Me*," Haven answered.

"But those guys are like PhD's and stuff," the witch said.

"Trust me, I don't need a PhD for that," Thomas assured him. Then he gave Cain a questioning look. "Shall we?"

"Ready when you are," Cain agreed, though he wasn't as confident as he let on. Without John by his side, he was bound to trip himself up. For starters he didn't know any of the guard's names other than the man who'd recognized him: Marcus.

Not letting his apprehension show, Cain marched through the double doors and along the corridor, his colleagues following him. Strange, he still thought of them as his colleagues, his equals, although he was king now. Granted, not *their* king, since Haven and Thomas didn't belong to his clan, and Wesley wasn't even a vampire.

"Anybody else hungry?" Haven asked.

Only now Cain realized that he hadn't had any blood since they'd arrived in Louisiana.

"I brought a few snack bars, but I could do with something," Wesley answered.

Haven tossed him a get-real look. "I doubt they have human food here."

Cain set his foot on the first step. "Let's find out. Haven, I think you should be the one to ask whether they serve bottled blood here. If the question comes from me, they'll become suspicious of me. In the meantime I'll ask for human food to be ordered for Wesley."

"Agreed," Haven said.

They walked up to the first floor in silence. A guard stood at the top of the stairs and stepped aside quickly when he saw them.

"Your Majesty," the vampire greeted him.

Cain nodded and walked past him, while Haven stopped.

"My colleagues and I need some nourishment," Haven addressed the guard.

"Would you prefer packaged or fresh?"

"Packaged will be fine," Haven answered.

Cain turned briefly, casually calling out to the guard, "Bring sufficient for all of us." Then he motioned in Wesley's direction. "And have some human food ordered, too."

"Human food, sir?" the guard asked, looking confused.

"You heard me. Get it done!" Cain ordered, raising his voice, and continued walking down the corridor. If he remembered John's directions correctly, at the end of it lay the king's reception room, part office, part living area.

When he reached another double door, he stopped and cast his friends a sideways look. "This had better be it."

Cain pressed the door handle down and pushed the door inward. His three Scanguards colleagues followed as he entered the room.

They weren't alone. Abel sat at a massive desk with elaborately carved legs and trim. His brother's head instantly shot up.

Cain hesitated. It appeared that he'd opened the wrong door and barged into Abel's office without knocking. Searching for something to say, he merely stared at his brother who now shuffled the papers he was perusing into one stack and jumped up.

"I was just cleaning up for you," Abel said, and motioned to the chair. "Didn't want you to start your first day back with a disorganized desk." Then he dug into his pocket and pulled out a set of keys, placing them on the desk. "And here are the keys to everything, of course."

Cain's feeling of relief was instantly replaced by displeasure. It appeared that his brother only hesitantly wanted to relinquish the power he'd had during Cain's absence.

"Thank you," he forced himself to say and walked to his desk.

Abel stepped aside and let him take his seat. Cain laid his hands on the cool wooden surface. "I would like you to inform the members of the king's guard that I'd like to speak to them."

"All members?" his brother asked with a frown on his face.

"Yes, every single one of them."

"But they can't just leave their posts. They have responsibilities that—"

Cain narrowed his eyes. "Are you the king or am I?"

Abel appeared taken aback by his question and raised an eyebrow. "Whatever happened to you, it seems to have made you very irritable."

"You would be irritable too if you were trying to find out who was responsible for your abduction." Cain knew full well what the reason for his irritability was: the knowledge that his brother had touched Faye. It made it hard to be civil to him.

"I understand, of course."

"I'm glad of that," Cain said in a less commanding tone. "Then maybe you can arrange for the members of the king's guard to come and see me. One after the other." He motioned to the door, nodding briefly, then buried his head in the stack of papers on his desk, pretending to know what he was actually looking at. Only when he heard the door close behind Abel did he look up again.

"A bit presumptuous, your brother," Haven commented. Then he grinned. "But you're doing a heck of a job pissing him off. Frankly, I think you were born to be king."

Wesley chuckled. "Totally! You're like a natural!"

Cain jumped up from his chair and pounded his fist on the desk. "That's because I *am* the king!"

"Hey, what the fuck?" Wes complained.

Cain rubbed a hand over his face and took a calming breath. "I apologize. I didn't mean to lash out at any of you." He motioned to the door. "I just can't stand that prick!"

"Understandable under the circumstances," Thomas said evenly and took a seat on one of the large sofas. "But I would caution you to keep your feelings about him under wraps. He's bound to notice that you resent him—for obvious reasons—and until we've gotten a lay of the land and figured out who's still loyal to you, you don't want to draw his wrath on you."

As much as Cain wanted to dispute Thomas's words, he couldn't. As so often, the wise vampire had hit the nail on the head. It was important to refrain from starting an open war over a woman whose motives Cain wasn't even sure of. What if Faye was playing them both?

Slowly he lowered himself back into his chair. "What are you suggesting, Thomas?"

"Play nice with your brother for a while. It doesn't mean you have to trust him. In the meantime we'll launch the investigation into the attempt on your life. Somebody is bound to know something. And now that you're back, everybody will want to get back in your good graces. Let's turn that to your advantage," Thomas suggested.

"Very well," Cain said, when a knock at the door interrupted him. "Come."

A middle-aged vampire carrying a serving tray with several glasses of red liquid entered and inclined his head toward Cain. "Your Majesty, the blood you ordered."

"Thank you, uh." He wanted to address the vampire by his name, but couldn't. "On the coffee table please." When the man turned his back to bend down and place the tray on the table, Cain shot Haven a look. Luckily his friend understood immediately.

"What's your name?" Haven asked casually and reached for a glass.

The vampire straightened. "I'm Robert. I'm the master of supplies for the palace and have been so for many years," he said with pride in his voice.

Cain rose and walked to the seating area. "It's good to see you again, Robert."

"It's good to see you well, sir." Despite the friendly words, Cain sensed some apprehension rolling off Robert.

"Thank you, Robert."

The vampire nodded, then looked at Wesley. "I ordered human food for you. Should I bring it as soon as it arrives?"

"Oh, yeah, I'm starving here!" Wes confirmed.

With an acknowledging nod, Robert turned to the door and left. Cain joined his friends and snatched a glass of blood from the tray. He set it to his lips and took a sip. Within seconds, he'd emptied the glass. Instantly he felt better. So far his bluff had worked. Nobody had an inkling that he suffered from amnesia. And the way things looked at the moment, nobody would ever have to find out. Whatever obstacles lay in his way, he would manage to overcome them.

"Let's get to work."

18

Faye walked through the hallway and noticed several guards waiting outside of the king's office. The door to it was closed.

"Marcus," she called out to one of them, who immediately looked in her direction and gave a short nod. "Is Abel with the king?"

"No, I believe he's outside in the garden."

"Thank you."

Taking a deep breath, Faye walked through the entrance hall and opened the door to get outside, past the two guards who flanked the door. She might as well get this over with or it would be looming over her all night.

Outside humid night air greeted her. A million stars hung in the night sky and the moon was still almost full, bathing the palace's grounds in enough light that even a human would not have needed an artificial light source to find his way around.

Faye glanced around the veranda, but Abel wasn't sitting in any of the comfortable chairs that dotted the porch. She'd loved sitting here with Cain when he'd had a moment to take a break from his business as king. She'd cherished those short moments where he'd shared his vision for the kingdom with her, before withdrawing again to implement whatever changes he thought would bring the clan further into the twenty-first century.

With a sigh, she walked around the palace, remaining on the porch that wrapped around the entire building. Maybe Abel was at the back of it, enjoying the beautiful evening. Her light summer dress clung to her skin, though she couldn't entirely blame the Louisiana humidity for it. She knew she perspired for other reasons. It was anxiety that made her skin feel clammy.

The back porch was empty too, and Faye was about to turn back, when she perceived a movement from the corner of her eye. She shifted her gaze to the area that had caught her attention: the white gazebo that stood several dozens of yards out in the vast garden, surrounded by bushes to lend it some privacy.

Knowing that the guards rarely ventured there because Abel had declared the place his own personal domain, Faye stepped down from the porch and strolled along the walkway leading to it, the sound of her flat shoes absorbed by the soft moss beneath her feet.

Apprehension rose the closer she got to the gazebo. She'd practiced her speech while in her room, but now that she was about to face Abel, her throat was dry. She took a deep breath. With it, the scent of human blood filled her nostrils.

Abel wasn't alone.

Faye stopped in her approach, but it was too late. Abel had already lifted his head and spotted her. His fangs were extended and dripped with blood.

"I'm sorry. I didn't mean to disturb," she said hastily and attempted to turn.

"Don't go. I'm done anyway," he claimed and waved her to join him.

She crossed the remaining distance and took the three steps that led up to the gazebo. Comfortable benches lined the interior of the wooden structure, and on one of them a human woman was stretched out, her clothes disheveled and two puncture wounds gracing her neck. Abel had been feeding.

"Apologies," he said lightly, then bent down to the woman again and licked his tongue over the spot where his fangs had been lodged only moments earlier.

The woman didn't stir, though her eyes were open. She was under his thrall, made numb by mind control. Every vampire possessed this skill, although Faye herself rarely used it. She had little contact with humans, preferring to remain in the safety of the palace's grounds. And using mind control on another vampire was an undertaking fraught with deadly risk.

Abel wiped his mouth with a handkerchief and pointed to the girl. "Would you like some?"

Quickly Faye shook her head. She preferred the packaged blood stored in the refrigerated cellar of the palace. "Can we talk in private?"

"We are in private," he said with a sideways glance at the woman who'd provided him with sustenance. Whether willingly or not, Faye couldn't tell.

She'd always known that Abel had never given up feeding from humans directly, whereas Cain had substantially reduced the incidences of feeding from a human, and then refrained from it completely when she and Cain had become lovers. Almost as if he'd wanted to show her that he didn't need to feel the sexual high that accompanied a feeding. Instead he'd switched entirely to packaged blood, and then, that last fateful night when he'd disappeared, he'd taken Faye's blood for the first time. Not to nourish his body, but his heart.

Faye pushed the memory away, not wanting to be reminded of how happy she'd been then. And how different everything was now. Cain's rejection when she'd snuck into his bedroom stung as much as it was confusing.

She turned away from the human girl and Abel. "I'm sure what I'm going to tell you won't come as a surprise."

Faye heard him rise from the bench and take a step toward her.

"No, it doesn't."

"I still love him. I never stopped loving him, and you knew that when you asked me to marry you." She swallowed, trying to moisten her dry throat. "Had I known he was alive, you know that I would have never agreed."

Abel's hands cupped her shoulders and she flinched at the contact. "You don't need to say anything else, Faye. I know how you feel. And I'm not going to stand in your way."

Choking up, she turned around.

Abel smiled at her. "Oh, Faye, did you really think I would keep you to your promise? Of course, I'll release you. I would be fooling myself if I thought that you could ever love me the way you love him." Then he dropped his lids. "I just wish I could protect you from the heartache you're going to face."

"Heartache?" she echoed. "He's alive. He's back." She hesitated, wondering whether Abel referred to the coldness with which Cain had greeted her. "It will take a little while until everything will be like before."

Abel stroked over her hair as if comforting a child. She'd never seen him so gentle.

"He's changed. You've noticed it, too, haven't you?" he asked.

"A year in captivity can do terrible things to a person." She knew that from her own experience. "Whatever wounds he has will heal." And she would be by Cain's side and wait as long as it took. As long as there was hope that he still loved her, she would wait for him to come back to her.

Abel sighed. "I spoke to him last night before he retired. Brother to brother."

Faye lifted her lids and looked at him. "About what?"

"I told him about us."

His confession didn't come as a surprise to her. Cain had confirmed as much.

"He didn't demand from me that I break our engagement. It surprised me. You know him. You know what he was like before. You couldn't have chosen a prouder and more possessive man than Cain. When he congratulated me on our upcoming wedding, frankly, I was stunned."

Faye's heart started to beat uncontrollably. "But . . ." Why would he do that?

"I think he's changed more than we can know. I didn't ask him what happened. I think he wasn't ready to tell me. But . . ." Abel's gaze drifted past her.

Anxiety tore through her. "What?"

"I think there might be another woman," Abel finally said and met her eyes.

It felt as if somebody had plunged a knife into her heart. "No," she managed to choke out.

"Listen, Faye, I can't be a hundred percent certain, and I truly hope that I'm wrong, but the way his men talked . . . I shouldn't have eavesdropped, but Cain's strange behavior worried me." Abel dropped his hands from her shoulders.

Faye shook her head in disbelief. Cain had another woman? "No, that can't be." She didn't want to believe it.

"Maybe I misunderstood what they were talking about. But it sounded like they were discussing when to bring her to court and present her to the clan." Abel turned his back to her. "I'm sorry, Faye. I wish I had better news. I'm worried about Cain. Whatever happened to him during the last year, it might have changed entirely who he is. What if he's being unduly influenced by the men who're now his guards, or by the woman they talked about? I'm worried for the clan."

Faye barely heard the words, because all she could think of was what had happened in Cain's room. He'd punished her for not having waited for him and then he'd rejected her. He'd been so angry and mistrusting of her. She'd felt it in her bones. Just like she'd been keenly aware of the absence of affection in his gaze. Had he stopped loving her because he'd fallen in love with another woman?

A sob tore from her chest before she could suppress it.

"Oh, God, Faye, it pains me to see you hurt," Abel said.

A moment later she felt his arms around her, pressing her to his chest.

"Don't do anything hasty. Maybe I'm wrong and he still loves you, but I couldn't help but notice the indifference with which he greeted you yesterday."

So Abel had seen it, too.

"What am I going to do?" she sobbed.

"Give him some space," Abel counseled. "Show him that you're not pressuring him. I can tell you from my own experience that no man wants a needy woman. Don't show your feelings. It will only make things worse."

She nodded, desperately trying to dry her tears. By visiting Cain in his suite she'd probably already made a huge mistake, but she couldn't tell Abel about it. She needed no confirmation of her own stupidity.

Why hadn't she read the signs Cain had so clearly exhibited upon his arrival? Why hadn't she seen that his love for her had died?

19

"There's not much point in interrogating the guards who were with me yesterday."

Cain stared at Marcus who sat in the chair in front of his desk. "Meaning what exactly?"

"They're new recruits. That's the reason they didn't recognize you. They came to us after your disappearance. Abel hired them," Marcus informed him. "I apologize again for the attack, but from where I was I didn't see your face. Had I known it was you—"

Cain lifted his hand to interrupt him. "Well, that explains why I didn't recognize them either," Cain lied. "When we're done here, give Wesley their names. I'll have my men do a background check on them."

"But that's already been done," Marcus protested.

"Not by me." He motioned to Wesley, who was leaning against the wall, watching them. "Wes, you know what to do."

The witch nodded. "I'll take care of it."

Cain glanced to the other end of the room, where Thomas had set up his computer and was busy typing away on his keyboard. Haven had left the room and was canvassing the property, familiarizing himself with its layout and inhabitants.

"Now back to you," Cain said and looked down at the pad where he'd noted down the vampire guard's answers to his previous questions. "Why were you in the French Quarter the night of my abduction?"

"It was my night off."

Cain looked back at his notes and scanned them until he found what he was looking for. He tapped on the paper with his pen. "You said earlier that your regular night off is Wednesday. I was abducted on a Monday."

Marcus dropped his lids. "I will regret for as long as I live that I wasn't there that night. I shouldn't have done it. Maybe if I hadn't, I could have prevented it."

Cain narrowed his eyes, suspicion creeping up his spine like a snake. "Done what?

"I asked Baltimore to change shifts with me."

"Why?"

Marcus shifted uncomfortably in his seat. "The woman I was seeing back then begged me to visit her that night. And I was a fool in love not to be able to resist her. So I asked Baltimore to change shifts with me."

"Why Baltimore?"

Marcus shrugged. "He'd mentioned earlier that he wanted to attend some concert on Wednesday night and was pissed that you wouldn't let him have the night off. So I figured he'd be willing to switch. I'm sorry."

Surprised that he'd been such a strict ruler, not granting his guards a night off when it didn't seem to make a difference which guard was on duty, Cain leaned back in his chair and steepled his fingers. "Tell me something else, Marcus."

The vampire lifted his head.

"In your opinion, did I treat all of you, the guards, fair and just?" With bated breath he waited for Marcus's reply. Had he maybe been a bad ruler, and one of his guards had taken it upon himself to remove him? Who else could have had unfettered access to him and known where he was at all times?

"I never had any complaints."

"And the others?"

"Not to my knowledge."

"What's your opinion of John?"

"John?"

"Yes, the leader of the king's guard. What's your feeling about him?" Cain pressed.

"I would never say a bad word about him," Marcus replied quickly. "Nobody would."

"Why is that?"

Marcus shot up from his chair. "There's no need trying to trick me. No matter my feelings about John, you know as well as everybody else at court that insulting John would be insulting you personally. Even before you became king, offending one of you meant offending both of you."

Cain pondered Marcus's passionate statement. "Even before I was king, you say?"

Marcus cast him a guarded look, but answered nevertheless. "When you were leader of the king's guard, John was always there to back you up. That's why you made him leader of the king's guard when you became king a couple of years ago."

He'd been leader of the king's guards once? Cain had always assumed that he'd been king for a long time, but according to Marcus he'd only been on the throne for a short time before the assassination attempt.

"Thank you, Marcus. I appreciate your candor. On your way out, Wes will take down the names of the new guards."

Cain turned away and walked to the window, staring out into the darkness. How had he risen from leader of the king's personal guard to king? He'd assumed that he was from a royal line and had ascended to the throne because he was a member of the aristocracy. However, it appeared that he was a warrior like the guards around him. No wonder he'd felt at home with Scanguards. Protecting others ran in his blood. How long had he been a guard? And under what circumstances had he become king?

He turned away from the window and saw Marcus walk to the door. "One more thing, Marcus."

The man looked over his shoulder. "Yes?"

"Make a list for me of all the guards who were in my service while I was leader of the king's guards and are still in the court's service today."

"It will be on your desk shortly." Marcus opened the door and stepped outside.

Before the door could close fully behind him, another person entered: Abel.

"Hope I'm not disturbing, Cain, but I just wanted a quick word. May I?"

Cain waved his hand to invite him into the room. The door closed behind Abel who gave a friendly nod in Thomas's direction, then greeted Wesley. "I hope Robert's order of human food was appropriate."

"It was great, thanks," Wes answered.

"Excellent," Abel said and finally turned to Cain. "I know you're busy, so I won't take much of your time."

"What can I do for you?" Cain walked back to his desk and motioned his brother to sit down.

Abel declined the invitation with a movement of his hand. "I only want to share an idea with you. As you know, in a week, my coronation would have taken place, which of course under the circumstances is cancelled."

Cain felt his heartbeat kick up a notch, curious as to why his brother had to remind him that the rightful king's reappearance had upset Abel's plans of taking the throne. "Yes?"

"Well, a lot of the arrangements have been made, and we've already incurred considerable expenses for this large gathering. Many vampires have been invited and have made travel arrangements, and I was wondering—"

"You were wondering what?" Cain ground out impatiently.

"Why don't we repurpose the event and turn it into a welcome home celebration for you instead?"

Taken by surprise by Abel's suggestion, Cain was speechless for a moment.

"I mean," Abel added, "why not let the entire kingdom see that you're back? I'm sure they'll want to see it with their own eyes. It would be a wonderful opportunity to express their loyalty to you and know that everything will return to how it was. What do you say?"

Cain was touched by his brother's thoughtfulness and wondered if he'd misjudged him. His words seemed to suggest that losing the throne that had already been within his reach didn't upset Abel. "I think it's a great idea."

"Excellent!" Abel exclaimed. "And may I suggest one more thing?"

Cain encouraged him with a nod.

"Why not invite the Mississippi clan?"

"Uh," Cain said, hesitating, since he didn't know anything about a Mississippi clan. John hadn't mentioned them during the flight to New Orleans.

Abel raised his hand. "I know what you want to say, but hear me out. While you were gone they've reached out to us, wanting friendlier relations between the clans and lay to rest the border disputes we've had. I think inviting them to your welcome home party would be a generous show of our willingness to forgive their prior infractions and make peace."

"Hmm." Cain rubbed his chin in an attempt to look as if he was contemplating the matter. Which in a way he was. If there was truly another clan out there that his kingdom had had difficulties with previously, it might indeed be advantageous to bury the hatchet with them. It was hard enough to figure out who in his own clan was loyal to him. He didn't need a war with another clan on his hands.

"Fine," he finally said. "Invite them on my behalf and tell them they are welcome if they come in peace. I'm willing to discuss terms with them."

With every word, Cain felt more like a fraud. He knew he was winging it, faking it. When would his brother or another member of his royal household figure out that he had no memory of his former life? And when they did, what would they do? Would the assassin strike again, encouraged by the fact that Cain didn't know who to trust? And Abel, would he want to rip the reigns from Cain's hands, suspecting that Cain wasn't capable of ruling the kingdom because he suffered from amnesia?

But most of all, how would Faye react? Would she see him as weak, too?

20

Faye had spent a restless day in bed, trying to sleep, but sleep was elusive. She'd listened for any sound while everybody slept, but the sound of the door opening and Cain entering hadn't come. He had made no attempt to see her, neither after he'd finished interrogating his guards nor after he'd retired to his suite. It only amplified her belief that he had lost interest in her and was in love with somebody else.

Determined to act, she rose in the early evening hours and started what she knew she couldn't drag out any longer.

After organizing a few boxes, Faye now placed a handful of bras in one which she'd set on the chair at the foot of the bed, emptying out the top drawer of her dresser. She was about to close the drawer, when her gaze fell onto the trinkets sitting on top of the dresser. Mementos from her life with Cain, the few short weeks that they'd been happy together.

"What is this?"

Faye whirled around and saw Cain standing at the open door to her bedroom, his finger pointing at the moving box she'd been filling with her things.

Her chest tightened with longing. He looked as handsome as the night he'd left her bed and disappeared. As virile. As desirable. And she wasn't the only one who thought so. She'd always known that, of course. That's why Abel's suspicion that Cain had found another woman wasn't all that far fetched. Cain attracted women like mosquitoes swarming toward a bright light.

"Cain, I'm sorry. I will be out of here shortly," she said, avoiding his gaze.

"Out of here?" he repeated and stepped in the room, shutting the door behind him.

"Yes, I'll be moving out of the queen's quarters. It's really not appropriate any longer for me to be here." Not after Cain had rejected her not twenty-four hours earlier. She had to face facts, and staying in this room any longer and fooling herself that things would work out was stupid.

His face remained impassive, though his jaw seemed to tighten. "So you've decided to stay with Abel then."

Her forehead furrowed. Why would he think that? Hadn't she told him already that she didn't love his brother? "I broke off the engagement with him." It had been a great relief, despite the words of caution Abel had imparted on her.

Faye turned back to the dresser and gripped the handles, but before she could shut the drawer, Cain was behind her and captured her hands with his, immobilizing her.

"Then why are you packing?"

His breath ghosted over her skin, making her shiver. She wanted nothing more than to lean back against his strong chest and let him catch her, but instead she remained stiff and unmoving. She couldn't allow herself to be weak. It would only make it harder to leave.

"Because it changes nothing. I have no right to live in this suite anymore."

"I see." He released her hands and stepped back.

Faye pulled a deep breath into her lungs, hoping it would strengthen her, but it had the opposite effect. It made her only more aware of his presence and of what she'd lost.

She changed the subject. "I'm happy that you're alive and have returned to us. Your clan needs you."

"How about you?" Cain asked unexpectedly.

"I'm not important now that you're back."

"Why do you say that?"

Faye sighed. "Because it's the truth. I don't belong here. It's time I realized that and moved on."

Cain's hands on her shoulders turned her to face him. "You're planning to leave the kingdom?"

She nodded, her heart getting heavier by the second. "Not this minute, of course. I have to make arrangements first. If it's all right with you, I'll stay another week or two until I've sorted things out and know where to go."

"You can't just leave."

A sad smile stole onto her lips. She appreciated that he was decent enough to make an attempt at convincing her to stay. "In the end it will be better for all involved." She would never be able to bear it to have to meet the new woman he would eventually install in the palace.

"Better for whom?" he ground out.

Surprised at his harsh tone, Faye looked at him and noticed the tempest that seemed to rage in his eyes.

"I'm sorry. I can see that my presence upsets you, and that's the last thing I want."

"It's not your presence that upsets me, but your words," he corrected her. "Why do you want to leave?"

"Isn't that obvious?" she asked. Because to her it was. "You made it clear to me when I came to you that you don't want me anymore."

Cain studied her with his dark eyes. "It's not that simple." He shoved a hand through his hair and turned away from her. "I've been away for a long time. I'm not the same man anymore."

Her heart bled for him. What horrors had he endured during his captivity?

"Much happened while I was gone. Things I can't explain right now."

Faye pressed her lips together so she wouldn't cry. As much as she wanted to know what had happened to him so she could help him heal, she couldn't bear the thought that he'd confess that he'd met another woman and fallen in love with her.

"I can't pretend that the last twelve months didn't happen, don't you see that, Faye?"

She nodded to herself. "That's why it's better that I'm leaving now," she concluded. "So you can be free to do as you please." So he could bring the woman he loved. "To start a new life."

"A new life."

Faye pushed back the tears that became more urgent with every second. "I'm sorry, Cain, I need to . . . I have to . . ." Unable to complete her sentence, she tried to dash past him, but his hand clamped over her upper arm and pulled her back.

"I want my old life back," he said, his eyes boring into hers as if she had the key to it.

Cain wasn't the same man anymore. She could see that now so clearly. He'd changed. Whatever he'd been through had made him more inscrutable. Where she'd previously been able to interpret his state of mind, she now met with an obsidian wall that was as impenetrable as Fort Knox. And as well guarded as the White House.

Cain was hiding his feelings from her.

No, she wouldn't be his toy to play with as he pleased. She'd loved him too much to allow him to destroy her love for him.

With her last ounce of strength, she ran past him, fleeing her room without another glance back.

Cain cursed and swiveled on his heel. Seeing her with tears in her eyes felt like somebody had driven a stake through his heart. He couldn't deny that he felt something for Faye, that despite the misgivings he had about her, he was drawn to her like to no other woman. To hear that she wanted to leave had felt like a punch in the gut.

He couldn't allow it. Faye had to stay.

Cain ran out the door, chasing her down the corridor. He followed her scent up the stairs and through the entrance hall. The two guards at the door tossed him surprised glances, but he ignored them and ran past them.

The humid night air hit him as if he'd stepped into a sauna. His eyes scanned the grounds. He spotted her as she ran past a copse of trees. He sprinted toward her, reaching her within a few seconds. He captured her in his arms and turned her to him.

"Please let me go, Cain!" she begged.

She struggled for a moment, but then all resistance seemed to drain from her, and sobs filled the silence of the night.

"I can't let you go," Cain said and turned her to him, holding her close and pressing her head against his chest.

A few yards away, under the copse of trees, he noticed a bench. He lifted her into his arms and walked to it, lowering himself onto it with Faye in his lap. He pressed her head against his chest and caressed her hair.

"Don't cry." He placed kisses on her head, wanting desperately to soothe her sorrows. "I'm sorry for having upset you. I didn't mean to. Please, Faye, don't leave."

She lifted her head. Pink tears ran down her cheeks, and he wiped them away with the pad of his thumb.

"I can't stay. It hurts too much."

He pushed a strand of her dark hair behind her ear and stroked his thumb over her soft skin. "Tell me what hurts," he said softly.

She lowered her lids, avoiding his gaze. But he didn't allow it and lifted her chin with his thumb and index finger and made her look at him. "Please help me understand you."

He gazed into her eyes. Was all this an act she was putting on for him so he would take her back now that she'd broken it off with Abel, or was what he saw the real Faye? Did she really want him for his own sake, or was she coming back to him because he was king?

And did it even matter? Wasn't it enough to have a woman like Faye by his side, in his bed?

"It hurts too much to have lost your love."

He sighed. If he were a different man, he would tell her now that he loved her whether he did or not. But he couldn't profess something he wasn't sure was the truth. "A year is a long time. We've both changed, Faye. We need time to readjust."

Her lips trembled. "You're punishing me because I accepted Abel's proposal. You feel that I betrayed you."

Cain shook his head. "I'm not punishing you. I'm trying to understand why you decided to marry him when you don't love him."

"I know what it must look like. But it's not like that. I didn't do it for myself."

Curious, he said, "I don't understand."

"As queen I would have had influence."

Cain closed his eyes. So she wanted the power her position as queen would have afforded her. He felt the blood in his veins turn to ice. How could he be drawn to a woman like that? A woman without a heart? Was that truly his destiny? Had he loved a heartless woman in his past life? What did that make him? A heartless man?

"Your brother is less lenient a ruler than you are," Faye continued. "Somebody has to make sure the members of our clan were treated fairly."

Her words made him open his eyes and furrow his forehead.

"They need somebody to look out for them."

The implication of her words finally sank in. But could he trust her words? "You were doing this for the clan?"

"I wanted to continue what you'd started."

Cain brought his face closer to hers. Was she telling him the truth?

Her breath bounced against him and he inhaled her scent. A vision of two naked bodies entangled in silk sheets appeared before his eyes. Soft moans and sounds of pleasure drifted to his ears.

"And now that I told you my reasons, please let me go. I can't stay here, not when you're going to bring another woman here to make her your queen."

"What?"

Faye tried to get off his lap, but he didn't let her. He needed to find out what she was talking about.

"Cain!"

Cain whipped his head in the direction of the voice. Haven was marching toward them.

"I'm sorry to disturb," Haven started.

"Not now!" Cain ground out, while Faye scrambled to get off his lap. This time he couldn't stop her.

"You said you wanted to be notified the minute John is back."

Cain jumped up. This was extremely bad timing. "Where is he?"

"Waiting for you in your office," Haven announced, casting a quick glance at Faye.

Cain turned to her and took a step closer. He lowered his voice. "We'll talk about this later. Don't make any hasty decisions."

When she didn't answer, he turned to Haven.

"Let's go."

21

Putting aside Faye's odd statement about another woman, Cain stormed into his office. John stood near the fireplace, while Thomas leaned against the backrest of the sofa, watching him.

Behind Cain, Haven closed the door and remained standing there.

Jaw tight, Cain walked up to John. "Where the fuck were you?"

"I apologize, but I had to attend to an emergency," John responded, his face unreadable.

"You left me on my own in those tunnels! And we had to come here without the benefit of your guidance. This had better be some fucking big emergency. You should have told me!" Cain ground out.

John dropped his head. "I couldn't. You wouldn't have approved."

"Explain yourself!"

"I have a human lover. In the French Quarter."

"What's that got to do with what I approve or don't approve?"

"The leader of the king's personal guard isn't supposed to have a private life, let alone be involved with a human. You never approved of vampire-human relationships."

"And how the fuck would I have known that?" Cain stabbed his finger into John's chest. "Amnesia, remember?"

"I'm sorry, I just assumed that your feelings and preferences would still be the same, no matter whether you remembered anything about your past life or not. It's part of your character."

"Well, guess what: I don't care who you sleep with! But I do care about you doing a disappearing act on me without an explanation!"

John gave him a stunned look, as if he couldn't believe his ears. "You *have* changed."

"Don't stall! Why did you leave?"

"My lover was in trouble."

Cain narrowed his eyes in suspicion. "What kind of trouble?"

"She was attacked by several thugs and injured. She needed my blood to heal."

Cain contemplated John's words. "Why didn't she go to a hospital?"

"They stabbed her in the womb. She was scared that the doctors wouldn't be able to save her." He looked down at his feet. "She wants children. Giving her my blood guaranteed that she healed completely. At the hospital she would have had only a fifty-fifty chance. I couldn't risk them performing a hysterectomy."

Stunned by his confession, Cain blew out a breath. "Are you blood-bonded?"

John shook his head. "No, but I was planning to once Abel was on the throne and I had passed on my knowledge to him. I knew he had another man in mind to become the leader of his personal guard. It would have freed me from my duties. I could have taken a wife then."

"And now that I'm back?" Cain asked, calmer now.

John looked straight at him. "I'll remain in your service. Nothing will change."

"And the woman?"

"She's healed."

Cain shook his head. "No, I meant, what will happen between you and her?"

"I will have to end it with her."

"Why did I not want the leader of the king's guard to have a wife?"

"You weren't the one to make this rule. The kings before you established this restriction. They wanted to make sure that their personal guard has no divided loyalties."

"A little old fashioned, don't you think?" Cain asked and motioned to Thomas and Haven. "Both of my friends here are blood-bonded. And it hasn't diminished their capacity to execute their duties."

"You mean you would consider changing the rule?" John stared at him in disbelief.

"Consider it abolished. Every man has a right to happiness."

John's chest lifted, and he tried to say something, but seemed to stumble over his own words. "I don't know what to say," he finally uttered. "Had I known . . ."

"Well, then we're in agreement. And the next time there's an emergency, I need to know immediately, no matter what you might assume my reaction may be. And I'd like to meet the woman. What's her name?"

"Nicolette."

"Good, now about my welcome home celebration."

John's forehead furrowed. "What celebration?"

"My brother is throwing me a party in a week. It should have been his coronation, but instead it'll turn into a welcome home party for me. It'll give me an opportunity to meet all my subjects. I'm counting on you to help me. I don't want people to get suspicious when I don't know who they are."

"Of course," John said quickly. "I'll be by your side all the way."

"Good." Cain patted him on the shoulder. "That's all for now."

"Thank you." John walked to the door and left.

A moment of silence followed, before Cain turned to his two friends. "Contact Eddie and have him and Blake check out his story."

"You don't believe his story about a human lover?" Thomas asked.

"Oh, the human lover I believe. But not the rest. The story was just a little too convenient for my liking. Have Eddie and Blake find Nicolette and get her to corroborate his story. Then ask them to come to the palace. We won't need them on the outside anymore. It's better if they stay at the palace. We need all the men we can get."

Thomas nodded in agreement. "I'll call him."

Cain walked to the door.

"What are you up to?" Haven asked.

Cain tossed a glance over his shoulder. "Finishing my conversation with Faye."

Haven grinned. "Didn't look like a conversation from where I was standing."

"And your point is?"

"I wasn't trying to make a point."

"What then?"

"Just giving you some advice which you'll probably ignore anyway."

"Which would be?"

"If you must use your dick, at least keep a clear head and watch your back. The assassin will strike when your guard is down. Don't give him that opportunity."

Cain shook his head. "My guard is always up."

"You didn't hear me approach when you were in the garden with her," Haven contradicted him.

Cain ground his teeth in frustration, knowing that Haven was right. "It won't happen again."

22

Faye was glad to find a distraction waiting for her when she reached the fully enclosed walkway that connected the palace to the old plantation kitchen. Like so many old plantations, the kitchen had been a separate building due to the fire hazard it represented. The vampires who'd first taken over the property had enclosed the walkway with drywall so they could reach the small freestanding structure during daylight hours without being burned by the rays of the sun. Few people ever used the kitchen, but Faye liked its cozy feel and often came here just to sit and read, or simply to think.

At the entrance to the walkway two strangers stood waiting. She immediately recognized them as vampires, but they weren't of the Louisiana clan. Even though she didn't know every member of the vast clan, their haggard looks led her to believe they had fled another clan. They weren't the first ones who'd come to her door to ask for help.

The man looked in his fifties in human years, the girl less than half his age, though Faye couldn't tell how many years they had been vampires already. When the girl pressed herself closer to her companion, her eyes darting around fearfully, Faye slowed her walk and raised her hand.

"Don't be afraid. You're welcome here."

The older man nodded at her. "We were told that you might be able to help us."

"I'm Faye. Where have you come from?" Faye asked and unlocked the door leading into the walkway.

"From Mississippi. I'm David, and this is Kathryn."

"Come." She motioned them to follow her. "I can give you blood."

"Thank you," David said and followed her with the girl in tow.

Faye marched into the kitchen and opened the refrigerator. "What happened to you?" She turned to look at them, noting their torn clothes and dirty appearances. As if they'd lived on the streets for days.

"The unrest in Mississippi continues," David explained, his voice sounding hoarse and dry. "We couldn't stay any longer."

"You look like you haven't had any blood in days." Faye grabbed two cartons of packaged blood and placed them on the table, before turning to the hanging cabinet and retrieving two glasses. "Take a seat, please."

Kathryn looked like she would collapse and followed Faye's invitation immediately, for the first time opening her mouth. "Thank you." Her scrawny arms reached for the container. She unscrewed the top, but instead of pouring it into the glass, she drank it directly from the carton.

Faye watched as she greedily devoured the liquid and glanced at David, who wasn't touching his container of blood. "Drink."

He reached for the carton and pushed it toward Kathryn. "Kathryn can have mine."

Surprised at his selflessness, Faye sucked in a shallow breath. "There's more." She retrieved another carton of blood from the refrigerator and handed it to the skinny older vampire.

David cast her a grateful smile and finally accepted the blood. Faye waited patiently until he'd had his fill. What horrors had these two endured to cause them to flee their clan? She looked at the girl. Now that her cheeks filled with color again, Faye could see that she was pretty. She closed her eyes for a moment, recalling the horrors she herself had experienced. Wanting to comfort the girl, she put her hand on her forearm, but Kathryn shrieked and jerked back, jumping up from her chair in panic.

"I'm sorry," Faye said quickly.

David stood up and slowly walked to the girl, who seemed frightened beyond comprehension.

"Everything is all right, little one," he coaxed and drew her into his arms. Then he looked over his shoulder. "I'm sorry, she doesn't trust anyone but me."

With pity in her heart, Faye looked at the girl. "What happened?"

Slowly, David led the girl back to the table and they both sat down. "The different factions in Mississippi are committing terrible acts. Those who try to flee and are captured are defanged, trying to prevent them from escaping again." He opened his mouth wide.

Faye recoiled, slapping her hand over her mouth. Where the vampire's fangs should be were gaping holes. "Oh, my God!" No wonder the two of them were starving. Without fangs they couldn't hunt for blood. They were dependent on handouts.

"They make sure the fangs don't grow back during our restorative sleep by implanting a pea-sized ball of steel. It's covered with a tiny spec of silver, just enough so the wound will never heal."

"What is this?" a male voice suddenly thundered from the door.

Faye's gaze shot to him, as did those of her guests. Baltimore, Abel's personal guard, filled the entire door frame and glared at her, his finger pointing at the empty containers of blood.

David and Kathryn had already jumped up from the table and retreated into the far corner of the kitchen. Faye now rose from her chair, slowly and deliberately. She wouldn't allow Baltimore to intimidate her.

"None of your business," she shot back. "Get out!"

But the bully didn't heed her warning and stepped inside the kitchen. "I see, we're handing out blood again." He motioned to the two needy vampires. "We have nothing for you here, do you understand? Go begging someplace else!" He took another step.

Faye jumped in his path. "Leave them alone. I can give them as much blood as I want to! Your intimidation tactics aren't working!"

He narrowed his eyes at her and growled. "You fucking bitch!"

When he grabbed her and pushed her back against the table, she was utterly unprepared for the assault.

"Abel forbids it!" Baltimore lifted his arm again to strike.

Faye jerked her leg up to knee him in the balls, but hit air when the hulky vampire was pulled back and tumbled. When he fell backward, her eyes fell on the man behind him: Cain, his fangs extended and murder in his eyes.

"Abel is not the king! I am!" Cain tackled Baltimore and pinned him to the ground, a silver knife pointed at his jugular. "You touch my bride one more time, and you'll find yourself with a stake in the heart."

Cain pressed the knife closer to the other vampire's skin, making it sizzle. The scent of burned hair and flesh permeated the kitchen.

"And now, you're going to get up and leave my property. If I ever lay eyes on you again, you'll regret it."

Cain jumped up and waited until Baltimore got to his feet. His jaw clenched tightly, he glared at Cain, then glanced past him at Faye. The threat in his look was clear. He blamed her for his fate and would harm her first chance he got. Only when Baltimore turned and left the room did Faye pull in a breath. Only now Cain's words truly sank in. He'd called her his bride. Did this mean he still wanted her after all, or had he simply used the term to make his point with Baltimore?

Cain turned to her, crossing the distance between them with two steps, and looked her up and down. "Are you okay? Did he hurt you?"

She'd endured much worse. "I'm fine." She studied his face, when a soft smile curved his lips upward.

"Good." Then he looked past her at David and Kathryn. "Would you introduce me to your friends, please?"

23

Cain stared at the two gaunt vampires, still reeling over Baltimore's audacity to prevent Faye's charitable act. He'd met Abel's personal guard briefly the night before, and knew that his brother would be angry for having him banned from the palace. Not that Cain cared much about that. Faye's safety and well-being were more important.

He'd seen red when he'd seen Baltimore touch Faye, and at that moment he'd felt a protectiveness toward her that demanded that he crush the vampire. Short of committing bloody murder in front of Faye and two strangers, he'd used all his remaining self control and banned Baltimore from the palace.

"This is David and Kathryn," he heard Faye say now and pointed to the two vampires huddled in one corner of the kitchen. David looked at him with apprehension, while Kathryn's facial expression was one of pure fear.

"I mean you no harm," Cain assured them quickly but didn't approach, sensing that such an action would only scare them more. Instead he turned to Faye. "Why didn't Baltimore want you to give our guests any blood?"

Faye's lips curled in displeasure. "Because Abel is against handouts. He's forbidden everybody in the palace to give away blood." She sniffed, her chest heaving with outrage. "And these aren't even the palace's supplies. They're my personal ones. I had every right—"

Cain put a calming hand on her forearm and squeezed it. "Yes, you did."

But Faye wasn't done yet. "A few days ago he wanted to punish Robert, because it was discovered that a few pints of blood had gone missing from the cellars."

"What did he do to him?"

Faye dropped her gaze to the floor. "Nothing."

Cain felt his forehead furrow. "But you said he wanted to punish him."

"He did. I stopped him. Because he said . . ." She paused.

Cain shelved her chin and forced her to look at him. "Faye, please."

She took a breath before she answered. "He said if I were his queen, he'd be a more lenient king."

Cain's heart clenched. "That's how he got you to say yes?"

Faye didn't nod. She simply closed her eyes.

Without a word, he pulled her into an embrace. It was all so clear now. What Faye had told him earlier was true: she wanted to be queen to help her people. Each of her actions confirmed it. And her charity even extended to vampires outside the clan. She was kind to strangers and brave to stand up to bullies like Baltimore. Cain felt his chest fill with pride.

When Faye's arms came around him to squeeze him tightly, he welcomed her action. He pressed a kiss on the top of her head, when his eyes wandered back to the two vampires.

Reluctantly, he released Faye and addressed the two strangers. He noticed their torn and dirty clothes and realized that blood wasn't the only thing those two needed. "How may we help you?"

David bowed. "If it's not too much trouble, if you could provide us with shelter, only for a day or two, until we've rested sufficiently."

Cain nodded. "What happened to you?"

Faye put a hand on Cain's arm, making him turn back to her. "It's awful, Cain. They're fleeing their clan because of the awful conditions there." Then she lowered her voice as if she didn't want the two strangers to hear what she had to add, even though their vampire hearing would allow them to pick up her words anyway. "They were defanged. They have no way of hunting for blood. We have to do something."

Even without Faye's imploring look, Cain would have helped the two, but knowing that Faye wished to help them made the matter even more urgent.

"Are any of the cottages on the property currently vacant?" he asked her.

"One is empty because we were planning on renovating it, but it's livable in its current condition."

"Good." He looked at David. "I hope you'll stay longer than just two days. Where are you heading?"

David shrugged. "As far away from Mississippi as possible."

Cain's heart stopped. "Mississippi?"

"That's where our clan is."

Cain balled his hand into a fist and slammed it onto the kitchen table, making both David and Kathryn shrink farther back into their corner. "Damn Abel!"

Faye let out a stunned breath. "What is it?"

Cain clenched his jaw. "He convinced me to invite the Mississippi clan to my coming home celebrations to make peace with them." He sucked in a breath and pointed at the two vampires. "How can I make peace with a clan that does *this* to their people?"

"Why did you even agree to invite them?" Faye asked. "You know they don't share our values."

Should he have known this? Obviously the old Cain would have been aware of this. "I thought things had changed while I was gone. Abel suggested giving them another chance." Though it appeared now that maybe he shouldn't listen to anything Abel was suggesting.

"Nothing's changed," Faye replied. "They're just as cruel as they always were."

He'd have a word with Abel later. He motioned to David and Kathryn. "Let's get you settled so you can rest." Then he looked at Faye. "Will you show me which cottage is available?"

"Come!" she encouraged the two strangers and turned to the door.

As they all walked outside, Cain reached for Faye's hand. Her head immediately whipped to him, and her face indicated surprise.

He smiled at her while he brought her hand to his lips and pressed a soft kiss on its back. A hesitant smile was her reply. In companionable silence they walked around the palace toward the long driveway. Cain glanced at the cottages along the way and let Faye take the lead, while he enjoyed her warm hand in his.

"This is it." She pointed to a small wooden cottage that looked like all the others and walked to the entrance door, then turned to him. "I don't have a key."

For an instant Cain froze. Then he remembered the set of keys Abel had handed him on his first night back and pulled them from his pocket. He looked at the different keys but didn't know which one fit the lock of the cottage. When he hesitated, Faye pointed to one of the keys.

"This one."

"It's been a long time," he deflected, hoping she didn't find it odd that he couldn't remember which key to use, and unlocked the door.

The inside of the cottage was simple, but functional: two large rooms, one furnished as a living room, one as a bedroom, plus a small bathroom with a tub.

"I'll have one of the servants bring linen and towels," Faye said. Then she looked at the girl who was glancing around and making hesitant steps into the interior. "And I can bring you some clothes, Kathryn."

At the sound of her name, the girl spun around. Her breaths came irregularly, but when Faye just remained standing where she was, Kathryn started to visibly calm down. "Thank you."

David stretched his hand out to Cain. "I'm very grateful for your kindness, Your Majesty."

Cain took his hand and shook it. "Don't thank me. This is Faye's doing, not mine." From the corner of his eye he noticed Faye cast him a soft smile. "Rest. I'll have one of my people bring you everything you need."

Then he turned to the door and walked outside. Faye joined him a moment later. He took her hand. "Come."

Once out of earshot of the cottage, he addressed her again. "I didn't want to ask in front of them, but how were they defanged? Any injury would heal during their restorative sleep. Their fangs would grow back within a day."

Faye sighed. "Normally, yes, but these monsters implanted them with metal pellets where their fangs would re-grow and coated them with silver so that the wound can never heal. The constant pain must be excruciating."

Cain shuddered at the thought. "There must be something that can be done."

"We'd need a surgeon, but we don't have one. We have to bring them to a human surgeon, but it will be risky."

"That won't be necessary." Because Cain had just come up with the solution.

Faye turned to him, pleading, "But you can't let them continue to suffer like this. The girl is numb with pain. I can feel it."

Cain took her hands and drew her closer. "They're not going to suffer much longer. I know a physician. She's a vampire. I can bring Maya here to operate on them. Everything will be fine."

Faye's eyes widened. "Maya? Is that the woman you love?"

"Maya? God, no! Maya is a friend. And she's bonded to a magnificent man not even I would want to cross." Cain brought her clasped hands to his mouth and pressed a kiss on them. "Faye, there's no other woman. Why would you think there is?"

"But I heard that you fell in love with another woman."

"Who said that?"

Faye looked away, but he didn't have to be a genius to figure out who had put that bee in her bonnet.

"Abel?"

She turned her face back to him. "He said he'd overheard your men talking about a woman you wanted to bring back here."

"That's bullshit!" Anger about his brother's latest manipulation churned up in him.

"But why would he say that?"

"Because he wants to drive a wedge between us!" It was the only explanation. "He wants you back." Cain let out a bitter laugh. "And why wouldn't he? What man wouldn't get addicted once he's had you in his bed?" The dreams he'd had told him that he was addicted to it, too.

"But he's never had me!"

Cain froze. "What?"

"He never touched me. He wanted to but I couldn't . . ."

He raised his hand and caressed her cheek. "You remained faithful to me," he murmured, unable to believe his fortune. Leaning in, he brought his lips close to hers. "I want to get to know you again. Will you show me what it was like between us before I disappeared?" He touched her lips, giving her every chance to withdraw if she wanted to, but she didn't pull back.

"Oh, Cain, I missed you so much."

24

He'd given Marcus instructions to take care of the two newcomers, and now Cain closed the door to Faye's suite behind him, flipping the lock. His gaze traveled to Faye who stood near the fireplace and didn't move.

He didn't care that there was *king business* waiting for him. What he was about to do was more important than ruling a kingdom.

"Thank you for helping those two vampires," she murmured.

He walked to her with steady steps although his heart was thundering. "I want you to know that I didn't do it in order to get you into my bed."

Faye laughed softly and motioned to the bed. "That's my bed, not yours."

"Same difference." Having reached her, he braced his hands at either side of her head. "If I remember well, it never mattered much to me which bed I slept in as long as you were with me." At least that much he knew from his dreams.

"And sometimes it didn't even matter to you whether it was a bed." She glanced down at the bearskin rug at her feet.

Had they made love there before?

"Why don't you show me what you like best?" he suggested.

Her lips came closer, and her breath bounced against his mouth. "You know what I like best."

Cain wished he could remember, but no memory was forthcoming. So he did the only thing he could. He captured her lips and kissed her. Her lips yielded to him, parting at the slightest pressure, a soft sigh escaping her mouth, while one of her hands slid to his nape, sending a shiver down his spine and into his tailbone. A corresponding bolt traveled to his groin and ignited him there.

He'd hoped it would be like this ever since the moment she'd appeared in his dreams, but he'd never expected Faye's passion to engulf him so fully that he lost all sense of reality. This could only be a dream; nothing could feel so good in real life. Yet holding Faye in his arms and devouring her lips like a man dying of thirst felt more real than all of the dreams he'd had about her combined.

He felt his heart roar to life as if it had been dormant since the beginning of time. It beat against her chest, providing the echo to Faye's heartbeat. Just as rapidly as his, her heart thundered inside her ribcage trying to escape. His hand moved south to capture it, to finally feel her warm flesh in his palm. Soft flesh greeted him, filling his hand to its capacity. His thumb stroked over her peak, feeling it harden under his caress. But the fabric of her summer dress was still in his way, still preventing him from making contact with her skin.

Cain ripped his mouth from her, panting heavily. "Oh, God, Faye!" He gazed into her eyes. They were heavy-lidded, the passion in them undisguised. It made him hungry just looking at her.

He squeezed her breast in his palm, then captured her other one with his other hand. Faye leaned her head back against the wall and moaned.

"It's not enough," he ground out and took hold of the fabric. Without thinking, he ripped the top of her dress in two, exposing her breasts.

Faye gasped, her eyes widening in surprise.

Cain dropped his gaze, drinking in the sight. She wore no bra, and her generous breasts spilled into his waiting hands. The contact of skin on skin made his cock throb uncontrollably, thickening further.

"God damn it, Faye, take my cock out before I explode!" he ordered before he dropped his head to her breasts and captured one nipple in his mouth.

He sucked on the delicious bud and licked his tongue over it, when he finally felt her hands on his pants, popping the button open. Then one hand pressed against the length of his shaft, while the other pulled the zipper down.

He felt release when the tightness of his pants made way for cool air as she pulled his pants and boxer briefs lower so they rested mid-thigh. Impatient, he ground his cock against her hands.

"Cain, my love!" she murmured and wrapped one hand around his iron-hard erection and slid down on him.

Her nipple popped from his mouth. "Fuck!" If she continued to stroke him like this, he would spill in her hand in three seconds flat. "Don't!" He breathed heavily, pulling himself from her grip.

"What's wrong?"

"What's wrong?" he repeated. "Faye, I'm going to come instantly if you do that to me."

"But I'm barely touching you."

He stared into her eyes, bringing his head closer to hers. "You're like a new woman to me. As if I've never touched you before. This might be over faster than we both want."

Her finger retraced his lips. "In that case we'll just have to do it again and again until we're both satisfied with the outcome."

Cain smiled at her. "So you're not gonna toss me out on my ass if I don't get it right the first time?" Because for him, this would be the first time he made love to her. He had nothing to compare it with other than his dreams. Yet Faye would compare him to the old Cain.

"My love," she murmured, shaking her head as if to reprimand him. "You've never gotten it wrong. You know my body better than I do."

He grinned. "Well, in that case . . ." He slipped his shirt over his head and tossed it on the floor. Then he took hold of her dress again and ripped the remainder in two.

His eyes wandered lower. "You're wearing panties today." In his last dream, she'd been bare.

"That's because I wasn't expecting this."

Cain clicked his tongue. "You should always be expecting it. Day and night. Because a woman like you should have her legs spread and my cock inside her twenty-four-seven."

Faye tossed him a coquettish look. "Then why are you still talking?"

"Good point," he acknowledged and took her lips again.

He remembered the dream where he'd taken her against the wall, but this wasn't how he wanted to take her for the first time. He needed her underneath him.

Kissing her hard, he lifted her into his arms and brought her down onto the bearskin rug before he released her, kicked his shoes off, and made quick work of his pants and socks. He wanted nothing to impede his movements.

Faye's hands reached for him to draw him down to her and he complied, sliding between her spread legs. Only her tiny panties now covered the precious spot at the apex of her thighs, yet didn't prevent the scent of her arousal from spreading in the room. His nostrils flared when they filled with the tantalizing aroma.

With his knuckles he rubbed against the fabric, making her jolt. "Easy, baby," he murmured. "I'll give you everything you need." Or die trying. But he wouldn't be rushed. He wanted to explore her, to get to know her body, to feast his eyes on her.

Had he really had a woman like her before when he'd still been the old Cain? When he'd had a memory? What a lucky son-of-a-bitch he must have been to have called a woman like Faye his own.

The knowledge that nobody had touched her during his absence filled him with satisfaction. And for that he would reward her now, so she would know how much he appreciated her loyalty and faithfulness.

His fingers slid under the fabric of her delicate panties.

"Hmm," she hummed, licking her lips and arching her back.

Encouraged by her receptiveness, he explored her moist flesh. She was soft and warm, her female folds drenched with her juices, her knees at an angle now to give him better access. By her reaction he knew that he'd done this to her many times. But for him it was all new. Exciting, thrilling. To touch a woman for the first time and learn what she liked, to give her pleasure, was an experience nobody could ever repeat. That he had this chance now, that he was able to start all over again with Faye, he was grateful for.

Cain bathed his fingers in her wetness before he dove farther south. Impatient to get a taste of what her muscles felt like when they would squeeze his cock, he probed at her entrance and drove his finger into her.

A gasp came from her. "Cain!" she panted. "Please, don't tease me."

Did she want more than just one finger? Already now she felt too tight for even one digit. Once he thrust into her with his cock, she would milk him in an instant.

"I'm not gonna rush this. You'll have to wait for my cock just a little while longer." Despite the fact that he himself could barely wait any longer.

Withdrawing his finger amidst a protesting mewl, he gripped her panties and pulled them down before discarding them on the floor. Finally he could feast his eyes on her. The sight made him salivate. Unable to resist, he lowered his head and brought his mouth to her pussy. His hands clamped over her upper thighs when he heard her moan.

"I haven't even started," Cain murmured, grinning.

"Then start," Faye begged.

She didn't have to tell him twice. He lapped his tongue against her soft female flesh and allowed the flavor to spread. Involuntarily he closed his eyes and let himself fall. Greedily he licked her, explored her, while Faye writhed underneath him, her hips lifting to grind against him, her lips issuing moans and sighs. Sounds of pleasure like the ones he remembered from his dreams echoed in his ears.

Intoxicated by her scent and her taste, he continued licking her, while he released one thigh, only to drive a finger into her quivering slit, so he could concentrate his efforts on a spot farther up. When he swiped his tongue over her swollen clit, she nearly lifted off the rug. He growled, letting her know that he wasn't done yet.

Faye put her hands on his head, caressing the short hair and sensitive scalp, sending a bolt of lust through his body and right down into the tip of his cock. Moisture dripped from its slit, and he knew he couldn't last much longer.

Cain lifted his head from her pussy and looked up. He met her eyes watching him.

"You're so different," she whispered and pulled him to her.

He couldn't let her think that something was different about him, so he gripped her hips and lifted himself over her, adjusted his angle, and plunged into her wet heat.

Faye's eyes closed on impact and a breath rushed from her lungs. "Yes!"

Her cry echoed his own as the sensation of her tight muscles clamping around his erection slammed into him.

"Look at me," Cain demanded.

Her eyes flew open and she pinned him. Slowly, he pulled back from her tight sheath and slid back into her, all the while looking into her eyes. Faye crossed her ankles over his butt and pulled him closer.

"I missed you," she confessed.

"All of me?" He plunged deeper into her, emphasizing his question.

"All of you." Her fingernails dug into his back, urging him to give her more.

Clenching his jaw to ward off his imminent climax, Cain began to thrust. Like a silk glove she enveloped him on every descent, and like a vise she pulled him back on each withdrawal. Her body felt like heaven on earth. Heat suffused his body as if the rays of the sun were shining on him, not burning but warming him, giving him a feeling of belonging.

He'd hoped making love to Faye would be special, but he hadn't expected it to be as earth shattering as it was. His muscles flexed and his hips worked frantically to deliver thrust after thrust into her intoxicating body. It seemed impossible to think that he'd once called Faye his own and had no memory of it. How could any man forget that he'd been with a woman like her, a woman who made him feel like the most powerful man in the world?

Every sigh and every moan she released fueled his drive to give her more, to show her that he would do everything to give her pleasure, to make her happy. And to keep her safe and never let her go again. And even though his mind had no memory of their prior lovemaking, his body seemed to remember now. His movements seemed to have a mind of their own, adjusting to the demands of her body, coaxing more pleasure from her.

Never for a second did he take his eyes off her face, reveling in the signs of lust and passion that reflected on it, and encouraging him to continue even when his body wanted to give into release. Only when Faye found her release would he grant himself his own. This sign of selflessness took him by surprise, because he hadn't seen this trait in his character before. Was she the one who brought it out in him? Was she the one who made him the man he wanted to be?

The aroma created by their bodies rubbing together filled his nostrils and brought his movements to a more and more frantic pace. Had Faye been human she would have perceived his movements as a mere blur, and the wildness with which he drove into her would have injured her delicate female flesh. But the vampire vixen beneath him had no such limitations. She reacted to him in the same out of control way. Her fingernails had turned into claws and were digging deep into his back, while her hips slammed into him with unrestrained need.

He felt her body tremble at each impact and her interior muscles start to clamp more tightly around his cock, an indication that she was close.

"Yes, baby!" he encouraged her.

The red tint in her eyes was more pronounced now and behind her parted lips he saw her fangs descend to their full length. Fascinated by the alluring sight, he growled like a beast and lowered his head, tilting it to the side to offer her his neck.

Faye's breath hitched.

The temptation of feeling her fangs in his neck was too strong to resist. He needed her to bite him, to drink from him. When he felt her lips connect with his neck, his heart did a summersault, and his cock jerked in agreement.

"Faye!" he rasped.

Like tiny pinpricks, her fangs drove into his neck, making him shudder. At her first draw on his vein, a bolt of lust shot into his balls.

"Fuck!" was all his lips could utter, before he felt his semen shoot through his cock and explode at the tip.

Then a corresponding shudder coming from Faye's body collided with his spasms as she reached her climax. He continued to press his neck against her lips, not wanting her to stop drinking from him, because every pull on his vein sent another thrilling shiver through his body and into his cock.

For seconds that turned into minutes, Cain continued to thrust his cock into her silken sheath, while Faye's fangs remained lodged in his neck.

25

Cain's arm wrapped around her as he pulled her into the curve of his body, his naked torso sliding against her back, his legs pressing against hers, his cock still semi-erect. His body was as hot as a furnace, his breath irregular and his heartbeat racing.

Faye's body felt boneless, yet she'd never felt better in her entire life. Though she knew the fact that he'd been gone for over a year had contributed to their lovemaking being more than amazing, she realized that Cain having allowed her to drink his blood had elevated the experience to a level she'd never thought was possible.

Cain's lips now nuzzled at her neck and his hot breath caressed her skin, making her shiver all over again.

"Hmm," he hummed, sending a tingling sensation down her spine. "Give me a few minutes, and I'll see whether we can improve on this." He pressed his groin against her backside.

Faye chuckled. "You must be joking."

"You think I can't?" he challenged.

"Oh, I have no doubt that you'll be ready again in a few minutes. You always are. But—"

"But what?" he growled, and the sound reverberated in her body like a soft caress.

"Not even you can improve on perfection." And that was exactly how it had been: perfect. As if the year-long separation had never happened. Yet, at the same time, something about him was different.

"Good." Cain pressed an open-mouthed kiss to her neck, while his hand gently stroked down her arm to her hand, where he intertwined his fingers with hers. "I've always loved you biting me while I make love to you."

Faye jolted, whirling her head to him and twisting from his embrace. "What?"

He gave her a puzzled look and opened his mouth to speak, but hesitated. "What's wrong?"

"Cain, this was the first time I drank your blood." Her heart pounded.

He blinked and pulled her to him, his hand cupping her nape, his thumb stroking below her ear. "Of course, baby, what did I say?"

She shook her head, confused. "That you've *always* loved me biting you. But I've never done it before."

He gave her a soft peck on the cheek. "You must have misheard. I said I loved you biting me." Cain nuzzled his face in the crook of her neck. "In fact, I've never felt anything better, baby."

She pulled away again. "And why are you calling me baby?"

"Don't you like it when I call you baby?"

"I do, but—" She hesitated. Was she going crazy and seeing things that were different about him because it had been such a long time since they'd been together? Or had he really changed so much?

"But what?" he coaxed, and pressed more kisses on her neck and cheek, while his hand traveled lower, palming one breast and squeezing it lightly.

"You used to call me your love."

He sighed and pulled his head back, looking at her. "I want to call you so many things, Faye. I'm overwhelmed by how you make me feel. I feel truly alive again in your arms. I know I've changed. I'm sorry."

At his heartfelt words, she felt tears rise into her eyes. She held them at bay and caressed his cheek. He turned his face to press a kiss into the palm of her hand.

"You must have gone through so much in captivity. Tell me what happened to you."

A slow shake of his head was his answer, then he turned his face away. "Please don't ask."

Slightly hurt by his rejection, she dropped her hand and made a motion to get up, but he held her back, pulling her against his body and lowering them to the floor again.

"Please understand. For so many reasons, I can't talk about what happened. I wish I could confide in you."

"But maybe it would help you get things off your chest," she suggested, hoping to change his mind.

"It's better this way."

"You made me talk about it back then, and it helped me." Sharing the details of her ordeal with Cain had been a relief.

"Back when?" he asked and slid his hand down her thigh.

Faye was glad that her face was turned away from him, so he couldn't see the big frown that now built on her forehead. Why would he ask that when he knew exactly what she was talking about? He had to know. Cain was the one who'd freed her. Her and the others.

"After you saved me."

He stiffened for a moment, making doubts rise in her. Why was Cain behaving so strangely?

He suddenly relaxed again. "Uh, yes, that." He sighed and caressed her thigh gently. "Faye, it's just ... I have to get used to talking to others again. All that time I had nobody to confide in. It's hard for me. Maybe it would help if . . ." He broke off.

"Help if what?" she encouraged him, putting her hand on his that rested on her thigh and squeezed.

"Maybe if you could talk to me, tell me about us, remind me of the things we shared."

"But you know all that."

"In my head, yes, it's all there. Our past, everything. But I missed your voice. All those sleepless days I was dreaming of listening to your voice telling me about our life together." He kissed her neck softly. "And perhaps hearing your voice will help me find my own voice again."

His kisses were pleading, wiping away her momentary doubts. Hadn't she too needed to find herself again after her imprisonment?

"Just before the old king died, remember when you lifted me up into your arms and carried me out of that hellhole?" she started and snuggled into his embrace.

"Yeah," he murmured.

"I knew then that there would never be another man for me but you."

Cain chuckled. "I made quite an impression, huh?"

Faye smiled wistfully. "You were covered in blood, and you looked like the devil himself. But you hadn't come to hurt me or the others. When I watched you open the cell, I shrank back into my corner, so afraid of you. Afraid that you were just one of the many who'd hurt us before. The smell of death clung to you. It made me shiver. But then you looked directly at me, and I couldn't escape your gaze. You were a warrior, and everybody yielded to you. So strong, so formidable, so fearless."

Cain's breath blew against her nape. "Was I all that?"

"To me you were." She paused. Retelling the darkest time of her life still hurt. But knowing that she was safe, safe in Cain's arms, soothed her pain.

"Tell me what happened." There was a strange tone in his voice, almost as if he was interrogating her and wanting to get to the bottom of an important question. She shook off the thought.

"But you know everything. You were there. You know what he did. I don't want to talk about the torture and the rapes. It's all behind me now. I've healed."

She felt a sudden tightening of his hand over her thigh, accompanied by Cain's breathing and heartbeat accelerating. When he spun her around, making her face him, she was shocked to see a mask of horror in his face, and pain sitting deep in his eyes.

"Faye," he murmured, moving his head side to side.

It looked as if he wanted to say something, but no words came over his lips for long moments.

"Nobody will ever hurt you again," Cain finally said, his voice choked up.

Then his lips were on hers and he kissed her more fiercely than before. She slung her arms around him and pulled him onto her, spreading her legs to make space for him. Hard and heavy, his cock rested against her center, but he didn't enter her. She took his head into both her hands and severed the kiss.

"Make love to me," she demanded.

Dark eyes looked down at her, the storm in them evident, though she didn't understand the reason for it. "I don't want to hurt you."

"Then love me."

Gentler than ever before, Cain slid into her in slow motion. And just as slowly, he pulled back. Her sex was lubricated not just by her own juices, but also by his semen, and Cain could have taken her even more fiercely this second time—which was how he'd often done it in the past—but instead his lovemaking felt as if he were touching a virgin.

She didn't understand what had brought on this change in him, but it didn't matter. Cain making love to her with such reverence, such tenderness, was new, and she welcomed every second of it.

"I missed you, Cain."

His mouth descended on hers and prevented her from uttering another sound for a very long time.

26

Bending over the desk, Cain slammed his fist on the wooden surface and glared at his brother.

"I don't care that Baltimore is your personal guard! I won't tolerate him on palace grounds any longer! That goes for everybody who treats my fiancée with disrespect." He pointed his index finger at Abel. "And your guard did more than that. He manhandled her! He's lucky to be alive!"

"You're overreacting. I'm sure it was a misunderstanding. Baltimore is a fine guard. He knows not to overstep his bounds."

"He did overstep. I suggest you pick another personal guard."

"You have changed, brother. A little disturbance like that would have never derailed you to the point where you put your own desires before the good of the kingdom."

Cain narrowed his eyes. "And how would having Baltimore remain here be for the good of the kingdom as you say?"

"He's a valuable and loyal guard. Are you sure we can turn men like him against us in this difficult time? Have you forgotten already that somebody out there wanted to kill you?"

Cain straightened, letting his brother's last words sink into him. "Kill me? It was a kidnapping, not an assassination."

Abel scoffed. "Well, same difference! You're no good to the kingdom either way—dead or kidnapped."

"At least on that we agree."

"Then reconsider your decision about Baltimore. You'll need men like him to protect you. He knows everybody. He'll be able to warn us if anything nefarious is going on. You need him."

Cain shook his head. "No. My decision stands. Anybody who hurts Faye will have to deal with me."

"Well, I guess that means you've taken her back despite my cautioning you about her motives."

At his brother's attempt to continue to show Faye as a gold digger, anger boiled up from Cain's gut. "Yes, I've taken her back. So I would advise you to keep your opinions about her to yourself."

Abel raised his hands in defense. "Now, now, since when are you so touchy? I'm looking out for you, Cain, as your brother, your closest advisor. We've been through too much together to let a woman come between us. I regret now that I gave into Faye's advances . . ."

Cain grunted with displeasure. "While we're on that subject, I would also advise you to stop alluding to things as if they were the truth."

Abel puffed up his chest and fisted his hands at his hips. "Are you saying I'm lying?"

Cain clenched his teeth. "I'm saying you should be careful what you say about Faye. Spread any more rumors about what she did or didn't do and I'll have to reconsider what relationship you and I will have in the future."

Abel leaned closer, his jaw tight, his eyes pinning him. "You need me, brother. Lots has changed during the time you were gone. You don't know who you can trust. And the men you brought with you, do you really think they can protect you? They haven't got the slightest clue about what's going on in the kingdom. Hell, they don't even know who's allowed on the palace grounds and who isn't. They can't protect you."

"Are you threatening me?" Cain ground out.

"I'm cautioning you. You have enemies. We all do. And it's unwise to leave yourself open to attack."

"While we're on the subject of enemies: why did you convince me to invite the Mississippi clan?"

Abel's forehead furrowed. "What has that got to do with anything? We need to make peace with them to safeguard the kingdom. You know that just as well as I do."

"Damn it, Abel, do you have any idea what those bastards are doing to their own people?"

"What are you talking about?"

"Last night two vampires came to us. They'd fled their clan in Mississippi."

"Those two down and outs who are housed in one of the cottages?"

How did Abel already know about them? Cain hadn't mentioned them to his brother when he'd informed him of his decision to ban Baltimore from the premises. "You've seen them?"

Abel shrugged. "Not personally, no. But one of the guards mentioned them."

Cain should have known. Nothing escaped his brother. This was his turf more than it was Cain's at the moment. But that was something he was planning to change. "Anyway, did you also hear what has been done to them?"

"How should I know?"

"They were defanged by their clan. Do you understand what that means?"

Abel showed little surprise. "I've heard of the practice. I'm sure there were grave reasons and they deserved it for whatever crimes they committed. Surely, you're not going to continue to give shelter to some criminal elements. Make them leave, before they draw us into a renewed feud with our neighbors."

"How can you be so callous?"

Abel shook his head. "I'm not any more callous than you. You know what's at stake. Why get into the middle of things that may jeopardize our plans? Taking sides has never been a good thing. And interfering in a neighboring clan's business will only cause more problems than we need right now."

"So you're still interested in making peace with Mississippi despite their brutal practices?"

"I won't be swayed by something so insignificant. I see the bigger picture, but it appears, my dear brother, that you've gotten soft during your absence. You'd better make sure nobody notices. Nobody likes a weak king." Abel turned on his heel and stalked to the door.

Before he reached it, Cain responded, "Nobody likes an evil king either."

A snort was Abel's answer before he shut the door behind him, leaving Cain to stew over their antagonistic exchange.

He turned to the window and stared out into the garden surrounding the palace. The lawn was illuminated by flood lights. Faye was outside, tending to some plants. He let his gaze wander over her body. In her tight jeans and equally tight tank top, her voluptuous curves were even more enticing. Clearly, other men had thought so, too. Just remembering the little she'd told him the night before made his blood boil. He hadn't dared ask any more questions, knowing his lack of knowledge of the events would have made her suspicious. Instead he'd made love to her again, making sure she knew that he would protect her now.

He knew he should return to the stack of papers—notes from his interrogations of the guards—to see if he could find any inconsistencies in their statements, but the need to take Faye into his arms was greater.

He opened the French doors that led to the wrap-around porch and stepped outside. When he jumped over the railing and landed on the soft grass below, Faye turned to look over her shoulder and smiled.

With long strides, he walked to her.

"Taking a break from your work?" Faye asked.

He pulled her into his arms. "I wish I didn't have to work at all and could spend the entire night in bed with you."

"Mmm." Her lips brushed against his. "But what would your subjects say if they found out how lazy their king was?"

"I wouldn't call it lazy," Cain deflected. "After all, I wasn't planning on sleeping. I would be engaging in plenty of strenuous activity."

When she laughed, he captured her lips and kissed her, first gently, but when her arms came around his neck and pulled him closer, he tilted his head to the side and slipped his tongue between her parted lips and tasted her.

Faye pulled her head back. "Cain, not here, everybody will be able to see us."

"I don't care," he murmured and tried to draw her back.

"But you do," she insisted. "You've never wanted anybody to see us being intimate with each other."

"I've changed my mind." He wanted everybody to see that Faye belonged to him.

She gave him a curious look. "Whatever happened to you while you were gone, it seems to have changed your outlook on many things."

What else had she noticed? "Is that a bad thing?"

"No, no, not at all. It's just that you used to carry the weight of the world on your shoulders, but now . . ."

"Now what?" With his finger under her chin he tilted her head up.

"You seem so much more relaxed, as if all your worries were gone. Which is so odd because being locked up for so long generally causes the opposite."

He caressed her cheek with his thumb. "Maybe I discovered during that time what's really important."

Faye smiled hesitantly. "Tell me what's important to you now."

He opened his mouth to answer when a door slamming made him snap his head to the side. Thomas, a concerned look on his face, was rushing out of the palace.

Instantly alert, Cain released Faye. "What's going on?"

"It's Eddie!" Thomas answered, already sprinting down the driveway that led away from the palace.

Having recognized the alarmed tone in his voice, Cain ran after him. As he closed in on Thomas, he shouted, "What's wrong?"

Thomas didn't even turn his head and continued running toward the end of the driveway. "Eddie needs help." Then he veered to the right and ran into the forest.

Cain followed, his hand already reaching to his belt where he kept his silver dagger in a sheath. Ever since arriving at the palace it had become his constant companion. He gritted his teeth. If the guards had ignored his orders to give his friends from Scanguards free passage to the palace, some heads would roll tonight. He'd advised them of Eddie's and Blake's imminent arrival, not wanting a repeat of how he, Haven, Thomas, and Wesley had been received.

A sound behind him made him whirl his head around.

"Fuck!" Cain cursed when he spotted Faye chasing him. He wanted her nowhere near any danger. "Go back to the palace!"

But she wouldn't be deterred and kept running his way. "Maybe I can help."

Not wanting to stop to argue with her, he continued running after Thomas who was now disappearing behind some trees. "Damn it, Faye!" He slowed briefly to give her a chance to catch up with him then accelerated again, and together they followed Thomas into the thicket.

A few minutes more, and Cain could smell the brackish water of the bayou, but it wasn't the only thing his superior sense of smell picked up. Human blood was in the air. Instantly on alert, he ran faster, his ears picking up sounds now. Grunts, splashing water, branches breaking. Evidence of a fight.

Cain tossed a concerned look at Faye who was still keeping up with him. "You should have stayed back."

"I'm nearly as strong as you," was her reply.

He doubted that. Yes, as a vampire female she was stronger than any human, but she was no fighter. She wasn't trained, not like him.

But before he could contradict her, his eyes perceived movements in the dark. He focused on it. Thomas had already reached the spot and now cursed, "Christ!"

Cain and Faye reached him two seconds later.

"Help!" Blake called out as he spotted them, while he was dragging himself out of the murky water, his legs kicking at an alligator whose massive snout with its fangs was snapping at him.

Cain's head whirled to where he heard water splashing and to his horror he saw Eddie engaged in a fight with another alligator, this one even larger than the one chasing Blake.

Thomas was already lunging toward the alligator whose mouth was veering toward Eddie's arm as the young vampire lost his footing in the shallow bank of the murky waterway and stumbled backward.

"You stay here," Cain ordered Faye and jumped toward Blake, grabbing him under the arms and pulling him from the reach of the attacking animal just as its jaws snapped shut, hitting air.

Cain blindly tossed Blake behind him and lunged toward the alligator, his hands having already turned into claws. With them, he dug into the animal's jaw, one from the top and one from the bottom, and ripped its mouth open. A row of deadly canines gleamed in the moonlight that filtered through the trees.

The animal thrashed, its tail whipping back and forth, whirling up the water and splashing it so high and far that Cain was instantly doused in the dirty liquid. But Cain didn't let go and continued to spread the alligator's jaw wider until he finally heard it snap and go slack. He'd disabled the animal's primary weapon, but its massive tail continued to thrash and was just as much a danger as its teeth.

Cain grabbed the alligator behind its head and pulled. Had he been human, he wouldn't have been able to move the easily three hundred pound animal even an inch, but with his vampire strength he swung the alligator into the air, making a hundred-and-eighty degree turn. The alligator's body slammed against a tree with such force that the trunk of the tree cracked.

Having temporarily dazed the alligator, Cain jumped onto its back, ripped its head upward and sliced his claws across the animal's throat. Blood spilled, the stench of it filling the night air. Cain tore at the head, ripping it off the body. Beneath him, the thrashing stopped. The alligator was dead.

Breathing heavily, his eyes searched for Blake. He found him sitting up against a tree stump, while Faye ripped one of his pant legs open, exposing a wound, where the alligator had gotten to him before Cain had arrived.

At the sound of another splash in the water, Cain whipped his head toward it and saw an alligator drop into the water, seemingly lifeless.

"Fuck!" Thomas cursed and reached for his mate. "Are you okay?"

Eddie breathed heavily, but nodded and waded out of the water, Thomas by his side. "There were three of them. I managed to kill one." He pointed to a spot on the banks where Cain now noticed another dead alligator. "But then these two attacked, and I tried to keep them off Blake."

Thomas pulled him into a hug. "Thank God you contacted me."

Eddie smiled at his partner. "Can't beat telepathy between blood-bonded mates."

"You scared the shit out of me."

"I'll make it up to you later." Eddie pressed his lips to Thomas's and kissed him.

Cain looked away and walked to Blake. He crouched down to him and looked at the wound. "Are you all right?"

A bolt of jealousy hit Cain when he noticed Blake only reluctantly pulling his gaze away from Faye.

"Pain's a bitch."

"We'll take care of it," Cain assured him. "Can you walk?"

"With a little help." Then Blake turned back to Faye. "Cain, don't you wanna introduce us?"

He'd rather not, but given the circumstance, he didn't have a choice.

"Faye, that's Blake. Blake, this is my fiancée." He glared at his human colleague, making sure he understood that she was off limits, but Blake didn't even look at him and already held his hand out to her.

"Bond," he said with a smile. "Blake Bond."

Cain rolled his eyes. Did Blake really have to lay it on that thick again? Did he not realize that his 007 routine wouldn't earn him any points in view of the fact that he'd only moments earlier screamed like a little girl?

"Faye Duvall." Faye shook his hand briefly.

Footsteps on the soft ground told him that Thomas and Eddie were joining them. Cain glanced at them. "That was bad luck," he said, nodding at Eddie.

Eddie scoffed. "I wouldn't call it bad luck." He glared at Blake. "I'd call it downright stupid!"

Blake straightened and thrust up his chin. "How was I supposed to know?"

"What happened, Eddie?" Cain interrupted.

Eddie pointed at Blake. "Stupidity happened. This idiot here says, *oh, let's take a shortcut. We'll just wade through the water. It'll save us a half hour.*" He let out a frustrated huff. "Shortcut my ass! I warned him not to go into the water when he couldn't see what was ahead of him. But, no, smartass Blake here had to know better, didn't he?"

Blake tried to pull himself up, but his attempt was shaky at best, and his face contorted with pain. "It wouldn't have been a problem if you hadn't shouted at me and woken up the alligators!"

"Woken them up? Don't you know anything? Alligators are nocturnal. They don't sleep at night! They hunt for food. And had I not saved your stupid ass, you would have been on the menu tonight! Next time I'll think twice about helping you when you disobey my direct orders."

Blake opened his mouth for another retort, but Cain slapped him over the back of his head.

"Another word out of your mouth tonight and I'm going to send you straight home. Are we clear on that?"

Blake's eyes shot to Cain. For a moment he thought the human would try to fight with him, too, but then Blake nodded silently.

"Good. Let's get back to the palace. And if you're behaving, then maybe one of us will even give you some vampire blood to heal."

"It sure ain't gonna be me," Eddie grunted. And by the look Thomas gave Blake, Thomas wouldn't be a willing donor either, since it was Blake's action that had endangered his mate.

Cain helped Blake up, putting one arm around his waist, and draping Blake's other arm around his shoulder while holding onto his wrist.

"Thanks, Cain," Blake murmured, all bravado now gone from his voice.

Maybe this incident would teach the kid some common sense. And instill some fear. Because without fear, there was no such thing as bravery.

27

Faye walked next to Cain as they made their way back to the palace, Cain helping the injured human, virtually carrying him when he became weaker from his injury. She'd ripped a piece of fabric from Blake's T-shirt and wrapped it tightly around the wound, stopping blood from gushing from the incisions the alligator's teeth had made.

Ahead of them, Thomas and Eddie walked hand in hand. She'd seen them kiss after they'd defeated the alligator and heard them mention a blood-bond. She'd never met a same-sex blood-bonded couple. Hell, she hadn't even realized that Thomas was gay when he'd first arrived at the palace. He didn't seem effeminate at all. Neither did his partner.

"How do you know all these people?" she now asked Cain.

He turned his head to her. "They're from a security outfit called Scanguards. They helped me."

"A security outfit? You mean they're actually professional guards?"

Cain nodded. "Bodyguards. The best money can buy."

The revelation stunned her. Somehow she'd suspected that maybe the men he'd brought with him had been imprisoned with him and they'd mounted an escape together, and that was why he now trusted them.

"How did they free you?"

"Let's not talk about that now."

Disappointed that he was yet again refusing to talk about anything related to his kidnapping, she pressed her lips together. After the day they'd spent in each others' arms, she'd thought that he'd finally open up to her and tell her what had happened to him. But again, she met with a wall of silence.

"So you're Cain's girl, huh?" the human suddenly asked, shifting his head so he could look past Cain's chest. He was a good looking guy, but from the interactions she'd observed so far it was clear that he was immature. He couldn't be older than twenty-five. Maybe in another ten years he would have grown into a real man.

Cain growled, and in Faye's ears it sounded like a warning. "Yes, she's mine. Any other questions?"

"Cain," she chastised softly, both thrilled that he'd called her his, and at the same time horrified that he would talk to Blake in such a menacing way. "Your human friend is just making conversation."

"He's not going to be a friend much longer, if he comes on to you once more," Cain shot back, then stopped himself as if he hadn't wanted to say it.

To calm him, Faye gently stroked her hand against his hip. His eyes immediately sought hers and began to shimmer golden. His vampire side was simmering right under his skin, ready to burst to the surface at any moment should he feel that somebody was threatening his territory.

"My love," she murmured under her breath.

The words seemed to soothe him, and he severed the eye contact and continued following the two gay vampires.

It took only a few minutes until they reached the driveway leading to the palace. Several guards were already rushing toward them, weapons at the ready. Clearly drawn by the scent of Blake's blood, they were expecting trouble and ready to meet it head on.

Before the guards reached them, Cain called out to them, "Stand down! They're friends."

The king's guards waited for their small group to reach them. "Was there an attack?" Lee, one of the more senior guards, asked, glancing suspiciously at Blake, his nostrils flaring.

"A little accident with some overly hungry alligators," Cain explained. "Escort us to the palace. We need to take care of my human friend here."

"Of course, Your Majesty."

Flanked by the guards, they marched to the palace and entered it.

"Where to?" Faye asked, looking up at Cain.

"Downstairs. Blake will be staying with Haven and Wesley." Cain glanced at Thomas and Eddie who were receiving curious looks from the guards. Cain didn't have to point out where Eddie would be staying.

By the looks the two lovers exchanged, it was clear that they couldn't wait to withdraw to their room.

"Back to your posts," Cain ordered the guards who'd accompanied them.

Faye walked ahead as Cain brought Blake downstairs and almost carried him along the corridor to the king's quarters, Eddie and Thomas following them. She opened the double doors wide to make way for the men behind her, then glanced at Cain. He motioned to the door on the right, indicating that it was Haven and Wesley's room.

She knocked and opened it before getting any reply. The room was empty.

"Here, on the sofa," she instructed, pointing to the large sectional that dominated the sitting room of the comfortably appointed guard's suite. While not as luxurious as the king's or the queen's suites, the king's guards' suites were homey. Considering that the king's guards had little private life, with the leader of the king's guard having none at all, each king had made sure that they were housed in rooms which spared no expense to make them feel at home. Each guard's room was therefore different and furnished to the taste of the guard.

Cain lowered the human onto the sofa. Blake let out a sigh of obvious relief at being able to get off his feet.

"I'll wash out his wound first, then somebody can give him vampire blood," she suggested. She had already turned toward the ensuite bathroom to get water and a towel, when Cain stopped her.

"I'll get it."

Surprised at Cain's willingness to help her, she smiled at him. "Thank you."

While he disappeared in the bathroom, she took a pillow and shoved it under Blake's head. "Here. That might be a little more comfortable."

Blake tossed a look at the open bathroom door behind her before thanking her with a smile.

From the corner of her eye, she noticed Thomas and Eddie waiting. She looked at them. "So who's gonna give him his blood?"

Eddie raised his hands. "Not me."

Thomas hesitated, but didn't get a chance to answer, because Cain's voice now came from the bathroom as he stepped out. "I will."

He walked to her and set a small bowl of water on the floor beside her, placed the towel on the armrest of the sofa, then crouched down next to the couch and loosened the knot of the makeshift bandage around Blake's leg Faye had made earlier.

"You don't need to do that," she said, and kneeled down next to him. "You're the king."

"He's my responsibility."

Faye put her hand over his and gently pulled it back. "I'm much better at that than you are." She held his gaze until he finally nodded and rose.

"Cain," Eddie addressed him. "A word, please."

"Excuse us. I'll be back in a moment," Cain said and followed Thomas and Eddie as they left the room. She heard them walk across the common area and open the door to the other guard's room, before turning back to Blake.

"Now let's have a look at your wound."

Cain shut the door to Thomas's room and looked at Eddie.

"You asked us to check out John's story," the young blond vampire started.

"Yes. What did you find?"

"I hacked into property records and searched for John's and his lover's names. John owns a little place in the French Quarter."

Cain nodded. "Makes sense. That's probably where this Nicolette lives. Did you check it out?"

"We did. Unassuming place, nice, but not flashy. She lives there, all right. We asked the neighbors."

"What about the girl? What did she say?"

"We didn't talk to her. She wasn't in."

"Didn't you wait around?"

"We did, but she didn't get back all night."

Cain rubbed the back of his neck. "Where would she be? John came back to the palace without her. I think I would have heard if he'd brought her to the palace grounds."

"There was something else really odd," Eddie continued, his forehead furrowing. "Maybe it's nothing."

"What is it?"

"Well, on the outside the house is a little run down, needs some paint on the windows and the shutters and stuff."

"So?"

"The door had just recently been replaced, and when I looked a little closer, I noticed that one of the hinges looked as if it had been bent and then straightened out again."

Cain tilted his head to the side. "As if somebody had kicked the door in?"

"Yeah."

"That might not mean anything," Thomas interjected. "There's plenty of crime in this city. Burglaries happen every night, I'm sure."

Cain contemplated Thomas's words. "You could be right, but I don't like it." He turned back to Eddie. "Did you mention any of this to the neighbors or ask them whether they heard any disturbances in the last few days?"

"I asked if they heard anything suspicious, but nobody did."

"I want you to go back and dig deeper. I want to know where the girl is. John said she was injured. So it doesn't make sense that she'd be venturing out in the middle of the night after just recently being attacked. She's human, and even though John healed her, any normal human woman would be wary about being out at night without protection after having been assaulted. Find out where she is."

Eddie nodded.

"We'll go into the French Quarter tomorrow night and make inquiries," Thomas said. "But first, I think we all need a shower to wash the stink of the bayou off us."

Cain turned up his nose. "You get no argument from me there."

He'd jump in the shower just as soon as he'd healed Blake with his blood.

28

Abel pulled into the alley and unlocked the car doors of his red Ferrari. He watched impatiently as the door opened and Baltimore slid into the passenger seat. Clenching his jaw, he waited until his guard slammed the door shut and turned his face.

"You fucking idiot!" Abel greeted him.

Baltimore lowered his head in a show of submission, but not even that gesture did anything to quench Abel's urge to hurt somebody.

"Do you have any idea what your stupid behavior led to?"

"I'm sorry, Abel!"

"Sorry doesn't fucking cut it! Imbecile!" He bent closer to his underling. "Did you have to go against her wishes? Was it necessary to attack her?"

Baltimore thrust his chin up. "I didn't attack her!"

Abel flashed his fangs. "I don't care what you call it! It doesn't change anything about the outcome! Now Cain has banned you from the palace grounds. You're no good to me out here! I needed you inside the palace walls."

"I couldn't know he was going to show up."

The flimsy excuse gnawed on Abel's nerves. "That's not the point! Besides, the way those two are right now, Faye would have gone to him anyway and told him what you did, even if he hadn't shown up. He's taken her back again, and with your stupid move you've probably made things worse and brought them even closer together. That wasn't my plan!"

"I understand."

"You understand nothing, you idiot! Or you wouldn't have done it. Now Cain trusts her again, or why did my spies report to me that he spent the entire day in her chambers, shacked up with her?" Abel slapped Baltimore across the face. "I wanted to isolate him, and what do you do? You drive him into her arms so he has an ally in the palace."

"But we've still got John."

"Just as well! We'll need him now more than ever, seeing that I can't rely on you doing your part. I'll have to rethink our approach." He leaned back in his seat and stared out the windshield. In a few hours the sun would rise again and bring him ever closer to the day of Cain's welcome home celebration. And if Abel hadn't set up a solid plan by then, the opportunity of ripping the throne right out from under him would slip through his fingers.

"Fuck! I'm not going to wait any longer to get what's rightfully mine. Do you understand me?" He didn't even look at Baltimore, because he didn't want an answer from him.

After a moment the idiot spoke anyway. "Maybe now is the time to call in some favors."

Abel turned his head and narrowed his eyes. "What are you talking about now?"

"There are several people still in the palace who will do whatever you ask of them, for fear that you'll make good on your prior threats if they don't."

Taking a few breaths, he contemplated Baltimore's words and had to admit that occasionally his personal guard did come up with possible solutions, though he wouldn't praise him for it right now. In his eyes Baltimore didn't deserve any praise for having screwed up part of his plan by getting himself banned from the palace.

"I'll think about it," Abel said instead and turned the key in the ignition. "Make yourself useful and relieve your men from their watch over John's lover. Stay with her until I contact you, and send the two guards back to the palace. I may need them."

Baltimore nodded dutifully and reached for the door handle.

"And another thing."

"Yes, Abel?"

"Have you spoken to the Mississippi clan?"

Baltimore's mouth twisted into a grin. "They were surprised to get your invitation, but they're happy to come and talk peace."

Abel chuckled. "Excellent. Have one of your men contact them anonymously to tell them that Cain is harboring two of their traitors."

Baltimore's forehead furrowed. "To what purpose?"

"I hired you for your muscles, not your brain, so leave the thinking to me. Now go. Don't contact me unless something goes wrong. I can't have Cain find out that I'm still communicating with you. Is that clear?"

Baltimore grunted his acquiescence and got out of the car. When the door shut, Abel jammed the car into reverse and raced out of the alley, then sped away as he hit the main road.

Only a few more days, and everything would fall into place.

And at the end of it, Abel would be king. Finally.

29

Faye snuck into the secret walkway, not wanting to be seen by Cain's guards. She'd made sure that Blake was recovering and left him in the care of the witch, Wesley. Having rid herself of the clothes that had gotten dirty in the bayou, she was dressed in only a robe.

Without making a sound, she opened the secret door leading into Cain's suite and eased it shut behind her. The sound of running water came from the bathroom, the door of which was ajar. On bare feet she approached and pushed it open farther.

Cain stood in the shower with his back to her. Water ran down his muscled back and sculpted ass. His strong thighs and calves were dusted with dark hair, his feet planted wide as he let the spray of the shower run over his head, his hands braced against the tiles.

She couldn't get enough of looking at his gorgeous naked body. When he'd fought the alligator a short while earlier, she'd watched in fascination how he'd battled the strong animal and defeated it with his bare hands. He'd looked ferocious, like a true warrior, and had reminded her of the night when he'd rescued her.

Seeing him fighting to save his friends had made the longing for him grow. She needed him, wanted him more than anything else in her life. She sighed.

Cain whirled around, his hands instantly forming into claws, but the moment his eyes landed on her, he visibly relaxed. A smile formed on his lips.

"You shouldn't sneak up on me like that." He stepped sideways, out of the spray of the shower.

Her gaze wandered over his nearly hairless chest. He was ripped, sporting a true six-pack. Farther down, a nest of dark hair surrounded his shaft. Long and thick, it hung there in a relaxed state. She licked her lips.

"If you don't want me in here, I can leave," Faye suggested, but made no motion to turn away. Instead she opened the belt of her robe and let it fall open in the front.

"Well, since you're here already," he hedged, "maybe you'd like to join me."

"I was hoping you'd say that." She pushed the robe off her shoulders and let it fall to the floor with a soft whoosh.

When she raised her eyes to his face, she noticed the hungry look with which his eyes devoured her. Lower, another reaction caught her attention. His cock was rising.

Slowly, without taking her eyes off him, she stepped into the glass enclosed shower and laid her hands on his chest. "When you were fighting that alligator earlier, I couldn't take my eyes off you."

His arms came around her, pulling her against his body. "Why's that?"

"You looked so strong, so formidable. Had we been alone, I would have asked you to make love to me right there," she confessed.

Cain grinned. "Well, look at that. My seductive vixen gets turned on by a little hand-to-hand combat. Is there anything else that turns you on?"

Faye slid one hand lower, moving it ever closer to his groin. "You naked in the shower." She slid her hand over his cock, reveling in his velvet smooth skin. "Your cock hardening at the sight of me."

"Keep going," he encouraged her, his hand now moving to her backside, stroking her suggestively.

"The thought of taking you in my mouth."

His breath hitched, and his eyes darkened with desire. "Is that what you came in here for? To suck me?" He rubbed his cock against her palm, and a groan left his throat.

"Only if you don't mind."

"You know I don't. So are you gonna tease me forever, or will you get on your knees and make good on your threat?"

She smiled, lowering her lashes halfway. "Are you commanding me as my king?"

"As your king, I'm powerless to command you. But as your lover, I beg you to put me out of my misery and let me feel your lips around my cock."

The fact that he wasn't commanding her but begging her surprised her. Previously when they'd played this game, he'd always played along by slipping into the role of the omnipotent king whose commands were to be followed. But now, suddenly, he was giving power over to her.

Faye looked into his eyes. So much had changed about him, yet so much was the same. The desire between them was still as potent as ever. No, even more so now. As if they were starting all over again. Everything was new and fresh, exciting and unknown. And utterly thrilling. Even now as she crouched down and brought her face level with his groin, anticipation coiled through her as if she'd never before pleasured him in this way.

"Please," Cain murmured and pressed himself against the tile wall at his back, placing his hands flat against the wet surface. "Let me feel you."

Faye slid her hands over his thighs, caressing his powerful muscles. She felt them flex under her touch. "You're beautiful." His cock stood fully erect now, the veined shaft tilting upward toward his navel. His balls had pulled up tight too, its two eggs visible beneath the skin.

With her index finger, she stroked over the tight sac, not stopping when she reached the underside of his cock.

Cain expelled a ragged breath. "Fuck!"

Ah, how she liked his reaction, raw and untamed. She would reward him for it.

Moving her face closer, she opened her mouth and let her tongue slide over the underside of his cock, taking her time to move to the tip to swipe over the purple flesh. From the corner of her eyes she saw his hands clench as if he was trying to get himself under control. But she wouldn't allow it. Cain would lose control tonight and be at her mercy. He would surrender to her.

Faye licked over the bulbous head once more before wrapping her lips around it and taking him into her mouth. Pumped full with blood, he was thick and long. She loved how hard he was even though she'd barely touched him. As if for him, this was new, too. Just like he'd said when they'd made love the day before. Maybe their long separation contributed to this sense of novelty.

When she suddenly felt his palm caressing her cheek, she glanced up at him. He was watching her, his eyes full of passion, his lips parted and showing his fangs.

"I don't deserve you," he said. "But, by God, I can't get enough of you."

She brought her hand around the root of his shaft and sucked him deeper into her mouth, while she licked her tongue over his hard flesh. Cain leaned his head against the tile wall, but continued to caress her cheek with his thumb. He wasn't forcing her to take him deeper by pulling her head closer. Instead, he simply moved with her movements, letting her guide him, not the other way around.

Feeling his cock in her mouth, hearing his moans and heavy breathing, and seeing the flexing muscles beneath her hands, sent shivers down her spine. A tingling spread over her entire body and reached her nipples, hardening them instantly. Farther below, the same tingling sensation made her clit vibrate. A thrill went through her. She felt powerful with Cain, because he was surrendering to her. He was giving control over to her, more than he'd ever done before. She loved this new side of him. There was something so soft about this tough warrior now. He was finally showing her something he'd always hidden from her.

The more she licked his cock, the louder and more frequent Cain's sounds of pleasure became. Like a symphony of lust they played off the walls of the shower, echoing her own. She couldn't get enough of him, of the powerful warrior, the magnificent king. But most of all she couldn't get enough of the vampire who was her lover.

"You've gotta stop, baby," he suddenly pleaded and gripped her shoulders with both hands, gently pushing her back so his cock slipped from her mouth.

"I'm not done." She looked up at him.

Cain pulled her up to stand and turned her so she found herself pressed against the shower wall, his hands already hooking under her thighs to lift her. "Oh, no, we're not done."

Spreading her legs as he lifted her and positioned himself at her center, he issued his command, "Now be a good girl, and guide my cock into your pussy."

Her breath caught in her chest. He'd never talked to her like that before, had always been almost polite in his utterances when they'd had sex before. Yet she found that she liked the way he spoke to her now. It aroused her more than she'd expected.

Without hesitation Faye took hold of his cock and brought it to her sex, placing it at the entrance to her wet core. When the head touched her nether lips, she moaned and leaned her head back, panting. But he didn't enter her immediately. Instead, he moved his hips upward and let his cock slide over her clit, lubricating it with her own juices. A shudder raced through her.

"Oh, Faye," he murmured. "Beautiful Faye."

Then he drew his hips back and lowered his cock to her female folds, probing, testing, until, after an agonizing eternity, his cockhead finally parted her flesh and drove inside her.

All air rushed out of her lungs as his thick shaft filled her and his balls slapped against her when he thrust into her to the hilt.

"Cain!"

Her insides went up in flames, igniting her clit and filling her entire body with pleasure. She felt her channel stretch to accommodate him and her hips undulate to beg him for more. Her hands gripped his ass now, her fingernails digging into his flesh to issue her demands.

"More! Harder!"

"Anything you want."

Cain's thrusts turned more ferocious, his chest heaving from the effort to hold her immobile against the wall, his breath coming in rapid pants. His jaw was clenched tightly, and his fangs had pushed past his lips. The sight made her heart beat even faster. She remembered how he'd bitten her just before he'd disappeared, and she'd never felt anything as exhilarating as the sensation of his fangs lodging in her skin and his mouth drawing on her vein.

Faye tilted her head to the side, offering him her neck.

He kissed her there, licked his tongue over her skin, while his cock pounded into her relentlessly. She felt his fangs scrape at her skin, making her shiver with pleasure.

"Tell me you love me," she demanded and cupped his head.

He ripped his head from her and captured her lips instead, drowning her request in a passionate kiss. As if something had angered him, he drove into her with even more force, his pelvic bone slamming against her clit so rapidly that she instantly exploded. An orgasm more powerful than she'd ever experienced crashed into her, just as she felt his cock spasm inside her. The warm spray of his semen filled her, lubricated her channel even further and allowed him to increase his tempo even more, until his thrusts finally slowed. He severed the kiss and leaned his forehead against hers, breathing heavily.

"I don't know how I ever got any work done as king with you around me."

Faye felt her forehead furrow. Cain had always put his duties as king first. She'd always known that and accepted it. But his words seemed to suggest otherwise. And what was even stranger was that while back then he'd always freely confessed his love to her and in the same breath excused himself to deal with king business, now the opposite was happening: he hadn't once said that he loved her, yet he was showering her with more attention than ever before.

Cain had changed. And she needed to understand why.

30

An urgent knock by Haven had ripped Cain from Faye's arms, and he'd dressed rapidly and dashed upstairs to meet him in the office. Cain was, however, grateful for the interruption. Faye had demanded to hear that he loved her when he'd been about to bite her and drink her blood, and in that moment he hadn't been able to go through with it. Neither with the bite, nor with a declaration of his love. It wouldn't have been fair to her. He couldn't take her blood or tell her he loved her while he was deceiving her about himself.

Yes, he'd never felt better than when he was with her. The sex was out of this world amazing, and his jealousy when another man so much as even looked at her was spiraling out of control. He knew he had feelings for her, emotions that were deeper than seemed possible after such a short time. But he knew he was also lying to her. He was keeping the fact from her that he didn't remember anything about her, yet pretended to her that everything was all right. It wasn't. And he didn't know how to tell her. Would she reject him if she found out? Would she think he was only half a man now, not the hero she came to make love to in the shower? Not the strong warrior she looked up to? Because if she rejected him now, he would be devastated.

Cain tried to push away the thoughts and opened the door to his office.

Haven wasn't alone. Robert stood in the middle of the room, flanked by Wesley and one of the king's guards.

"What's going on?" Cain asked, looking at Haven as he closed the door behind him.

"Simon, tell the king what you told me," Haven instructed the guard.

"I found a copy of the palace's blueprints in the supply cellar. It was hidden between the pages of the ledger Robert keeps. There was an envelope, too."

Cain looked at the papers in Simon's hands and pointed to them. "That it?"

Simon nodded and handed him the folded piece of the paper and the envelope. Cain unfolded and examined it. It was indeed a blueprint of the palace, indicating all entrances and exits on all levels, though to his relief it didn't indicate where the secret tunnels were located. He folded it again, then looked at the envelope. It was addressed to a PO Box in Gulfport, Mississippi.

Cain whistled through his teeth and stared at Robert. "Explain yourself, Robert!"

"I don't know how that copy got into my books. It's not mine!" Robert spat indignantly.

"Of course it's not yours," Cain ground out. "That's why it should have never been in your ledger. So what the fuck were you planning to do with it, huh?" He could venture a guess what Robert's plan had been.

"Nothing! I didn't make that copy. Somebody must have planted it in my things," Robert protested.

Cain shoved the envelope in front of his face. "Is that your handwriting?"

The clenching of Robert's teeth was indication enough that he was hesitant about answering the question.

"I asked—"

"It's my handwriting, but it's not what you think."

"What do I think?" Cain shot back.

"It's the new address of our blood suppliers. I was about to mail them a check."

"To Mississippi? Do you think I'm stupid?" Though Cain didn't know for certain, he assumed that his clan didn't get its packaged blood from Mississippi. He was certain that the neighboring clan would never tolerate Cain's clan infringing on their supplier. He hoped he was right.

"I received a notification that they moved their billing operation to Mississippi. For tax reasons."

Cain cursed and went nose to nose with Robert. "So you really do think I'm stupid. I'll tell you what really happened! You decided to cause trouble and sell sensitive information to a rival clan so they can attack us. What did they promise you? Money? Power?" Cain gnashed his teeth and felt his fangs extend.

"I didn't do anything of the like! I'm a loyal subject. I don't deserve your mistrust! Have I not served you loyally ever since you became king? Don't you know me at all?"

The words struck a cord. No, he didn't know Robert, and that was the crux of all his problems. He didn't know who to trust, who was loyal to him, or who meant him harm. Despite the interrogations of the guards and all the other staff at the palace, he and his friends from Scanguards hadn't gotten any further in the investigation of the assassination attempt. This was the first lead they had, and he wouldn't let Robert's passionate plea prevent him from doing what he had to.

"Lock him up downstairs," Cain ordered Simon.

Robert glared at him. "You're making a mistake."

"I'd rather owe you an apology if I'm wrong than wake up with a stake in my chest." Then he motioned to the guard to execute his command.

Robert didn't struggle when Simon escorted him out the door, but kept his head high. The door didn't shut behind them. Thomas and Eddie walked in, their heads turning to Simon and Robert.

"Hey, guys." Thomas pulled the door shut behind them.

"Hey, Haven," Eddie greeted his colleague.

"Good to see you, Eddie. Heard you had a little trouble with the local animal population."

"You could call it that. Or you could call it a clusterfuck by our incredibly stupid human colleague."

Haven rolled his eyes. "No need to say anything further. I've already heard it."

"No doubt Blake's sanitized version."

"Trust me, I've already put two and two together."

"How is Blake now?" Cain asked.

Haven shrugged. "Better. His leg wound is healing quickly thanks to your blood. He'll be like new in a few hours."

Cain nodded. "Good. We'll need every man we can get. Even Blake." He turned to Thomas and Eddie. "We just found Robert with a copy of the palace's blueprints and an envelope addressed to a PO Box in Mississippi. I can't help but suspect he was planning to sell the information to the clan in Mississippi. He's a traitor."

"That's a grave accusation," Thomas replied. "What's his defense?"

"He said somebody planted the documents, yet he admits that he addressed the envelope himself."

"Do you think he could have something to do with the assassination attempt?" Haven asked, hooking his thumb in his belt.

"It's entirely possible. He could have been the one to let the assassin in, and now he's trying it again."

"Do you want me to talk to him and see if I can get anything else out of him?" Thomas offered.

"Go ahead. You're better at this than I."

"Does it even make sense?" Eddie interrupted.

"Does what make sense?" Cain asked.

"Robert being involved in the assassination attempt." He shifted his weight onto his other foot. "See, if he already gave the Mississippi clan access to the palace a year ago to try to kill you, why would he have to send them the blueprints now? Wouldn't they already know how to get in?"

Eddie had a point. "Possible. But what if the Mississippians weren't behind the assassination then? What if he had somebody else help him then and, since they failed, he's now putting his money on the Mississippi clan?"

Eddie shrugged. "Maybe. But why switch camps? The more people you involve in something like that, the more likely it is that someone is going to talk." He looked to his partner for agreement.

Thomas nodded. "I'll have a word with him and see what I can get out of him. Do we have anything on him we can use as leverage?"

Cain rubbed his hand over his face. "I wish I knew. Talk to John and see what he knows about the guy. But only tell him what he needs to know."

"You don't trust him anymore, do you?" Thomas said.

"I have my doubts about him, though I can't fathom why he would first save me and then betray me. It doesn't make sense. When are you and Eddie going into the Quarter to follow up on his woman?"

Thomas looked at his watch. "Sun's up in a couple of hours. Not much point now. We'll go tomorrow night. In the meantime, I'll check out Robert."

"Agreed," Cain said and turned back to Haven. "Get the staff to organize a blackout van for sunset tomorrow. I want you to send Blake to the airport."

Haven put his hands at his hips. "Come on, you can't just send him home now. Didn't you just say we needed every man we can get? It's not fair to the kid. He meant well."

Cain sighed. "Don't get your dander up. I'm not sending him home. He's just gonna play chauffeur. At least that's something he's not likely to screw up."

Haven chuckled. "You know he hates being relegated to errand boy."

"I do. Let that be his punishment."

His friend laughed out loud. "You're way too soft on him."

Cain couldn't help but smile. "I just don't want Quinn to kick my butt when I'm too rough with his precious grandson." Besides, he didn't dislike Blake. He just wished the kid exhibited more common sense and less bravado.

31

Cain sidestepped the two vampires who were carrying a large potted plant across the hallway, while a female member of the house staff with a stack of table linens in her hands walked behind them.

"What's going on here?"

The woman turned her head and bowed briefly. "We're preparing the ballroom for your welcome home reception, Your Majesty."

Well, it appeared he had a ballroom, not that he'd had any time or inclination to inspect said room so far.

"Carry on," he dismissed her and marched to the entrance door, when he saw John come out of one of the doors on the other side. Cain motioned him to approach.

"Good evening, Cain," John greeted him politely.

"Evening, John. I see the festivities are coming along nicely." Though Cain wasn't interested in talking about the stupid party, it suited him fine as a lead-in to another subject.

"Yes, it's going to be quite an event."

"Looks like it." Cain paused for a moment. "Listen, I wanted to let you know that now that I've changed my mind about the leader of the king's guard not being allowed to be in a relationship, I figured it would be appropriate if you brought your woman—Nicolette's her name, right—to the party. I'm planning to announce some policy changes, and having you there with Nicolette would underscore my sincerity."

John stared at him, clearly stunned for a moment. "Well, uh, I don't—"

Cain put his hand on his forearm. "Don't say no. Bring her. I'd like to meet her. I won't take no for an answer."

"Of course, in that case. I'll make sure she attends. And thank you for the invitation." He nodded. "Excuse me, I have to go over the shift changes with the guards."

"Thanks, John. And, uh, thank you for not giving me a hard time about having moved Thomas and Eddie into your rooms."

"I expected it. I know you trust your men from Scanguards more than anybody here. Maybe in time . . ." He didn't finish his sentence.

"Yes, maybe in time." Then Cain watched the leader of his king's guard turn and disappear down the corridor.

He hoped that Thomas and Eddie would find out that everything with John and Nicolette checked out, so Cain could lay his worries about the leader of the king's guard to rest.

With a sigh, he opened the entrance door and looked down the long driveway, while the warm night air made his shirt cling to his body. A dark limousine was approaching, kicking up dust from driving too fast on the gravel road. When it finally came to a stop by making a dramatic turn to the side, gravel was whirled up by the back tires and landed on the steps to the house.

Cain refrained from rolling his eyes and instead walked down the steps to greet his visitors.

The door to the passenger area behind the driver's cab opened and Gabriel stepped out. He turned immediately to gallantly help his wife, Maya, out of the car. Cain had to smile. Gabriel was an old-fashioned kind of guy and a gentle soul, despite the hard exterior he displayed.

When he turned back, Cain had no problem making out the large scar that marred Gabriel's face, reaching from the top of his left ear to his chin. It lent him a dangerous air, and in his job as the second-in-command at Scanguards, it came in handy. He was both feared by his enemies and revered by his colleagues and subordinates—and sometimes also feared by them.

The dark beauty by his side was something special. A doctor in her human life, she'd been turned into a vampire against her will, but had found true love with Gabriel. The blood-bonded pair was utterly devoted to each other. It was therefore not a surprise that Maya hadn't flown out to New Orleans on her own, but had brought her husband along for company. Though Cain suspected that Gabriel was here for a different reason: to protect the woman he couldn't live without.

"Gabriel, Maya, I'm so glad you came," Cain greeted them now and shook their hands.

Any other woman he would have given a hug to say hello, but he knew Gabriel's sentiments about his wife being touched by other men, and finally Cain understood the feeling. He felt the same about Faye.

"So this is your place," Gabriel replied and cast an admiring look at the enormous property. "Who would have thought?"

"Everybody sends their love and congratulations," Maya added with a smile. "They're all very happy for you."

"Thank you." Cain's gaze drifted to Blake, who was getting out of the car. "Blake, would you get their luggage, please? I had a guest room on the second floor prepared for them."

Blake nodded and walked to the back of the limousine, opening the trunk, while Cain motioned to the front door. "Shall we?"

"Have you settled in?" Gabriel asked, sidling up to him.

Cain shrugged. "As much as I can. It's an adjustment."

"I bet," Maya commented, walking hand in hand with Gabriel. "But I'm sure you'll manage." She paused for a moment before changing the subject. "I'm anxious to see my patients. Are they in the house?"

"I put them up in one of the cottages on the property. They are somewhat frightened and I thought it would be best if they had a place by themselves. Particularly the girl is scared out of her wits."

"Pain will do that to a person," Maya agreed as they crossed the foyer and walked toward Cain's office. "I did a little research on the practice of defanging a vampire."

Cain looked at her from the side, curious. "And?"

"It's been employed sporadically over the centuries, but lately the practice has been largely banned. It's considered cruel and unusual punishment."

"Well, it hasn't stopped the Mississippi clan from using it on those two unfortunates." Cain entered his office and motioned Gabriel and Maya to take a seat on the couch. He took the armchair opposite them.

"What do you know about that clan?" Gabriel asked.

"Precious little. My understanding is that we've been at war with them for decades over border disputes, but that they're seeking a peace agreement. I'm afraid I can't see how making peace with a clan that treats its own people so cruelly is in the interest of my kingdom." Calling it his kingdom still sounded foreign in his ears. "Wouldn't it mean I condone what they're doing?"

Gabriel contemplated his answer before he spoke. "Maybe it could become part of the peace negotiations. You'll make peace with them if they abandon certain practices."

"Sure, but who's going to enforce those rules? The only reason we know about their crimes is because those two vampires managed to escape and survive long enough to find shelter with us. Had Faye not tended to them and given them what they needed, they might have perished and we'd never be the wiser."

Maya smiled at him. "And how is Faye? I can't wait to meet her."

"She's charming." More than that, Faye was everything he'd ever dreamed of and more. Every minute he spent with her made him want her more. And what she'd done to him in the shower the previous night had been out of this world. To feel her mouth on him had been more than amazing, it had been mind blowing.

Gabriel chuckled and exchanged a look with his wife. "It seems our friend is quite smitten with her." Then he looked back at Cain. "I'm happy for you. How about your memory? Is anything coming back?"

"I'm afraid not. Which makes certain things difficult. I don't know who I can truly trust without knowing what my history with them is."

"That's understandable," Maya agreed. "But it's also an opportunity."

"An opportunity for what?"

"To see everything with fresh eyes."

Cain sighed. "Right now, I'd settle for remembering just a few essentials, rather than having to worry every moment of the day that I'd trip myself up and make people suspicious that things aren't the way they should be. I can't afford to appear weak."

"And you're not weak." Gabriel's words were reassuring. "I've always told you that you were an exceptional bodyguard when you were in our service. We're sorry to lose you."

Cain laughed. "Are you trying to tell me that I'm fired?"

"I believe by taking on this job here you were subtly trying to tell me that you quit," Gabriel joked. Then he turned serious again. "You were a skilled bodyguard. You'll be a great king."

Cain looked toward the window. "Would you believe me when I told you that before I became king here, I was actually the leader of the king's guard? I guess that's why I did so well with Scanguards. I had prior experience."

"Doesn't surprise me at all. From the start you knew what you were doing. You didn't need much training at all. Though your willingness to take orders did lack toward the end," Gabriel said and winked.

"Must be the fact that I'm not meant to take orders."

"Guess so."

Maya sat up straight. "Hate to interrupt your reminiscing, but I'd like to see my patients as soon as possible and examine them."

"Of course."

"Is there a place where we can do that in private? I'll need access to water and blood, and a surface to turn into an operating table. My guess is that the operation will be painful, and without any means to sedate them I'll need help restraining them. Maybe strap them down."

"The old plantation kitchen may be suitable for it. There's water and blood supplies, and it's a little separate from the rest of the palace. It'll provide some privacy. I'll be happy to assist." Cain looked at Gabriel, who nodded instantly.

"I'll help with restraining them," Gabriel agreed.

"Cain, I'm sure you have better things to do," Maya said. "Why don't you get Thomas to do it. He might even be able to calm them down a little with mind control. He's the only one who can safely use his skill on another vampire."

Maya was right. Thomas was a master of mind control. "I'm afraid Thomas and Eddie had to go into New Orleans to follow up on a lead. They won't be back for twenty-four hours."

"Oh, that's a shame."

"What kind of lead?" Gabriel wanted to know.

"We're not sure yet. Just a hunch. I'll fill you in later." Cain rose. "Let me introduce you to David and Kathryn and have my staff set up the kitchen for you to use."

Both Maya and Gabriel also rose when the door was suddenly ripped open. Cain whirled his head to it and saw Faye storm into the room.

"How could you!?" she yelled at him, her face a mask of fury, her eyes glaring at him.

Stunned, Cain froze. What had he done now? "Faye."

She marched toward him, when she suddenly seemed to realize that he wasn't alone.

"Faye, these are my friends: Gabriel and his mate Maya. Maya is the doctor I told you about."

Faye took a deep breath and nodded toward them. "Nice to meet you." Then she looked back at Cain. "Can we talk? In private."

Her tone told him that this conversation couldn't wait. He glanced at his friends, but didn't have to say anything.

"We'll be unpacking in the meantime," Maya suggested and took Gabriel's hand. "Shall we, baby?"

With a concerned look on his face, Gabriel followed his wife and shut the door behind them.

Cain waited another few seconds, before he looked back at Faye. He'd never seen her this furious. "What's wrong?"

32

Looking at Cain's clueless expression, Faye fumed even more. As if he'd already forgotten what he'd done!

"You locked up Robert! As if he were your enemy! How could you?"

Cain stiffened visibly. "I'm afraid that's my business. I have to protect myself."

Faye felt tears of frustration well up and pushed them down. "Robert is my friend! He's an honorable man! He's not your enemy."

Cain widened his stance, bringing his hands to his hips as if he wanted to intimidate her with his physicality. "Then why was a copy of the palace's blueprints found in his possession, together with an envelope with an address in Mississippi?"

Faye instinctively took a step back and pressed her hand against her chest. "You think he's a traitor?"

"What else am I supposed to think given the evidence?"

She shook her head in disbelief. "Robert would never do that. He's loyal to you. It's all a mistake."

"The evidence doesn't lie."

"Robert wouldn't betray you. He was my support all this time. He was there for me when I needed a shoulder to cry on. He's not a traitor. You have to believe me. Somebody must have set him up."

"You sound like him. He claimed that somebody planted the blueprints."

"You must believe him," she pleaded.

"How can I do that when in the same breath he admitted to having addressed the envelope himself? Thomas compared the address with Robert's ledger. It's his handwriting. Without a doubt. He did this, Faye. You're wrong about Robert. He wanted to sell sensitive information to the Mississippi clan to help them attack me. Most likely assassinate me."

Faye shook her head, trying to drown out his words. "No! You're wrong. Robert hates the Mississippians. He despises their practices. No way in hell would he sell information to them."

"Please stay out of this, Faye. Clearly, it upsets you. Let me handle this." He reached for her, but she shrank back.

"Stay out of it? So that's how it's gonna be between us, is it?"

Cain narrowed his eyes. "What are you saying?"

"Don't pretend you don't know. Are you really that blind?"

He clenched his teeth and took a step toward her. "What is going on, Faye? Why are you behaving like this?"

"Because of how you're behaving. This relationship is a farce."

An expression of shock spread over his face as fast as wildfire engulfed a forest during drought season. "You can't mean that. You and I, we are amazing together. We have great—"

"Sex?" Faye spat, interrupting him. "Oh yes, we have great sex. But that's all we have." She scoffed. "We have fabulous mind-blowing sex and then you turn away and close yourself off as soon as I want to talk to you. You don't share anything with me. What happened to you while you were gone?"

Cain evaded her gaze. "It's complicated."

"See!" She pointed her index finger at him. "You're doing it again. You're shutting me out and refuse to answer any of my questions about what happened during the year you were gone."

Cain sighed. "Faye, please, baby—"

"Don't call me baby. It clearly means nothing to you. Because beyond sex, there's nothing between us. You don't give a damn about my feelings. You make no effort getting closer to me, and you thwart every single one of my attempts to understand you. What do you want from me?"

"Faye, you're my fiancée."

"I don't care about being your fiancée. I want to be the woman you love. I want to be your confidante again. But you're shutting me out. And I can't pretend any longer that I can live like this."

There was a hitch in his breath. "What are you saying?"

"I can't come to your bed and have you make love to me when you don't mean it. Hell, you can't even say that you love me, can you?"

Cain lifted his hand as if reaching for her, but dropped it again. His lips parted to speak, but no words came out.

"I knew it."

"But you must know how I . . ."

"What must I know? I know nothing, Cain, nothing at all. Because you're not telling me anything. All I know is that you can't tell me that you love me." And that thought hurt the most. Despite the physical intimacy they'd shared in the last few days and nights, emotionally they were farther apart than ever before.

"You're overreacting."

"Am I?" How dare he marginalize her concerns? "Release Robert, and I'll give you another chance to explain, but don't expect me to warm your bed again. I'm not going to marry a man who doesn't love me, no matter who he is. If you can't tell me that you love me and mean it, then you and I have no future together. Make your choice, because mine is made."

She turned abruptly and marched to the door. Her hand on the door handle, she hesitated for a moment.

"Don't do this," Cain pleaded.

"Those are the wrong words."

Her heart aching, she opened the door and left the room. Only once she had reached the stairs leading to the lower floor did she dare breathe again. By the time she reached her suite, tears were streaming down her face.

Cain didn't love her.

33

Cain had contemplated running after Faye the instant she'd charged out of his office. But what would have been the use? He couldn't say the words she wanted to hear. Not yet, not when he had to continue to lie to her about himself. Only when he could tell her about his amnesia and what had really happened to him could he confess his feelings for her. Doing it while he was still hiding the truth from her would cheapen the moment. And he didn't want to tarnish the one real emotion that he was finally certain of. The prospect of losing her had made it clear to him once and for all: he was in love with Faye.

How could he tell her that he loved her when in the same breath he had to continue to lie to her?

When he got word from Gabriel that everything was set up for the procedure on the two fugitive vampires, Cain was glad for the distraction.

The old plantation kitchen was set up like an operating theater—complete with sterile linens, stainless steel bowls, and sterilized instruments Maya had brought with her from San Francisco. The only thing missing was anesthesia. Unfortunately, vampires couldn't be put under with the drugs that worked so well for humans.

"Who wants to go first?" Maya asked and looked at David and Kathryn.

David had his arm around the girl, hugging her to him. "Do me first. But don't make Kathryn watch."

Kathryn clung to him, frightened. He looked down at her, his voice softer when he addressed her. "It will be all right, little one. You'll be safe with them."

Cain pointed to Blake who stood near the entrance door. "Blake can take her to the library in the meantime." He figured that since Blake was human, the girl would be less frightened of him than if somebody like Gabriel would guard her.

Kathryn glanced in Blake's direction. Cain noticed how Blake smiled at her encouragingly.

"There's also a big screen TV in there," Blake coaxed. "We can watch a movie, or play Xbox."

Cain rolled his eyes. He doubted Kathryn was into playing some stupid game on Xbox.

"Xbox?" she echoed.

Blake grinned. "Yeah, I'll teach you."

"Go with him, Kathryn," David encouraged her. "You'll be safe with him."

Hesitantly, she left the shelter of David's arms and walked toward Blake. When she reached him, she looked over her shoulder, seeking further encouragement from her friend, who nodded. A moment later, she left the room with Blake by her side.

Gabriel closed the door behind them.

"Lay down on the table, please," Maya instructed David. "It will hurt, I'm afraid. But there's nothing I can do about that."

"I know that." David glanced at Cain and Gabriel. "I suppose that's why you have two men assisting you."

Cain approached. "We'll be strapping you down on the table. I'll be holding your head immobile, and Gabriel will make sure you don't escape from the straps. We don't want to use silver." Though it would assure that the vampire couldn't move, Cain had no intention of inflicting even more pain on him than he'd already endured.

Nodding, David climbed onto the table which had been covered with a white sheet. While Maya slipped on some latex gloves, Cain and Gabriel proceeded to put leather straps across David's legs, thighs, and torso, and tie them underneath the table. When he was secured, Cain looked at the patient.

"Ready?"

David swallowed hard. "Ready."

"I'll make this as quick as I can," Maya promised and picked up stainless steel pliers from a tray next to the table. "I'll first test how tightly the ball is lodged in your gums, okay?"

David blinked his eyes in acquiescence, while Cain placed his hands to either side of his head and gripped him firmly to hold him in place.

Maya bent over her patient. "Open wide."

Suddenly the door was ripped open and everybody snapped their heads in its direction.

"Wait!" Wesley stormed into the room, kicking the door shut behind him. "I've got something to numb his pain."

David tried to rear up from the table, but the leather straps prevented him from lifting anything except his head. "Witch!"

"Stay calm, David," Cain assuaged him. "Wesley is a friend. He means you no harm. He's here to help." However, Cain had his doubts that the witch was capable of what he claimed.

Wesley walked to the table. "I put together a potion. It should work on a vampire."

"Should?" Maya asked skeptically.

"It will," Wes corrected. "It'll put him into a bit of a trance and make him less aware of what you're doing."

Maya exhaled. "And if it doesn't work?"

Wes shrugged. "If it doesn't, then it just doesn't have any effect. It can't hurt him. Promise."

"It better not tint him red," Gabriel interjected.

"What?" David asked, confused.

Wesley stared at the patient. "Don't listen to him. Some people here will just never let me forget my mistakes, no matter how much I've improved my witchcraft."

"Improved?" David tossed a quizzical look at Cain. "He's an apprentice?"

Cain shifted his weight from one leg to the other. Pointing out to David that Wesley wasn't exactly an expert in his field wouldn't help in this situation. Maybe for once it was better to cut the kid some slack. "Wesley is an accomplished witch."

Suddenly a smile formed on the older man's face. "You're a terrible liar, Your Majesty." Then he glanced at Wesley. "Well, do your thing then and let's hope it won't kill me."

Triumphantly, Wesley removed a vial from his shirt pocket. "You'll all need to step back for a moment, so you don't inhale it, too."

Cain took a few steps back, as did Maya and Gabriel. Then Wesley opened the vial and held it under David's nose. A green colored mist rose from it.

"Just inhale deeply," Wes instructed in a soothing voice.

The vampire did as told and pulled in a deep breath. His eyes closed and suddenly his head rolled to the side. He was unconscious.

"Oops." Wes looked up, a sheepish look on his face.

Cain charged at him. "What the fuck did you do now?"

"I suppose the potion was a little stronger than I thought. Don't worry, he's just out for a little while." He motioned to Maya. "Better start right away. I have no idea how long it's gonna last."

"That's just great," Gabriel grumbled. Then he pointed to the door. "Better get out of here. He might not be too happy to see you when he comes to."

"*If* he comes to," Cain added.

"You're such pessimists," Wes complained and turned on his heel. "Call me when it's all done and I'll take care of the girl, too."

When the door closed behind him, Maya took up the pliers once more. "Well, let's do it then."

Cain took both sides of David's head again and turned it to face upward.

"Spread his jaw open," Maya instructed.

He gripped the vampire's jaw and pried it open, then reached for the metal rectangle which was the size of a candy bar and wedged it between David's teeth on the left side of his mouth, making sure his mouth remained open and Maya could freely access the right side.

Cain watched as she set the pliers at the spot where the small metal ball that the Mississippi vampires had implanted was visible. She tried to grip it with her instrument, but it slipped without finding purchase.

Maya looked up. "I can't get a grip. I'll have to cut it out instead."

She set aside the pliers and reached for a scalpel instead. The moment she made the first incision into the gum, the air filled with the scent of the vampire's blood. Cain turned his head away, but he couldn't prevent his fangs from lengthening as a reaction to the smell.

"That's better," he heard Maya mumble. "Just a little bit more." She grunted and Cain felt David's head in his hands move.

"Shit, he's coming to," Cain warned her. "Quick!"

"Gabriel, the pliers."

Instantly, Gabriel jumped and handed her the pliers while taking the scalpel from her hand.

A moan came from the patient now.

Cain noticed David's eyeballs move underneath his lids. "It's wearing off too quickly."

"Got it!" Maya called out and pulled.

Blood splattered as Maya ripped the ball from the vampire's mouth and tossed it in a bowl.

"Now the other side."

Gabriel already switched the scalpel for the pliers in her hand, while Cain hastily moved the metal block in the vampire's mouth to the other side.

The incision on the left seemed to take Maya less time, and moments later she was already gripping the second ball with her instrument.

When she ripped the ball out, David's head reared up and his eyes shot open at the same time. A pain-filled scream tore from his throat while blood splattered all over his front and the metal block slipped from his mouth. His eyes were glaring red, and he jerked at his restraints.

"It's over, David, it's all good," Cain tried to calm him and gripped his shoulders, pressing him back down onto the table.

The vampire's chest heaved, but finally his eyes connected with Cain's gaze, and he blinked.

"Are they out?" he asked, his speech sounding a little muffled.

Maya smiled at him. "Yes, they're both out. Let's get you some human blood so you can heal."

David closed his eyes and sighed. When he opened them again, he looked calm again. "Thank you. All of you."

"Did you feel anything?" Maya asked.

"Only when you pulled just now."

"Good."

David looked around the room. "Where's the witch?"

"We sent him outside. I figured you might not want to see him after this," Cain said.

"Bring him back. And make sure he gives Kathryn a larger dosage of his potion. I don't want her to feel any pain."

"You got it," Cain agreed.

34

While both Kathryn and David were resting after their procedures, and Maya and Gabriel watching over them to see if their fangs would indeed grow back during their restorative sleep, Cain paced in this office.

Faye's staunch belief in Robert's innocence made him doubt his own suspicions. Though Thomas had talked to the prisoner, he hadn't been able to make him admit to the treasonous act. Robert had continued to declare his innocence.

Did he have anything to lose by talking to Robert himself?

Cain charged out of his office and nearly bumped into Abel in the hallway.

"Whoa, Cain, where are you off to in such a hurry?"

"Going to see Robert in his cell."

"Ah, the traitor. Do you want me to come with you?"

Cain was already walking past Abel and didn't even turn his head when he responded, "No!" and continued on his way into the lower level of the palace. By now he knew the layout well enough to find the cellblock without having to ask anybody for directions.

One guard—Cain recognized him as Simon—sat at a table in the anteroom to the cells. He jumped up instantly when Cain entered.

"Good evening, Your Majesty."

"Evening. Open Robert's cell and let me in."

"Of course, sir." Simon unhooked the keys from his belt and motioned to a heavy iron door at the end of the corridor.

Cain walked to it and waited until the guard had unlocked and opened it. "Lock it after me. I'll let you know when I'm done."

He stepped into the dim interior and heard the door shut behind him with a loud thud. His eyes perceived Robert instantly. He sat on a small cot in the corner, his back stiff and his gaze locked onto Cain.

"To what do I owe the pleasure?" Robert said with a good dose of sarcasm in his tone.

Cain didn't let that show of defiance deter him. "Faye is pleading for your release."

A spark ignited in the older vampire's eyes. "Ah, Faye, she still believes in the good in people, doesn't she?"

"Is she wrong in doing so?"

"Sometimes she is."

"And this time?"

Robert gave a slow shake of his head. "This time her instincts are right. I'm not a traitor. What I told you is true. Somebody set me up."

"And why should I believe you?"

"I can't help you there." Robert shrugged.

"That's not very helpful."

"Why are you really here? If Faye had managed to convince you, you'd be releasing me now." He glanced at the door. "But it doesn't look like you're letting me go. So, if she couldn't convince you of my innocence, there's no reason for me to try. You and I, we always had a bit of a rocky relationship. If you trust anybody in this place, it's Faye. It's always been that way, ever since you rescued her."

To have Robert confirm Cain's trust in Faye felt reassuring. "A rocky relationship, huh?"

Robert smiled. "Yeah. I never approved of the way you disposed of the old king."

Cain instinctively took a step back. "Disposed of?" What was Robert suggesting?

The captive dropped his eyes to the floor. "My apologies if you think that's not the right word for what you did. No matter whether he deserved it or not. But you slaughtered him; you let him suffer like an animal before you put him out of his misery." Robert made a dismissive movement with his hand. "Well, it's all water under the bridge now. You got what you wanted, didn't you? And now you're king. And guess what, you find it just as difficult to make the right decisions as any of your predecessors."

The words hit him hard. Had he, Cain, really killed the previous king? No, that couldn't be. He wasn't an assassin. He was honorable man with ethics. Not a murderer, and for certain not a man who inflicted undue pain. He didn't torture people.

"You're mistaken."

"Why deny it?" Robert asked, meeting his eyes. "Everybody suspects it, though only few know with certainty."

"That's enough!" Cain ground out between clenched teeth.

"See, you can't even take the truth, but you expect me to accept being falsely accused. I'm innocent. Faye believes in me."

Cain looked away and tried to clear his mind. He didn't want to dwell on Robert's revelation that he was a king slayer, because wouldn't that mean that he, Cain, was evil?

"Faye says you're her friend."

"She needed a shoulder to cry on when she thought you were dead."

"I thought Abel would have been that shoulder."

Robert scoffed. "Abel? She was avoiding him as much as she could."

The words only reinforced Cain's suspicion that Abel had been trying to drive a wedge between him and Faye, even though it appeared that Cain had driven that wedge in himself now by not coming clean with her. It was something he needed to do, or he would lose her. But Faye had given him one other condition to fulfill: she wanted Robert's freedom.

Cain looked back at his prisoner, staring long and hard at him. Could he take the risk to believe in Robert's words and free him? Maybe it was time to take that leap.

"Guard!"

***

"Guard! Open the fucking door!" Cain yelled from behind the heavy cell door.

Abel felt like rubbing his hands together and only refrained from it because it was a childish gesture. However, it didn't make him feel any less giddy. The timing was perfect. And even though this had not been his original plan, he couldn't have planned it any better himself.

Cain was in the cell with Robert. This was the perfect occasion to pin Cain's murder on Robert and thus still implicate the Mississippi clan. Everybody knew that Robert had been found with incriminating materials he'd wanted to send to the rival clan. Nobody believed his claim that the blueprints had been planted. Nobody but Abel, because Abel had been the one who had slipped the papers into Robert's ledger and made sure one of Baltimore's men would find them there and report it.

It had all worked like clockwork, though Abel had only done it to draw suspicion on the Mississippians, so that once Cain was found dead when the rival clan arrived for the festivities, it would be easy to point the finger.

But the solution that lay in front of him now was even easier. All he would have to do was kill Cain himself, pin it on Robert, then execute him and declare war on the Mississippians.

Abel made a motion to Simon, the guard who was stationed in the cellblock. He was loyal to Baltimore. Simon walked up to him and Abel bent closer, talking quietly into his ear and giving him instructions as to what to do.

Simon nodded obediently and walked to a cupboard. He unlocked it and took out a small-caliber handgun. He screwed the silencer onto its front end.

"Loaded?" Abel whispered.

"With silver bullets."

Abel took it and cocked the gun. He loved the sound that echoed against the stone walls. "Do you have a stake?"

"Yes, sir."

"Good. Make sure it's found in Robert's cell once we're done." Even though Abel was going to shoot his brother with a silver bullet which would incinerate him from the inside out, the end result would be the same. Nobody finding Cain's ashes would be able to tell whether he'd been staked or shot. All Abel had to do was to remove the bullet and the casing from the cell before he sounded the alarm. Nobody would hear the shot.

"Ready?" Abel asked.

Simon nodded and slipped the key into the lock, then turned it silently. At Abel's nod, he pushed the door open.

Abel aimed into the dark, his trigger finger twitching.

But he didn't pull the trigger.

The cell was empty.

Stunned, he turned to his accomplice. "What the fuck?"

The vampire guard looked just as surprised. Only moments earlier, Abel had heard Cain call out to the guard to be let out of the cell. But Simon hadn't opened the door.

Abel had to think quickly. If Cain and Robert had escaped somehow, it wouldn't take long until they were coming back around the other side, exposing his plan. He had no time to wonder how they'd done it. He had to cover his tracks. This instant.

"Sorry about this," Abel said, looking at Simon.

The shot was muffled by the silencer, hitting Simon in the forehead. Slowly the vampire disintegrated into dust.

Abel cursed. He was back to square one, and would now patiently have to wait until he could execute his original plan. So much for golden opportunities.

35

In the tunnel, Cain turned to Robert. "Take off your shirt."

"What for?"

"So I can blindfold you." After all, even though he'd found the entrance to the tunnels that John had mentioned and had managed to get himself and Robert out of the cell before somebody had thrown the door open, Cain wasn't about to reveal all his secrets to Robert. He couldn't allow him to actually see the tunnels. It was bad enough that he now knew about them.

"One word about the tunnels, and I'll stake you myself."

Robert took off his shirt and handed it to Cain. "You have my word."

Had Cain not heard the cocking of a gun through the door as well as some low whispers, whose origin he couldn't discern, he and Robert would have been sitting ducks. Dead sitting ducks. Who the would-be assassin had been, he didn't even want to speculate about at this point.

As soon as Robert was blindfolded, Cain took him by the elbow and guided him through the labyrinth until he reached the secret walkway that led to the king's suite. He let himself in, dragging Robert with him. When the piece of artwork snapped back into place in front of the hidden door in his room, he turned Robert around his own axis several times.

"Now you can take off your blindfold."

When Robert did so, his eyes roamed the room. "What now?"

Cain had already marched to the door, but stopped himself before he reached it and rushed to the bedside table. He bent down and pulled a gun from the drawer and holstered it, when his eyes fell on something beneath his bed. A cell phone. His hand instinctively went to his pants pocket, but his cell phone was where it was supposed to be. Not having time to investigate this any further, he rushed to the door and opened it.

"Haven?" he called out.

A moment later, his Scanguards colleague popped his head out of his room, his cell phone pressed to his ear. "Yeah?"

"I need you, now!"

"Gotta go. Kiss the baby for me. Love you," he said into the phone then disconnected the call and rushed toward Cain. "What's wrong?"

"I believe somebody made another attempt on my life."

"Shit!"

"Get your gun." Then he turned to Robert. "Stay here."

Haven returned to his room and was back two seconds later, his gun in his hand. Behind him, a sleepy looking Wesley emerged. "What's going on?" His clothes looked rumpled.

"Go and make sure Faye is in her suite. Then guard her with your life."

Not waiting for his answer, Cain charged down the hallway, heading for the cellblock, Haven on his heels.

When he entered the anteroom to the cells, Cain already knew he was too late. The door to Robert's cell stood wide open, but the cellblock was empty. The guard was gone, and so was whatever visitor he'd had. His eyes fell on a cupboard whose door was still swinging as if somebody had slammed it, but failed to let it snap shut. In the cupboard, several guns hung on hooks.

Cain walked to it and sniffed. One of them had been fired recently. He could still smell the residue.

"Shit, look at that!" Haven called out to him.

Cain turned and saw him crouching down near the door to the cell. When he approached, Cain could see what his friend was looking at. A fine layer of ash. Amidst it lay a cell phone and some coins. The keys still stuck in the door.

"Somebody killed the guard."

Cain nodded and tilted his head toward the cupboard behind him. "One of those guns was fired. And I'm sure once we examine it, we'll find out that there are no fingerprints on it."

"Let's give it a whirl anyway," Haven suggested.

"You and Gabriel check it out. Then go get Robert and bring him to a safe place." After this attempt, Cain was certain that Robert had been framed as he'd claimed. "I have to talk to John."

Cain turned on his heel and left. He found the leader of the king's guard in his new room on the first floor. When Cain ripped the door open, an only half-dressed John reared up from his bed.

"Cain!" John set his feet on the floor and jumped up. "What do you need?"

"I need to know the truth. Did I assassinate the old king?"

Clearly stunned, John blinked. "How do you—?"

"—know? Robert alluded to it. Is it true?"

John looked down at his bare feet. "Yes."

"Why the fuck didn't you tell me?"

John lifted his head. "It wasn't important."

"It wasn't important? I'm a murderer, an assassin!"

"And it's always haunted you. That's why I didn't tell you. I didn't want you to go through the same thing again. You blamed yourself for how savagely you killed him, despite the fact that the old bastard deserved everything that he got."

All air rushed from Cain's lungs. "I slaughtered him, didn't I?" Was that what he was, a man without scruples? A cold-blooded murderer?

John nodded. "When you saw what he'd done, you flew into a rage. And when you saw his victims, when you saw Faye, there was no stopping you."

"Faye?"

"She was one of the unfortunates he'd locked up in a part of the cellars that's now been filled in with debris. You found out that the old king liked to make it a sport to capture vampires from other clans and torture them. Faye was one of them."

Cain rubbed a hand over his face. "Oh, God."

"I didn't want you to have to think about all this again. I needed you to have a clear head."

"Who else knows I killed the king?"

"Your brother, of course. He was your second-in-command when you were leader of the king's guard. A few others knew, Robert included. But the rest of your subjects only suspect it was you."

"There must be members of my clan who hate me for it."

"No doubt, but the few who know for certain never breathed a word about it, and the others won't raise a hand against you."

"They're afraid of me, aren't they? Afraid that I'll kill whoever rises against me."

"Every king has his enemies."

"And I have more than my fair share. No wonder somebody wants to get rid of me." Cain paused, taking a breath before asking the question that was most important to him.

"And Faye? Does she know?"

"She knows. She watched you when you delivered the death blow."

Cain jolted back, shocked at the revelation. "Why would I let her watch?"

"You wanted her not to be afraid any longer. You wanted her to know that you'd slay any dragon for her."

Cain dropped down onto the bed. Faye knew all his secrets, had seen him at his most savage, yet she still loved him. She was stronger than he could have ever guessed. If she had stood by him when he'd killed the evil king, would she stand by him now when he laid himself bare before her?

36

Faye heard the knock at the door to her suite and stopped pacing for the first time in the last two hours, ever since Wesley had come to see her and told her to remain in the safety of her own rooms until he told her otherwise. She hadn't protested. Past experience had taught her to heed warnings when their bearer issued them with a glint of fear in his eyes. And the witch had looked alarmed enough to make Faye follow his command without question.

Her heart pounded into her throat when she answered, "Come in."

Her eyes on the door, she watched it open. None other than Cain stepped inside and closed the door behind him. He remained standing there, his eyes searching hers then running them over her body as if to assure himself that she was all right. That action made her even more nervous. Her hands clasped in front of her stomach, she took a hesitant step toward him.

"What's going on?"

Cain motioned to the sofa in front of the fireplace. "I think you should sit down."

So the news was bad. Really bad. Nobody ever asked another person to sit down for good news. "I'd rather stand."

"Fine." She saw him swallow hard, before his mouth opened again to speak. "There was an attempt on my life."

Faye gasped and instinctively pressed one hand against her chest. "Oh, God, no!"

"I'm all right."

"What happened?"

"I went to see Robert in his cell to talk to him. When I called the guard to unlock the door, I got no reply. But I heard a gun being cocked."

Her feet carried her to him, and her hands reached for him, finding hold in his shirt. "Cain! Oh, no!" The thought of Cain's life being in danger cut off her air supply. "Who was it?"

"I don't know."

Faye tilted her head to the side. How could he not know? He'd clearly survived. "But you must have killed him. Otherwise, how would you be alive?"

"I managed to escape through the tunnels."

Stunned, she stared at him. While she was aware of the tunnels and the secret passage way between her and the king's suite, she didn't know all the other underground routes. Cain had only shown her the one entrance she needed to know. "There is an entrance to the tunnels in the cellblock?"

"It saved my life."

Suddenly her breath hitched. "And Robert?"

Cain stroked his hands over her upper arms. "Robert is safe." He dropped his head. "I want to apologize to you. You were right. Robert isn't a traitor. After what happened in the cell, I firmly believe that Robert was set up, maybe even to lure me down there to him so the assassin could get rid of me and blame Robert for it. I can't know for sure."

Relief traveled through her. Cain had taken her advice after all and given Robert a chance. But relief wasn't long lasting, because her advice had landed him in this dangerous situation. "I'm so sorry, Cain. If I hadn't put such pressure on you to see Robert, this wouldn't have happened." She felt tears well up in her eyes and tried desperately to push them down.

"It's not your fault. You did the right thing. I was wrong about Robert."

"What are you going to do now? Where's the guard that did this?"

Cain shook his head. "The guard is dead. Most likely killed by whoever is behind this. My men are looking for the assassin, but we don't have much hope. He didn't leave any clues. We found a weapon that was most likely used to kill the guard. Haven checked for fingerprints, but there were none."

Faye searched his eyes. "He's going to try again and again until he succeeds, isn't he?" How would Cain ever be safe?

"We have to assume that. That's why I'm here."

Her forehead creased at his odd statement. "What do you mean?" Was he suspecting her after all, even though he'd said it wasn't her fault? Her heartbeat drummed in her chest. "You can't believe that I'm—"

"Faye." He pulled her closer. The intensity in his gaze rendered her immobile. "When I was in that cell about to be assassinated, all I could think of was you, and that I would never get a chance to tell you the truth if I died."

"The truth?" she heard herself echo.

"About me and what really happened during the year I was gone." Cain took a breath. "I lied to you, Faye."

Instinctively, she tried to pull away from him, but his hands wrapped around her upper arms and didn't allow her to escape.

"But I can't go on lying any longer." He closed his eyes for a moment.

Speechless, she stared at him.

"I think you'll want to sit down for this." He released her. "Please."

Her entire body numb, she walked to the sofa and sat down, her back remaining stiff. Was he going to tell her now that there had been another woman after all?

The sofa cushions depressed when he sat down close to her, his body turned sideways to face her, his hands reaching for hers, holding them gently.

"I wasn't kidnapped a year ago. An assassin made an attempt on my life and injured me. John saved my life, but the head injury was bad. When I came to, I had no memory of my life. I didn't know who I was. I had complete amnesia."

Faye gasped.

"John made the decision to smuggle me out of the palace via the tunnels and stage my death to keep me safe. I believe he did the right thing under the circumstances. I was in no state to defend myself against another attack."

Faye pressed her hand to her lips. "Oh my God!"

"That's not all."

What else could there be? "You're back now. You can fight whoever is behind this."

The sad smile Cain gave her made her heart clench with pain. "Faye, I haven't recovered from the amnesia."

Not understanding, she shook her head. "What do you mean? Any non-mortal injury a vampire has will heal over time. And you came back. So you must remember."

Cain sighed. "For the last year, I've been working as a bodyguard for Scanguards. They became my friends, the only friends and family I remember. My memory still isn't back. I don't know why the injury never healed." He looked into the fireplace. "Faye, I don't remember you. I don't remember loving you. I remember nothing of my old life. Nothing about us. That's why I couldn't tell you what you needed to hear from me."

A sob tore from her throat. He didn't remember loving her? "Cain," she whispered, but her voice broke with another sob. So it was true then; he didn't love her anymore and had only been pretending. "The last few days. They were a lie," she said, talking to herself.

Cain turned his head back to her and clasped her hands once more. "Not all of it. I may not remember our love, but that doesn't mean I don't feel it."

Her eyelashes rose and her eyes widened while she sucked in a breath.

His loving gaze pinned her. "I was given a second chance, Faye. A second chance to fall in love with you all over again. When you came to my room after my return, for me it was the first time I'd ever kissed you. Everything was the first time for me. To make love to you here in front of the fireplace, to feel your lips around my cock when you came to me in the shower. I got to experience your passion, your tenderness for the first time." He shoved a hand through his short hair. "But when you pressed me to tell you that I love you, I couldn't say it. I couldn't lie to you and profess my love when I didn't trust my own feelings. I can now. Because now I've seen what kind of woman you are. You're good and generous. Loyal and faithful even when you thought me dead."

Regret suddenly flashed in his eyes.

"I'm so sorry, Faye, but you have to know this: I slept with other women. I didn't know you existed. Had I known, I would have never touched another woman." Cain dropped his head. "None of them meant anything. In my dreams it was always you."

While it pained her to hear that he'd been with other women, she couldn't really blame him. Without any knowledge of his former life, how would he have known to be faithful to her? Faye put her hand on his forearm. "Don't blame yourself. Tell me about your dreams."

Cain looked up, a tentative smile on his lips. "Several months ago I started dreaming about you. About us. Making love. I saw everything so vividly, I thought it was real. That's why I had to come back when John came to see me last week and told me about you. About the fact that Abel had proposed to you. I knew I had to fight for you."

"And for your kingdom," she added.

He shook his head. "I didn't come back for the kingdom. I came back only for you. What I felt in my dreams became reality. *You* became reality. And the way you treated those strangers and helped them, truly revealed your heart to me. And your trust in Robert only cemented what I already knew."

Cain lifted his hand to her cheek and caressed it. "I can say it now, because I know it's true. I love you, Faye, and no matter what happens, I'll never again forget that I love you."

A single tear escaped her eye and ran down her cheek, leaving a hot trail in its wake. "Cain." It was all she could say.

"Will you take me back?"

Through tears in her eyes, Faye nodded, but words failed her. Instead she reached for him and pulled him closer, leaning her forehead against his.

"Help me remember, my love, and I promise I'll do anything in my power to become the man you once loved."

She pulled back a fraction and took his face into her hands. "Oh Cain, but you *are* the man I love. That will never change."

A moment later his lips were on hers, and her heart opened to welcome him home.

37

Faye's lips gave Cain all the reassurance he needed to take the next step. The final step. He had no doubt that if his own life was in danger, so was Faye's. And there was only one way to make certain that he could truly protect her.

Reluctantly, he severed the kiss before it turned too heated. Breathing heavily, he pressed his forehead against hers. "Blood-bond with me. Right now."

Faye gasped and drew away from him, but only enough to look into his eyes. "Now?"

"This instant. So I'll always be able to protect you." Their bond would allow him to sense when she was in danger, just as she would sense if he found himself in a perilous situation and reached out to her. Together they would be stronger than as individuals.

"Yes. My love."

A smile formed on his lips. "My queen."

He stood and lifted her into his arms. Her hands laced behind his neck, and she brought her lips back to his to kiss him. Finally, he could let himself go. He'd told her everything, and she'd forgiven him. Nothing stood in their way now, nothing but their clothes.

Cain knew that Wesley was still standing guard outside the door of the queen's suite, ready to alert him should any trouble arise. But he hoped no immediate trouble would ensue to give him a chance to make the next few hours with Faye a lasting memory. It would be the start of their lives together. The beginning of eternity.

He laid her down on the bed, simultaneously ridding himself of his shoes, before slipping hers off her delicate feet and dropping them to the floor.

"I need you," Faye murmured and reached for him, pulling him on top of her.

"So eager," he whispered back.

"I've waited for you for so long."

Cain brushed a strand of hair from her cheek. "I'll never again make you wait for anything. I promise. From now on, you'll always come first."

"But your kingdom—"

He put his finger over her lips. "My kingdom isn't half as important as my love for you."

She smiled up at him. "You *have* changed. A year ago the needs of the kingdom were more important to you than anything else."

"I must have been a fool." Cain lowered his lips to hers and took possession of her mouth, wanting to show her what he felt for her, how she got under his skin.

Her mouth was yielding, inviting his invasion and welcoming him with firm strokes of her tongue against his and the strong press of her lips against his mouth. Her hands cupped the back of his head as if she wanted to make sure that he didn't withdraw ever again.

Finally he could explore her without regret, without guilt about the lies he'd told her. Only the truth existed between them now, and it made being in her arms so much more perfect.

"I love you," Cain murmured between taking a breath and capturing her lips again for a deeper kiss, drowning out whatever reply she had for him.

No words were necessary now, because he could feel the depth of her devotion to him in the way her body pressed against him, the way her hips ground against his pelvis, asking silently to make her his. Just like her tongue danced with him in a mating dance as old as time itself.

Faye tasted like a rainbow after a long downpour. The scent of her skin filled his nostrils and drove a spear of anticipation through the core of his body. He was already aflame. Her kiss alone could do that to him, turn him into a man who could think of only one thing: making the woman in his arms his forever. In that instant, he reveled in the fact that he was an immortal being, a vampire, for whom the words *I'll love you forever* really meant forever. And he counted himself lucky to have found Faye, to have saved her, so that she could save him in turn.

Even if he never gained his memory back, it didn't matter anymore, because he had Faye back. She was his memory, his life. Nothing else mattered.

Slowly, with gentle movements, Cain started to peel away layer after layer of her clothing, first her T-shirt, then her jeans. Then he allowed her to do the same to him, to strip him of his shirt and his pants. He stopped her when she reached for his boxer briefs.

"Not yet." He didn't want to rush this, and though his cock was already tenting the front of his boxer briefs, he wasn't ready to let the beast out of the cage. He wanted to savor this moment.

"Didn't you just promise never to make me wait again?" Faye coaxed.

He couldn't help but chuckle. "Oh, I'm not going to make *you* wait, just myself. I will shower you with pleasure this instant."

Faye slid her hand onto his nape and pulled him back down to her. "I like the sound of that."

He brushed his lips against hers in a feather light touch, while farther down, he moved into the "v" of her thighs, his groin resting against her pelvis. Even through the fabric of their underwear, he could feel how wet she was, how ready for him.

Cain inhaled, taking the tantalizing scent of her arousal deep into his lungs. His gaze wandered from her face down to her neck, where he saw her vein pulse as if to lure him to her. Soon, he'd drive his fangs into that very spot and take her blood to form an unbreakable bond with her.

Without haste, he hooked his thumb underneath one strap of her bra and slid it off her shoulder. He did the same with the other one, then pushed the cups down, away from her breasts, exposing her rosy peaks to his view. Rock-hard, they greeted him. He dipped his head and sucked one pert nipple into his mouth, swiping his tongue over it.

His eyes closed without his doing, and his body delighted in her taste and the texture of her flesh. Her moan sounded in his ears and confirmed that he gave her what she wanted. Eager to please her, he licked and sucked her beautiful breast, while his hands busied themselves to free her from the garment. When he'd finally opened the clasp, he tossed the bra aside.

He switched to her other breast, paying the same attention to it as to the first. His hands now free, Cain squeezed her breasts in concert with his sucking motions, and earned more moans and sighs for his efforts.

Faye's back arched off the bed as she thrust her voluptuous bosom deeper into his mouth, demanding he suck harder.

The temptation to do more than just lick her was too strong to resist. He allowed his fangs to scrape against her warm flesh and felt her shiver from the contact.

"Yes!" she cried out, her voice a symphony of passion and need.

The vampire inside him responded to it with a growl.

"Screw it," he cursed, releasing her breast. He couldn't wait. He'd wanted to, but he had no control over the beast inside him that demanded his mate. "I'm sorry, Faye, I need you now."

Their eyes met when she looked down at him. "What took you so long?"

With one jerky movement he rid himself of his boxer briefs then reached for her panties. The thin fabric ripped instantly though he barely touched it. Maybe the fact that his hands had turned into claws had something to do with that.

With all barriers gone, he adjusted his cock, bringing its tip to Faye's quivering slit, and plunged into her. Her heat imprisoned him instantly, robbing him of his breath. Her legs wrapped around him, her ankles locking him into a tight vise, making escape impossible. She'd imprisoned him. And he couldn't imagine a more heavenly prison to find himself in.

Cain undulated his hips and began to slide in and out of her inviting body. This was where he belonged. Just like in his dreams, he could sense their connection, the love they shared; only now it was real. *She* was real.

"I'll always love you, Faye," he murmured, gazing into her green eyes that had already started to change color.

With every second that their bodies moved in synch with each other, her irises turned from a vibrant green to a deep orange, to a glowing red. She was all vampire now, her primal needs at their height.

"Show them to me," he demanded, and gazed at Faye's lips as they parted.

Razor-sharp fangs peeked from her upper gums. The sight sent a jolt of desire through him, making his cock jerk impatiently. His eyes shifted, homing in on the vein that pulsed at her neck. He felt his fangs itch more urgently now, eager to drive into her flesh.

Sucking in a steadying breath, he locked eyes with her once more. "You're mine." No sooner had the words left his lips, did he press his mouth onto her neck and pierce her soft skin with his fangs.

Beneath him, Faye arched into him, rubbing her body against his.

Her sweet blood spread on his tongue and ran down the back of his throat. He swallowed greedily, taking her essence into him. Then he felt her lips on his shoulder, just below where it connected to his neck. At the contact, a shudder charged through his entire body. Then her fangs touched his skin, and inside him the fire raged more violently.

Trembling with need, he waited for her fangs to finally pierce his skin. When they lodged in his flesh and he felt her drawing from his vein, pleasure shot through his blood vessels and drove more blood to his cock. It hardened more than it seemed possible, and the tempo of its relentless movements quickened.

Perspiration now covered his skin, making him slide even more smoothly against her. Faye's breathing too had accelerated, and her sighs and moans became more pronounced, just as her movements turned more demanding.

Yes, he loved this woman, loved her with every fiber of his being. And as he took more and more of her blood into him, just as she took his blood, he could sense the changes happening in their bodies. He could feel the vines of love wrap around them to bind them together, to make them one. Their hearts now drummed with the same beat, their breaths filled their lungs with unerring synchrony. And farther below, where they were joined by his cock inside her, another heartbeat drummed steadily, driving them higher with every second.

Cain swallowed down Faye's intoxicating blood and let himself go. A wave of pleasure washed over him, catapulting him to a place where only love and ecstasy existed. Faye's body spasmed at the same time, her pussy gripping him tightly and milking every last drop of semen from him.

His orgasm was more powerful than he'd ever experienced before, but something else was even more amazing. He could sense her now. He was in her mind, in her thoughts, in her heart. Warmth wrapped around him, protecting him like a soft cocoon, just like he was protecting her. They were one, free to share their love, their thoughts, and their hearts with each other.

I love you, Cain, he heard her words echo in his mind, though her lips hadn't moved.

Always, he responded by sending her his thoughts.

Then something white flashed in front of his eyes, shot through his head like a spear and made him jolt backward. Pain shot through his head. He pressed his hands against his temples, trying to stop his skull from exploding.

"Cain! Oh God, what's wrong?" Faye's panicked voice brought him back to earth.

Slowly he released his head. The pain was gone as quickly as it had come, but it had left something with him.

"I remember everything. Faye, I remember us."

38

Fully dressed, Cain took Faye's hand and looked at her. Faye had given him his old life back. His memory was fully restored. He remembered every moment of their time together, their love, their plans for the future. But he also remembered what had happened in the night of the assassination attempt. And that knowledge demanded that he act immediately.

"God, I wish we could stay in bed and celebrate our bond, but—"

Faye put her finger on his lips. "You don't have to explain anything, my love."

He pressed a quick kiss on her lips, contentment filling him. To know that there was a person who instinctively understood what was going on inside him was a blessing.

Cain opened the door into the hallway. Wesley still stood at his post outside the queen's suite and immediately straightened when Cain and Faye stepped out.

"Wes, get Gabriel and Maya and have them come down to my suite. Immediately."

Seemingly alarmed by the curt command, Wes asked, "What's wrong?"

"I think I know who the assassin is." Still holding Faye's hand, Cain rushed past him, heading for the king's suite. He ripped the double doors open and entered the foyer. "Haven? Thomas?"

A sound came from the room Haven was occupying with Blake and Wesley, and Cain stalked toward it. The door opened before Cain reached it.

"Cain?" Blake stared at him.

"Is Haven up?"

"He went back to the cells to see if he could find any other evidence about the assassin."

"Get him. Now!"

Blake pulled his cell from his pants pocket and tapped it. "Uh, shit, I'm out of juice. Forgot to charge it." He shoved it back into his pocket. "Back in a jiffy."

When Blake hurried toward the double doors leading into the corridor, Cain called over his shoulder, "Thomas back?"

"They're on their way. He and Eddie should be here any moment," Blake answered as he ran outside.

Alone with Faye now, Cain turned to her and pulled her into his arms.

"Why do you think your memory suddenly came back?" she asked.

"I can only assume that your blood did that to me. It was one of the last things I did that night before I was attacked. I drank your blood for the first time. Perhaps it triggered something in me that made everything rush back."

"I'm so relieved that you have your memory back." Faye smiled at him, though her smile faded quickly and her face became serious. "But I'm so sorry about—"

"What's so urgent?" Gabriel's voice came from the open door, interrupting their conversation. Behind him Wesley appeared, too.

Cain released Faye and waved Gabriel and the witch to enter. "Thank God you're here. Where's Maya?"

"She went to check on her patients to see whether they are fully healed yet. Shall I get her?"

Cain shook his head. "That's fine. Let her take care of them first. We'll fill her in later." He listened for any sounds coming from the corridor. "Let's wait for Haven and Blake, so I don't have to go over it twice."

Gabriel tossed him a concerned look. "Are you okay?"

Rubbing a hand over his head, Cain searched for an answer. He was okay. More than that. Having bonded with Faye had made him whole again. But remembering the events of the last night of his old life now forced him to take action. Swiftly and without mercy. Before he could find the right words to answer Gabriel's question, Haven and Blake stormed into the foyer.

"Shut the door," Cain ordered Blake, who followed his command instantly.

All his friends looked at him expectantly, nobody saying a word.

"Something's happened," Cain started, and glanced at Faye. "Faye and I blood-bonded."

Several mouths opened, obviously to congratulate him, but he raised his hand to stop them. "Thank you. I'd celebrate with you, but there's no time right now. I have my memory back. I don't know how, but I assume it has something to do with Faye's blood. In any case, it doesn't matter right now why I remember, just that I do."

"That's great news!" Haven said.

"It is. But that's not everything. I think I know now who is behind the assassination that caused my amnesia."

Haven took a step toward him, stunned. "It's Abel, isn't it? That bastard."

"It's not him. It's John," Cain interrupted.

"John?" The question wasn't just asked by Haven, but also echoed by Gabriel, Blake, and Wesley.

"But that can't be," Blake protested. "He saved you and came back for you."

Cain glared at his human friend. "Then why did he send me into a trap?"

"Hold it," Gabriel cautioned. "Tell us exactly what happened back then. Don't leave anything out."

Cain felt Faye squeeze his hand in reassurance and exchanged a quick look with her. "Faye and I were in my suite. It was around sunset when I got a text message. It was from John. He asked me to come to the plantation kitchen, alone. He wrote that he'd uncovered a conspiracy and that I could trust nobody. And that we had to act quickly before the guards involved in it could cover it up and destroy all evidence."

Faye nodded, addressing the men from Scanguards. "I knew something was seriously wrong when Cain got the text message. He said that heads would roll that night before he rushed out of the suite. It was the last time I saw him alive that night."

"And you're sure it was John texting you, not somebody else?" Gabriel wanted to know.

"Absolutely. It was his name on the caller ID. It was John luring me there."

"What happened when you got to the kitchen?"

"It was empty. John wasn't there. When I turned to leave, a vampire I'd never seen attacked me. We fought."

"Were you armed?"

Cain nodded. "Yes, but I never got a chance to even draw my weapon. He was strong. I knew it was a fight to the death. I'd thought I'd gained the upper hand, but then a second person appeared. It was John. I turned my head, and saw him. I told him I knew it was him, and then he aimed his gun at me and pulled the trigger. I felt the impact in my skull and everything went dark."

Haven shook his head. "A silver bullet would have killed you. Yet you're not dead. And apparently the remains of a vampire were found there."

"That's true. Even though nobody in the palace remembers hearing any shots, we found the ash," Faye said, putting her hand on Cain's forearm. "It was unmistakable. And since both you and John are alive, the assassin must have died. John must have killed him."

"Yes," Cain bit out, "to cover his own ass, so nobody could testify against him."

"Then why didn't he kill you, too, if that was his intention in the first place?" Gabriel challenged.

Cain shrugged. "Maybe he got cold feet in the end and couldn't do it. And when he realized that I'd lost my memory, he simply carted me off to another part of the country with me being none the wiser." While it was a possible explanation, there was however none for why John had then come to bring him back to the kingdom. Cain sighed, frustrated. He knew something didn't add up. However, one memory was crystal clear in Cain's mind: John had aimed his weapon at him and pulled the trigger. "I have to confront John. I need to know the truth."

He stared at his friends and issued his orders without hesitation. "Gabriel, Haven, you two come with me. Blake, Wes, stay with Faye." Cain stalked to the door, but it was opened before he reached it.

Thomas and Eddie marched in. "Hey," Thomas greeted them, his eyes glancing at the assembled. "Did we miss something?"

"Cain has his memory back."

"Excellent!" Eddie exclaimed and smiled.

Cain nodded. "Yes, and I believe that John was the one trying to kill me. He lured me into a trap with a text message where I was ambushed by the assassin."

Thomas and Eddie exchanged a quick glance, before Thomas whistled through his teeth. "Well, that would explain why Nicolette has disappeared. We can't find a trace of her. He must have stashed her away somewhere, expecting trouble."

"You sure?" Cain asked.

"Absolutely. She hasn't been seen since the night we arrived in New Orleans. We followed every lead, and used a little mind control on the neighbors to make sure we got the truth from everybody. Nobody saw anything, which makes me think that John made sure to wipe the memory of anybody who'd seen him usher Nicolette away."

Eddie scratched his neck. "But if John is behind this, don't you think it odd that he brought you back?"

"We've been over this already before you got here," Cain answered impatiently. "He probably got cold feet in the end. Who knows?"

"You sure John lured you into the trap?" Thomas pressed.

"The text was from him."

"Let me have a look at the cell. Do you have it?"

Cain shrugged. "What's the use of it? I remember clearly that it was from him. Besides, he shot me that night."

Thomas raised an eyebrow. "Just covering all angles. Do you have the phone?"

"It wasn't with the things we found with the vampire's remains that night," Faye interrupted. "I don't know where it is. Maybe John destroyed it because it could have led back to him."

"No, he didn't. Last night I saw something under the bed in my suite. It must have fallen down and been kicked underneath it the night of the ambush. I never took it with me. I was in too much of a hurry." And according to Faye, nobody had used the king's suite since.

"Give me thirty seconds." Thomas was already charging into the king's suite to retrieve the cell phone.

Mentally Cain shook his head. Looking at the phone wouldn't serve anything but to confirm that John had sent the message and set the trap for him. But he also knew that Thomas was thorough and always insisted on verifying all information presented.

Impatiently, Cain tapped his foot when Thomas came back, the cell phone in his hand. "Got it." He already pressed the *on* button, then cursed. "Shit! Battery's dead."

It didn't surprise Cain. After all, the phone had been under that bed for over a year. "I'm not gonna wait any longer." He motioned to Gabriel and Haven. "Let's go."

He almost bumped into Marcus when he ripped the door open to rush outside.

"Excuse me, sir," Marcus said, breathing heavily. "I thought you should know: the delegates of the Mississippi clan have been spotted about a half hour away. My scouts believe they're armed and hostile."

Cain cursed. "Fuck!" This was bad timing. He stared at the guard. "Make sure everybody is at their post. Reinforce the perimeter."

He turned to his friends. "Gabriel, I need you to stall them when they arrive. Take Eddie with you. Marcus, you'll take your orders from Gabriel. Haven, Wes, Blake, you're coming with me." He cast a look at Thomas then at Faye. "Thomas, protect Faye. And nobody utter a word about the two Mississippi clan members out in the kitchen." Cain stared down Marcus. "Do you understand me?"

Marcus nodded quickly.

"Go!" Cain ordered him. The moment the guard was hurrying down the corridor, Cain addressed Gabriel again, "Warn Maya to keep her patients out of sight. I don't want any confrontations. Not right now."

Gabriel nodded. "I'll take care of it."

Then Cain stormed into the corridor, his three friends following him.

39

The guards' common room across the entrance hall, where the guards received their orders and hung out between their shifts, was humming with activity. Guards were suiting up, strapping on their weapons and getting ready for a confrontation with the Mississippians. Cain stopped at the open door and let his eyes wander over two dozen vampires in the room, until he spotted John.

"John!" he called out to him.

The leader of the king's guard looked over his shoulder, his face tense. "Yes, Cain?"

"A word. My office."

John frowned. "Can't it wait? I'm getting the men ready. Haven't you heard? The delegates of the Mississippi clan are on their way. And they don't look friendly. I expect an altercation."

Cain clenched his jaw. "My office. Now, John!"

Several heads snapped in Cain's direction, staring at him in stunned silence. Waiting for John to comply with his orders, Cain glared back at the men. "What are you looking at? Get ready."

The men hurried to continue with their preparations, while John marched out of the room and into the hallway.

"What is this about?"

Cain didn't answer and simply walked across the foyer into his office. At the door he waited for John to catch up with him. He motioned him to enter, then followed him and closed the door. Haven, Wesley, and Blake were already waiting for them, and Blake now moved in front of the door, blocking it.

John cast a curious glance at the human before turning his head back to Cain.

"I have my memory back," Cain announced without preamble, watching John's facial expression intently.

To his surprise, his personal guard appeared pleased about that fact. His words only underscored that impression. "That's wonderful! What happened?"

"That's not important right now," Cain cut him off.

Clearly taken aback by the brusque tone, John's forehead pulled into a frown, but he didn't comment any further.

"I know what you did, John. I remember every second of the night I was nearly assassinated." Cain paused, waiting for John's face to show that he was caught. But it appeared that John was a better poker player than anybody else Cain had ever met. "What have you got to say for yourself, John? Why did you do it?"

"Do what?"

Cain shook his head. "I never expected this from you. We were friends. I trusted you." They'd always had each others' backs when they'd both been guards. Cain had trusted this man more than he'd ever trusted his own brother. This betrayal felt like a stab in the gut.

"What the fuck are you talking about? If you have your memory back then you know what happened."

Frustrated about John's refusal to confess his crime, Cain lunged at him and slammed him against the wall, pinning him there. "You lured me into a trap, and then when the assassin couldn't finish me, you aimed your gun at me and pulled the trigger. Damn it, you shot me!"

"I didn't shoot you!"

Cain flashed his fangs at him. "Stop lying and stand by your actions like a man, and not like a sniveling weasel. You betrayed me!"

"Never!" John ground out.

"You lured me into that trap."

"No!"

"Then you're denying that you sent me a text message that night to inform me about a conspiracy?"

"What?" John's forehead creased and his mouth twisted in disbelief. "I never sent you any text message that night."

"I have proof!"

John pushed against him, causing Cain to release him. "You have no fucking proof, because there is no proof. Because I didn't do anything!"

"Give it up, John. I found my old cell phone. I can prove it was you!"

"Then show it to me! Because you've got nothing. I'm innocent! I came to rescue you!"

Cain scoffed. "By fucking shooting me? That's a funny way of rescuing me."

John continued facing off with him stoically, his jaw tight, his shoulders stiff. "Show me your proof and I'll show you that you're wrong. I aimed at the assassin, not at you. I killed the assassin to save you. You have to believe me."

Cain searched his former friend's eyes. Was he lying? Or was there really something to his claim that he was innocent? Cain had thought that having his memory back would make things easier, but it didn't. Knowing his history with John, how they'd fought side by side, how John had stood by him to defeat the old king and save the imprisoned vampires, Faye included, made it impossible to condemn John outright.

Cain sucked in a long breath. "Follow me."

***

Faye looked over Thomas's shoulder as he powered on the cell phone that was currently connected to a charger. Thomas sat at the little desk in his room and had already booted up his computer and was typing away on it until the screen of Cain's old cell phone finally lit up.

"Well, let's have a look then," Thomas said calmly as he picked up the phone and swiped across it with his finger. He looked up at her. "No password. Interesting."

"I'm sure he had a password on his phone previously," Faye replied. She'd seen Cain enter it many times, though she didn't know the combination.

She watched as Thomas swiftly opened the message app and navigated to the last message the phone had received. "Here, that must be it." He pointed to it.

Faye read it. It was exactly like Cain had told them. He'd received a note that he should come to the old plantation kitchen to find out about a conspiracy. Her eyes drifted to the top of the small screen. "John," she read aloud.

Thomas nodded, a disappointed look on his face. "I'd hoped Cain was wrong."

Faye shook her head. "I always blamed John after Cain's presumed death. I blamed him because he didn't keep him safe for me. But that John is actually behind this is so hard to believe. They were such good friends."

Thomas hummed to himself, as if contemplating something. "That's odd." He paused and scrolled through the messages. "The older messages make no sense. I wonder—"

A sound at the door had Faye whip her head around. Maya stood there, opening the door wider.

"I'm sorry, Faye, but I need you."

"We're just checking out Cain's old cell phone," Faye said, wanting to hear what was startling Thomas.

"My two patients are scared. They're getting ready to run. We've gotta convince them to stay here, or they'll run right into the arms of their clansmen. You need to help me."

"Shit!" Faye cursed. She had already stepped toward Maya when Thomas gripped her arm.

"I'm supposed to protect you."

She shook her head and motioned to Maya. "I'm a vampire, Thomas. I can protect myself. Besides, Maya is with me. I'll be fine."

Thomas stared at her, but seemed clearly distracted by the cell phone in his hand. "Fine. Maya, make sure Faye stays safe, or Cain will have our hides for breakfast."

Involuntarily, Faye had to smile at Thomas's words. Cain had always been overly protective of her, and she had the feeling that now that they were blood-bonded, his need to protect her would reach new heights. A blood-bonded vampire protected his mate with his life.

"I heard congratulations are in order," Maya said as they hurried along the corridor.

"Yes, thank you. Finally, I have Cain back."

"I'm very happy for you both. A blood-bond is a wonderful thing."

Faye smiled at the young woman who was so beautiful she could have had any man she wanted. Yet she'd chosen Gabriel, whose scarred face had repulsed Faye when she'd seen him the first time. Well, it was none of her business. She pushed the thoughts out of her mind and concentrated on the task ahead: to keep David and Kathryn safe.

When Maya wanted to turn toward the stairs leading up into the main foyer, Faye took her by the arm and motioned in the other direction. "We'll take the service stairs. They're closer to the kitchen."

Quickly she led Maya toward the service stairs which seemed deserted, just like she'd expected. The majority of the staff and the guards would be in the front of the house, preparing for the arrival of the Mississippians.

"How did the operation go?"

Maya tossed her a sideways glance and smiled. "I think it went well. Their fangs haven't fully grown in yet, but from what I could see when I examined them just after sunset, the roots are there, and in David's case I can see a little bit of a tooth already. I think it's working. Maybe another two or three sleep cycles and plenty of blood, and they'll be healed."

Faye sighed with relief. "I'm so glad. I'm really grateful to you for doing this. We don't have any doctors here. Well, none who're vampires anyway. And I couldn't really bring them to a human doctor. It would have been complicated."

"That's quite all right. I was happy to do it. I'm still learning so much about our race. I look at it as research."

"Research?" Faye asked curiously.

"I was a doctor when I was human. Urology. I did a lot of research at a university hospital before my turning."

"And now?"

"Oh, I still do a lot of research, but I've switched my field to female reproductive medicine."

"Vampire females?" Faye shook her head. "But vampire females are infertile. Everybody knows that."

Maya winked at her. "It's not quite as simple as that."

"What are you saying?"

"That not everything is black and white. I'm close to developing a treatment that will allow vampire females to conceive from their blood-bonded mates."

Faye stopped at the top of the stairs they'd just reached. "What?" Was this woman really saying that one day it could be possible for a vampire female to birth a child? Her thoughts immediately went to Cain. Could she and Cain one day become parents?

"Well, to put it in lay terms, it's not impossible for a vampire female to conceive, but the problem has always been that the fetus can't grow in the womb, because the vampire body rejects the fertilized egg as an injury and heals it during the vampire's restorative sleep."

"And how are you going to prevent that from happening?"

"The same way human doctors prevent a human from rejecting an organ that was transplanted into them. By lowering the body's natural instinct to heal itself."

"But that's impossible."

Maya smiled. "I'm close to a solution. I can sense it." Then she looked around. "Which way?"

Still thinking about Maya's words, Faye pointed to a door. "Through there."

Moments later, they were in the enclosed walkway that connected the main house with the plantation kitchen. Just in time, as it turned out: David and Kathryn were getting ready to leave.

Their eyes filled with fear, Maya's patients looked at them.

"We're so grateful," David started, "really, we are. But we can't stay any longer. They'll find us and kill us. You have to let us go."

Maya pointed toward the outside. "They're already coming up the driveway. You can't go out there now. You'll run right into their arms."

A sob tore from Kathryn's chest and she wrapped her arms around David, holding onto him as if hiding her face in his chest would prevent her from being found. Faye's heart went out to her. She'd been frightened like that too once. She knew what the girl was going through.

"I have another solution," Faye said. She knew she should talk to Cain about it first and get his approval for what she was about to do, but the lives of these two vampires depended on her acting without delay.

She reached for Kathryn. "I'll keep you both safe."

40

Cain charged into Thomas's room, John and the others behind him. Thomas looked up from his computer.

"Is the cell phone working?"

"Yeah, it's juiced up."

Cain looked around the room, suddenly alarmed. "Where's Faye?"

"She's with Maya."

"I told you to watch her. With the Mississippians right at our doorstep—"

"Don't go all apeshit on me. You're not the first vampire who's suddenly acquired a mate. She and Maya know what they're doing. They're just making sure the two escapees won't run into our unwelcome visitors."

Cain hesitated for a moment, but instinctively he knew Thomas was right. He couldn't watch Faye twenty-four-seven just because he didn't think he could continue living without her.

Faye, my love, are you all right? He sent the thoughts to her via their telepathic bond.

It took only seconds before warmth spread inside him and he felt rather than heard her response. *Of course, I'm all right. Is anything the matter?*

Satisfied that their mental connection was working, he sent her another thought. *Everything is fine.*

Then he jerked his thumb back at John while addressing Thomas. "Show him the text message. Show him how he lured me into the trap."

Thomas stood up from the desk and unplugged the charger from the phone. Then he swiped over the screen and navigated to the right spot. "By the way, there was no password on it. I'd call that a security risk."

Cain felt his eyebrows snap together. "I always had a password on my phone." He remembered it clearly.

Thomas handed the phone to John. "Here. That's the message."

John stared at the screen and read it. Then his head shot up and he glared at Thomas. "What is this? Are you trying to set me up?" He stabbed his finger at the display. "I never sent that message!"

"Says right there," Thomas replied pointing to the top of the display, where the caller's name appeared. "John. Are you denying that's you?"

"It must be another John. It's not me!" John turned to Cain, his eyes pleading. "You must believe me."

Disappointed that John still didn't want to fess up, Cain took the phone from his hand, pressed the contact button in the top right corner of it and then the call button. "Do you need another proof?"

The phone rang. And rang.

Cain brought it to his ear, when he suddenly heard a click and somebody breathing. He stared at John in disbelief. John hadn't moved, hadn't pulled his cell phone from his pocket, yet somebody had picked it up.

"Hello?" Cain said into the phone, but the call was abruptly disconnected. He pointed at John. "Who's got your phone?"

John dug into his pants pocket and pulled it out. "I do." He swiped over the display and unlocked it with his password, then navigated to the call app, before holding the display up for Cain to see. "No call from you." He motioned to the phone in Cain's hands. "I don't know who you just called, but it wasn't me."

"Did you change your number in the last year?" Cain asked, trying to make sense of the situation.

"My number hasn't changed."

Cain exchanged a look with Thomas. "How is that possible?"

Thomas sighed and rubbed the back of his neck. "I thought the earlier messages in this thread seemed odd."

"What do you mean?"

"They didn't sound like they were addressed to a king from his guard."

Cain looked at the display once more and scrolled back up through the messages, scanning them quickly. Then he looked up. He remembered some of them. "That can't be."

"What?" Haven asked, stepping closer.

Cain lifted his head. "The earlier messages are from Abel."

Several gasps echoed in the room.

Cain looked at Thomas. "How's that technically possible?"

Thomas reached for the phone and tapped something on it. "Easier than you think." He held up the phone, now showing the entry for the contact *John*. "You can change a contact's name whenever you want to. Let's say you made a typo when you originally entered it. So you just go back in, and change the name."

"Shit!" John cursed, drawing all eyes on him. "So that's how he did it! He got hold of your phone, cracked your password, and changed his contact info to mine so that when he sent you that message to send you into a trap, it would look like it had come from me."

"Easy to prove, too," Thomas continued. "The phone number will still identify Abel." He pointed to the screen. "Is that his number?"

Cain almost bumped heads with John when they both bent down to read it.

"Yes," Cain confirmed.

John nodded in agreement.

"He probably counted on being the first to get a hold of the phone after your death and would then have erased his message to you and changed the contact info back," Thomas guessed. "But you didn't have the phone with you when you walked into that trap."

"My brother wants me dead."

Thomas shrugged. "Wouldn't be the first time one brother tries to kill another for the throne. The entire English royalty dealt with that kind of thing on an ongoing basis."

"But this one is not going to succeed," Cain said with determination.

***

Abel shoved his cell phone back into his pocket.

"Shit," he cursed under his breath.

The call had come from Cain's old cell phone, which Abel had always thought had been destroyed. In fact, he'd searched for it after Cain's supposed demise in order to erase all evidence that could lead back to him. But he'd never found it and had eventually forgotten about it.

But now Cain had it. And it had been Cain who'd made the call. He'd recognized his brother's voice.

Did this also mean that Cain was on to him? Abel had to find out, because his entire plan depended on his brother remaining in the dark so that John could execute the orders Abel had given him.

Easing the door to his suite shut behind him, Abel stalked across the corridor and into the connecting hallway that led to the other side of the palace's underground living quarters, where the king's and the queen's suites were located. He treaded lightly, not wanting his footsteps to be heard by anybody.

Frustration churned in his stomach. He'd waited for this opportunity for so long, and now that he was so close to his ultimate goal, he couldn't allow anything to stand in his way.

Silently, Abel opened another door and peered into the dim corridor. Through the sliver between door and frame he saw a guard pass on his way toward the stairs leading to the first floor. Several seconds passed until the guard was outside of earshot, and Abel could enter the hallway without being seen. Quickly he approached the double doors to the king's suite, ready to dive into the next closet should anybody come. Luckily, several supply closets were lining the hallway.

But he didn't have to resort to such hide-and-seek measures. The double doors were ajar. When Abel peeked through the slit, he couldn't see anybody in the luxurious reception area, but he heard voices from the room to his left: the door to the suite of the leader of the king's guard, which was now occupied by that interloper, Thomas, and his gay lover, stood open.

Abel wanted to snort, but didn't dare make a sound. What a disgrace to the vampire race to have two vampire males engaging in sodomy!

And under his roof! How could Cain allow such a thing? Cain wasn't fit to be king if he tolerated such disgraceful acts in his palace.

Abel shifted to bring his ear to the gap between the two doors to listen more closely to the conversation, while holding his breath.

"Before you do anything, Cain . . ." It was John who spoke, hesitating for a moment, before continuing, "Abel has me by the balls."

Abel jerked back, wanting to curse, but no sound came over his lips. Instead he pressed them together. John was going to betray him, revealing what he was supposed to do for Abel, despite the fact that this would mean death for his lover.

Abel balled his hands into fists. There was no time to lose now.

Change of plans.

He turned on his heel and rushed in the direction he'd come from.

He had to act quickly and save what he could. Now the gloves would come off and he'd go for the jugular.

No more being Mr. Nice Guy.

41

John dropped his head. "He's holding Nicolette captive to force me to do his bidding."

Cain expelled a breath. "Fuck!"

Similar curses came from his colleagues.

"I'm sorry, Cain." John lifted his head, his eyes now displaying regret and pain. "He's going to murder her the moment he finds out that I won't kill you. He's going to make her suffer."

Seeing John's anguish, Cain felt his heart go out to his old friend. He was willing to sacrifice the woman he loved for his king. "It doesn't have to come to that. We'll get to Abel before he can do anything."

John shook his head, his hand trembling as he lifted it. "I'm supposed to kill you when the Mississippians are here. So he can pin it on them and start an all out war. As soon as he realizes that I'm not executing his orders, he'll order Baltimore to kill Nicolette. We'll never get to her in time."

"War with the Mississippi clan? Are you sure?"

"He didn't say outright, but it's obvious, isn't it? If he pins your murder on them, all your subjects will be behind him to avenge you."

Cain put his hand on John's shoulder, squeezing it. "I appreciate what you're sacrificing by telling me the truth, John. I do. And I'll do everything in my power to save Nicolette."

John closed his eyes, his jaw clenching now, his chest heaving as if to hold back tears. When he opened his eyes again, they were rimmed with tears. "I've fought with this decision ever since I was confronted with it. Every minute since Abel captured her. She's tied up in some hut somewhere in the bayou, scared. I promised her that nothing would happen to her. That I'd come back for her." A tear ran down his cheek. "But that won't happen now. Because I can't kill a man that I've loved and admired ever since I met him. Because of you, I can't save the woman I love." John's jaw set in stone. "And right now, I hate you for that, Cain!"

Before Cain could react to the tearful confession, John's hand went to the inside of his jacket. In lightning speed, he pulled a stake from it.

Cain jumped to the side, but instead of John lunging at him he jerked the stake toward his own chest.

"Noooooo!" Cain cried out and barreled toward John, slamming his fist against John's arm. The impact loosened John's hold on the stake.

At the same time, Haven tackled John from behind, while Thomas kicked John's legs out from under him, making him tumble to the floor.

Moments later, Haven and Thomas had John pinned flat to the ground. Cain crouched down next to him. "That's not a solution, John! Do you hear me? We'll get Nicolette out of there."

"How?" John spat, anger and desperation evident in his entire body.

Cain had never seen a man in so much emotional pain and hoped that he would never have to go through what John was going through this moment.

"Uh." Wesley cleared his throat, making Cain snap his head to him and toss him a quizzical look.

Wes raised his finger as if he were in second grade, asking for permission to speak up in class. "Is Nicolette human?"

John turned his head, an impatient look on his face. "Why is that important?"

"Well, it is, because I assume you don't know her exact location, right?"

"When I was brought to see her, they blindfolded me and then did the same when they released me. I only know it was some hut in the bayou. Maybe forty-five minutes from the palace."

Wesley nodded. "Well, since she's human, it shouldn't be too hard to find her. I can *scry* for her, which I couldn't do if she were a vampire."

John made a motion to sit up, and Cain nodded to his friends to let go of him.

For the first time, a hopeful glint appeared in John's eyes. "Can you really do that?"

Wesley nodded proudly. "I'm a witch. Of course I can."

John sighed. "And once we know where she is? We might still be too late."

Cain reached his hand out to his loyal guard and helped him up. "At least this way we have a small chance. We can send a few guys there clandestinely, while you continue to pretend you're doing what Abel wants you to do."

"Uh, actually," Wesley threw in, drawing everybody's attention back on him. "We have more than just a small chance. Once I have Nicolette's location, I can put a protection spell on her so that whoever is guarding her won't be able to harm her."

"I recall you mentioning on the way here from San Francisco that you were working on one, not that you had actually perfected it," John said with a good dose of skepticism in his voice.

Wes rolled his eyes. "I've had plenty of time to work on my craft. So why does everybody here constantly doubt my abilities?"

To Cain's surprise, Blake slapped his colleague on the shoulder, grinning. "Maybe it's time to redeem yourself and show them all that you're not just a fuck-up."

Wesley exchanged a look with Blake that appeared almost conspiratorial. "Maybe you're right. Let's show those vamps what the rest of us are made out of. Wanna assist?"

Blake chuckled. "As long as you don't turn me into a pig in the process."

Wes clicked his tongue. "Speaking of pigs, Blake, do me a favor. The next time you want to borrow one of my potions, ask me first, instead of messing with my stuff."

"Huh?" Blake appeared utterly clueless.

"Well, never mind. I see why you have the need to arm yourself with some magic to defend yourself. Next time just ask first." Then Wesley turned away from Blake and motioned to John. "I need something that belongs to Nicolette so I can scry for her. Do you have something she wore, or a lock of hair, something with her sweat or her scent on it?"

John reached to his neck and pulled a chain out from under his shirt, revealing a small vial dangling at its end. "Will her blood work?"

"You've gotta be kidding me," Wes said, already reaching for it. "That'll make it so much easier."

Cain glanced at the vial with the red liquid inside. "You carry her blood with you? Why?"

"I need to feel her close. You understand that, don't you?"

Cain nodded slowly. He understood. Because John had not been able to blood-bond with the woman he loved due to the previous rule that the leader of the king's guard wasn't allowed a private life, he'd resorted to the next best thing: to always have her blood around him to be reminded of her.

Cain took John's arm and clasped it. "Once this is over, I promise you'll get to make her yours if that's what you desire."

John locked eyes with him, and in that moment their old friendship was restored.

Then Cain turned to Wesley. "How long will the spell last?"

"Twenty-four hours."

"Good. That should be sufficient time. Get to work. Make it quick. Blake will help you." And he hoped that the witch knew what he was doing. For all their sakes. "The rest of us, let's get Abel and take him down."

The cell phone in his pocket rang, and Cain impatiently pulled it out, glancing at the display. He answered it. "Yes, Gabriel?"

"You'd better come up here."

"Stall them."

"I'm afraid I've stalled as long as I could."

Cain cursed. "I'll be there in a minute." He disconnected the call and looked at his friends. "Your orders stand. Find Abel and prevent him from making any phone calls to alert whoever is guarding Nicolette. And be subtle so nobody is aware of what you're doing. We don't know which of the guards are loyal to my brother. I don't want anybody to warn him that we're on to him."

Not waiting for a response, Cain charged out of the room and ran up the stairs. When he reached the upstairs foyer, he could already sense the tension that rendered the air so thick he could have cut through it with a knife.

Two guards blocked the entrance door and immediately stepped aside when Cain approached.

On the porch, Gabriel and Eddie stood, two more guards at their sides, their backs turned to the palace. Cain marched between them and stared at the six vampires who stood on the driveway just below the steps. Behind them three black SUVs were parked, and the tinted windows made it impossible to see how many more vampires were inside. Or how many others were hiding in the forest bordering the palace's grounds.

Cain took a quick look around. Several of his guards were standing watch along the driveway and the grounds, pistols at the ready and waiting for orders.

The visitors from Mississippi were similarly armed, carrying their weapons on their belts in a show of aggression.

Cain stepped down the stairs and walked up to their presumed leader who appeared surprised at seeing him but caught himself quickly. "Victor. Since you're leading the charge, I assume you're representing your king?"

Victor, whose skin was the color of milk chocolate, chuckled. His eyes were of a vibrant blue-grey, evidence of his mixed race heritage. "I *am* the king."

"I see." It appeared that there had been an unexpected change in leadership in Mississippi.

"What's good for the goose is good for the gander," the vampire responded with a smirk.

Cain acknowledged the reference to having killed the king of his own clan without flinching. "You're a day early. My welcome home celebrations don't start till tomorrow night. So what do you want?"

Victor snorted. "Isn't that obvious? You're harboring two traitors, and I've come to collect them."

"I'm afraid I can't help you there."

"Can't or won't?"

"Take your men and leave. We have nothing to discuss."

Victor clenched his teeth. "We have plenty to discuss. But first hand over the traitors." He glanced at his men. "Or we won't be using words but deeds to make our position clear. If you want peace between our two kingdoms, don't undermine my rule by harboring traitors."

Despite Victor's words, Cain knew that the Mississippi clan hadn't come to make peace. They were using the fact that Cain sheltered the two defanged vampires as a reason to stamp out any peace negotiations in their infancy. But right now, Cain couldn't afford this distraction.

"They're not here." Cain motioned to the guards behind him. "Show our visitors the way off our property."

Victor narrowed his eyes when his gaze suddenly strayed past Cain and a grin spread over his face.

Cain turned his head and saw Lee, one of the guards on the porch, tilting his head toward the side of the palace where the plantation kitchen was located. Cain ground his teeth in displeasure.

"It appears somebody has spotted my errant clan members," Victor said pointedly and marched past Cain. "Shall we see where they're hiding?"

Not having a choice now, Cain followed Victor, his eyes silently communicating with Gabriel to cover him. Confidently Victor walked to the enclosed walkway that connected the plantation kitchen with the main house and opened the door.

"May I?" Victor asked almost politely.

Cain sensed the other men as well as his own guards follow him. "After you."

"Well, let's see who we have—" Victor marched into the kitchen.

42

"This way," Faye whispered to David and Kathryn as she ushered them through the corridor and cast a look over her shoulder to verify that the two vampires were remaining close to her.

In a few moments they would be at her suite, and from there she could smuggle the two out of the palace and get them to safety by using the tunnels. Cain would be furious for revealing the location of the tunnels to strangers, but she didn't feel that she had a choice. She'd seen the delegates of the Mississippi clan through the windows. They'd been heavily armed, and she was sure they wouldn't give up until they'd recaptured the two unfortunate defanged vampires. And with their fangs still not having fully grown back, the two would fare poorly in a fight with their clansmen.

At the next bend of the corridor, she stopped and peered around the corner. Her breath caught in her throat. Abel came running and ripped the door to her suite open, storming inside without looking left or right. What did he want in her room? And he hadn't even knocked! This wasn't good.

She couldn't bring David and Kathryn to her rooms now to use the entrance there. Abel couldn't know about the tunnels. After everything that had happened and all the things Abel had done to keep her and Cain apart, she knew instinctively he couldn't be trusted. What was she going to do now? If the Mississippians found the two defanged vampires, they would imprison and torture them. Death would be certain to follow.

Faye turned to them, pressing a finger to her lips to command them to remain silent, when a thought pierced her mind. The prison cells. Cain had escaped from there via the tunnels. She knew which cell he and Robert had been in. It couldn't be too hard to find the entrance to the secret tunnel.

She motioned David and Kathryn to follow her as she rushed in the other direction, away from her suite. Since nobody was currently locked up in the cellblock, she didn't expect any guard to be on duty there. Besides, they would all be upstairs, trying to hold off the Mississippians.

Careful not to make a sound, Faye turned the next corner and reached the entrance to the cellblock. She peeked inside. It was empty. A sigh of relief came over her lips.

"Come."

David and Kathryn hesitated when they saw what they were entering. Kathryn froze.

"Don't be afraid. There's an exit through there." Faye pointed to the cell that Robert had occupied. "Trust me." She walked to the open door and took a step inside, nearly tripping at the threshold. She looked down and saw that the wood had worn down over time and was loose, creating a tripping hazard.

Faye glanced back. The doors to the other two cells were open, too, and behind the last one was another small room the guards used for supplies. She entered the cell fully and looked over her shoulder.

Hesitantly, David and Kathryn followed her to the entrance of the cell and waited there, clearly afraid to step inside the dim interior. Faye didn't press them immediately. After all, she had to find the entry point to the tunnel first anyway, and there was no need for the two to wait inside the cell they so clearly feared until she'd managed to locate the tunnel entrance.

"Wait there," she instructed them and went to work.

Methodically, her hands swept over the walls of the prison cell, feeling every indentation, every groove, testing them, before moving on to the next section. She knew what she was looking for: a series of indentations that would fit her fingers, allowing a certain sequence of pressure which would unlock the mechanism to open the secret passage. She knew both the doors in her and in the king's suite were opened that way, and she had no reason to believe that this one functioned any different.

Inhaling the stale air in the room, she tried to remain calm. Rushing would only lead to her not noticing the indentations she needed to find.

"Are you sure there's an exit?" David whispered from the door.

Faye cast a glance over her shoulder. "Yes, there has to be." Cain had used it. And if he'd found it while still suffering from amnesia, so could she.

She felt her heart pound in her chest, beating rapidly against her ribcage. Memories of her own suffering at the hands of a cruel king resurfaced and made her double her efforts. She had to help these vampires. Nobody deserved to suffer like they had.

Her index finger slipped into a groove. She froze. Then her thumb found purchase.

"There," she whispered to herself and pressed against the stone wall, feeling something click. She stepped back, a feeling of accomplishment already spreading within her.

"Somebody's coming," David suddenly whispered.

Faye whirled her head around and saw how David grabbed Kathryn. Faye rushed toward him, but he was already dragging Kathryn toward the far end of the cellblock where the supply room was located. At the sound for footsteps growing louder, Faye froze for a split second. She was about to dive after David and Kathryn to hide in the supply room with them, when she remembered the door to the tunnel. She spun on her own axis and saw that it was now fully open. Anybody stepping into the cell would see it. She dove back into the cell, but her foot caught on the uneven threshold and she tripped.

Reaching out her hands, she fought for balance, when the person entering the cellblock reached her.

An arm caught around her waist and she was jerked back.

"How fortunate."

The cold voice in her ears made her blood freeze in her veins.

"Abel," she managed to echo, pulling herself up to standing. She quickly turned in his hold, hoping to block his view so he couldn't see the open door to the tunnel.

But when she saw his face, she knew it was too late.

"Well, well, well. So that's how he got out."

Faye's breath hitched. Abel's words could only mean one thing. He'd been the one who'd tried to kill Cain. "It was you!"

Before she could do or say anything else, Abel shoved a vial at her mouth and forced the contents down her throat. The bitter liquid sent a shock through her system, making her spasm involuntarily. Then her movements slowed and though she tried to push against him and refuse to swallow, her body wouldn't follow her mind's command.

She concentrated, collecting her strength to send a mental message to Cain, but she couldn't form any thoughts.

"Gotcha now," was the last thing she heard Abel say before darkness engulfed her.

***

"Oh, hello, can I help you?" Maya's voice cut off the Mississippi vampire.

Cain entered the kitchen behind Victor and looked around. Only Maya was present. He sighed in relief. The two defanged vampires were gone, as was any evidence of the operation that had taken place the night before. The place looked spick and span, a hint of bleach still in the air. It appeared Maya had scrubbed the place down to get rid of David's and Kathryn's smell.

Victor turned back to him and stared to the door where others were gathered, tossing the vampire who stood there an annoyed look. Cain didn't have to turn around to see who he was communicating with. Lee had already outed himself as being loyal to Abel by giving Victor a hint at where he could find the two traitors.

"Well, it appears I was mistaken," Victor said calmly and nodded. "We'll be on our way then."

Cain stepped aside. "A misunderstanding, I'm sure."

"This is not over."

"It is for now."

Without another word, Victor left the kitchen. As soon as he was out of earshot, Cain glared at Lee before issuing his order to Gabriel. "Tie him up."

"But, Your Majesty . . ."

Gabriel grabbed him and took him away.

Looking at Maya, Cain asked, "Where are they?"

"Faye is trying to get them off the property."

"How?" he asked, his heart already thundering.

"She didn't say."

"Fuck!" he cursed, guessing what Faye was planning. She was going to get them out through the tunnels.

Faye! he called out to her via their bond. *Faye, where are you?*

But there was no reply. No wonder. She had to know that he was furious at her for revealing the most closely guarded secret of the kingdom. But that wasn't even the reason his heart was pounding like a jackhammer: Faye was taking a risk by navigating the tunnels on her own. She wouldn't know which exit to surface at and could still run right into the hands of the Mississippians. While they were leaving the property now, Cain was certain they had some of their men stationed in the forest to keep watch on them. If they caught Faye trying to smuggle out the two defanged vampires, they would capture her.

"To the queen's suite, Gabriel, Eddie!" he ordered and ran back into the palace. Inside, he charged down the service stairs and ran along the corridor as if the sun were on his heels.

Meanwhile, he sent his thoughts to her. *Faye, don't take the tunnels. Come back! It's too dangerous.*

But there was no reply.

I won't be angry. Please just come back.

Still, there was no reply.

The door to Faye's suite stood wide open. Cain charged in, Gabriel and Eddie on his heels. It was empty. Without a thought for the confidentiality of the tunnels, he touched the mechanism to open the hidden door in full view of his two friends. As soon as the door opened, he squeezed through it and entered the passageway.

"Faye!" he called out to her, his voice echoing in the confined space.

He inhaled deeply. He could only smell his own and Faye's scent, indicating that no strangers had entered the secret passageway that led toward the tunnels. Stunned, he froze while Gabriel and Eddie stepped into the corridor.

"What?" Gabriel asked.

Cain turned to him. "She didn't take this route."

"Then which way?"

"I don't know." He'd never revealed the other secret doors that led into the tunnels, though he'd planned to do so once she was queen. But he'd never gotten the chance. "She doesn't know any of the other secret passages."

"How many are there and where?"

"Shit!" Cain cursed, suddenly realizing that she knew of one other entrance. "The cell. I told her how I escaped from the cell. She must be using that entrance to the tunnel." But with some luck it would take her a while to find the mechanism that opened the door. It would slow her down and give him a chance to stop her.

Gabriel and Eddie were already charging out of the queen's suite, Cain now chasing them. Cain ran faster, passing them at the next turn and racing ahead of them toward the cellblock. He reached it moments later.

The door to the cell he and Robert had been in was open. Cain barreled inside. It was empty, but an odd smell lingered. It reminded him of something, but he couldn't put his finger on it.

His eyes wandered to the place where the secret door was hidden, but it was closed. Had Faye not been here yet? Or had she simply closed it behind her to make sure nobody found it? It was the more likely scenario.

Desperate to stop her, Cain walked to the wall and laid his hand over the hidden mechanism.

"Your Majesty, wait!"

He swiveled and saw David hurry into the cell. Cain breathed a sigh of relief. Faye hadn't made it into the tunnel yet.

"Oh thank God!" Cain let out, almost wanting to hug David. "Faye?" He looked past the older vampire to search for her. "Where is she?"

David lowered his lids. "Somebody took her."

Cain's heart stopped and inside him the beast roared. "Who? Who took her?"

"Your brother. I heard her say his name."

"Fuck!" Why hadn't she called out for help to him? Why hadn't she used their telepathic bond to communicate that she needed help?

He sucked in a shaky breath and with it the bitter smell that lay in the air. He recognized it now. "Wesley's potion."

He stared at Gabriel and Eddie who were now crowding into the cell.

"He knocked her out with Wesley's potion."

Cain whirled to the secret door in the stone wall. "I have to save her."

43

Even though Cain had been able to figure out which branch of the vast tunnel system Abel had taken by following his brother's and Faye's scent, he'd lost their trail when they'd surfaced in a wooded area about three miles from the palace.

Cain cursed and turned to John. The leader of the king's guard looked agitated and Cain knew why.

"Abel will have had ample time by now to arrange for his jailor to hurt Nicolette," John said, his eyes pleading.

"Wesley put the protection spell on her, didn't he?"

John nodded. "But we have no way of knowing that it worked. Please, give me a couple of men, and let me free her. Wesley has her location." He shoved a hand through his dark hair. "And who knows? Maybe Abel is on his way there himself. Baltimore was guarding Nicolette when they caught me and, knowing that you banned Baltimore from the palace after he got back, we must assume Baltimore returned there again and relieved his men. He's Abel's closest confidante. If anybody knows what Abel is planning, then it's Baltimore."

Even though Cain knew that John would say anything to make his case for a swift rescue of his lover, he couldn't deny that John had a point about Baltimore. If anybody knew where Abel could be hiding, or where he was heading, it had to be his right hand man.

It was the only lead they had. Faye was still not responding to his telepathic calls and he had to assume that she was still unconscious from Wesley's potion, though it was strange that the witch's punch was having such a lasting effect. With the defanged vampires the potion hadn't lasted longer than fifteen minutes. The thought that Abel had more than just knocked her out made a chill creep into Cain's bones. He didn't want to think of what Abel could have done to her.

"Let's make this quick."

It took twenty minutes before two dark SUVs headed into the bayous. One of them carried Cain, John, Wesley, and Eddie. Gabriel, Blake, and Haven rode in the other. Thomas and Maya stayed back in the palace to maintain order and control.

"Has Thomas started grilling the guard who indicated to the Mississippians that the two defanged vampires were in the kitchen?" Cain now asked.

Eddie nodded. "He's just started."

"What will that serve?" Wesley asked.

John, his entire body coiled with anxiety, answered in Cain's stead, "I've always suspected that Lee is loyal to Abel. Most likely he was told to give David and Kathryn's hiding place away to cause trouble. In fact, Abel only invited the Mississippian as a diversion." He sought eye contact with Cain. "And to make sure he can claim the throne as soon as you were dead."

Cain nodded, immediately understanding what John alluded to. "If he could blame the Mississippians for my assassination, there would be outright war, and he would become king instantly without having to wait out the mourning period once more."

Wesley whistled through his teeth. "Nice brother you have."

"We can't choose family," Cain agreed. "But we can choose our friends."

"How many more guards do you think are on Abel's side?" Wesley, who drove, asked.

Cain shrugged. "Hard to say. Simon for sure, but he's dead. He was the one on duty in the cellblock when Abel came for me and Robert. But when we escaped through the tunnels, Abel must have realized that he had to cover his tracks and couldn't rely on Simon not giving him up to save his own life. So he killed him."

"Lee's a coward," John added. "He'll give up whoever else is loyal to Abel. We'll clean house when we get back."

Cain nodded to John. "I should have never doubted you."

A sad smile crossed John's face. "You had every right to. I was compromised. I understand now why the leader of the king's guard should never have a family. Why he should—"

"Don't," Cain interrupted. "Everybody has a right to happiness. I'm not going to deny you yours. I want you to remain the leader of my king's guard. And my decision stands. I'll do away with the old rules." Lots of things would change in his kingdom soon. Just as soon as he had Faye back. Because, without her, he couldn't go on.

There was silence in the car for a while and all Cain could hear was the engine, the breathing of his friends, and his own heartbeat.

"We're almost there," Wesley announced and pointed to the GPS in the car. "There's a bend in a few hundred yards. We'll have to park here, otherwise we'll risk getting seen from the hut."

"Pull over here," Cain instructed.

The moment the car stopped, Cain opened the door and jumped out. His friends followed him. Behind them, the second SUV came to a stop. Gabriel, Haven, and Blake got out.

"This it?" Gabriel asked, pulling his gun from the holster.

Wesley pointed to a spot in the distance. "The hut must be about five, six hundred yards past that bend."

"I suggest we split up. Gabriel, take Haven and Wesley and approach from the back. Make sure nobody escapes that way. John, Eddie, and I will take the front."

"What about me?" Blake asked.

"I need you to stay with the cars and alert us if Abel is approaching. His red Ferrari is hard to miss. Have you programmed in all our phone numbers as a group?"

Blake nodded. "Any text message will go to all of you simultaneously."

"Good, let's do it. And I want Baltimore alive. He's no good to us dead. Is that clear?"

All nodded in silence.

With John and Eddie by his side, Cain cut through the thicket, avoiding the dirt road that led up to the hut. He treaded carefully, deftly avoiding any broken branches that might make noise that could be heard in the rickety shack just becoming visible through the trees. It was no larger than five by five yards, with a roof that probably leaked and a door that could be kicked in by a five-year-old.

Cain inhaled deeply as he approached, trying to ascertain if Abel had been here lately. But he could smell neither his brother's scent nor Faye's. The various smells coming from the bayou close by were too strong. And only in an enclosed space would Faye's or Abel's smell have lingered. Out in the open the scents vanished too quickly.

Cain paused for a few moments, motioning Eddie and John to do the same, while he waited for Gabriel and the others to get into position. When he saw Haven wave to him from the side of the hut, indicating that they were ready, he nodded to John.

Cain noticed him suck in a deep breath. Then John's fangs extended and he pulled his silver knife from its sheath.

"Don't kill him, understand me? No matter what he's done," Cain cautioned, knowing that John would be unpredictable if any harm had come to his lover.

Sneaking up to the hut, Cain and his friends made no sound. At the door, they stopped for a moment. Cain listened for sounds from the inside and heard a mumbling voice. He concentrated.

"You fucking bitch! I'm gonna get you." It was Baltimore who spat the words between loud thumps.

A panicked look crossed John's face, and a split-second later he ripped open the door and charged inside. Cain was on his heels, watching as John barreled toward Baltimore who was crawling on the floor, poking under the bed with a broomstick.

Baltimore was flat on his back so fast, John's knife at his throat, that Cain barely had a chance to enter the hut. Cain looked around, searching for the woman. He bent down to look under the bed. But there was nobody, though the smell of a human lingered.

"What did you do with her?" John ground out, driving the blade of his silver knife a half inch into the soft spot underneath Baltimore's chin. Blood trickled from the wound. "Where is she?"

Baltimore glared back at him. "Fucking bitch!"

John growled.

From the corner of his eye, Cain saw his friends charge into the hut.

"You got him?" Gabriel asked.

Cain looked over his shoulder, when John cried out once more. "What the fuck did you do to her?"

"Wes?" Cain glared at the witch. Had Wesley failed again?

Wesley approached. "The spell worked, I'm telling you. She must have escaped."

"I'm going to kill you, you fucking bastard, if you hurt her!" John yelled at Baltimore, then glared at Wes. "And you're next!"

A movement from under the bed suddenly caught Cain's eye and he snapped his head to it. A rat came running out and ran straight to John, jumping onto his thigh. John rocked back on his haunches, but kept his knife at Baltimore's throat where it continued to make the vampire's skin sizzle.

"Oh, fuck," Wes suddenly said and crouched down. He pointed to the rat.

Cain exchanged a quick glance with him. Then his eyes went back to the rat. "You've gotta be kidding me, Wes. Really?"

Wes shrugged. "Oops."

Cain put his hand on John's shoulder. "John, she's fine. Nicolette is safe." He motioned to Haven and Eddie. "Tie Baltimore up."

As the two Scanguards men took care of Baltimore, forcing John to remove his knife from the vampire's throat, Wes reached for the rat, which was still sitting on John's thigh.

"Come on, Nicolette."

The rat turned its head to Wesley.

In disbelief John stared at the rat, then at Wesley. "Oh, my God, what have you done?" His jaw dropped. "Are you telling me this is Nicolette?"

Wes tossed him a sheepish look. "Sorry, just a little mishap."

"Mishap?" John ground out, murder in his eyes. "You turned my woman into a rat!"

"Kept her safe, though, didn't it?"

"And now? Fuck, what am I gonna do now?"

Wes stretched out his palm and the rat walked onto it. "No worries. I can turn her back." More quietly, he added, "I think."

"You think?" John lunged for the witch, but Cain jumped in between them.

"Let him try."

Wesley placed the rat on his lap and reached into his jacket pocket. He pulled out a small vial. "This should work."

"What is it?" John asked, clearly suspicious.

"Sort of a reversal potion. Makes whatever last spell somebody is under go away. You know, like the undo button on a computer."

Cain rolled his eyes.

Wesley opened the vial and dropped a tiny amount over the rat. A moment later, he landed flat on his back. A beautiful dark-skinned woman was sitting in his lap.

"Nicolette!" John cried out and snatched her from Wesley, pulling her into his arms. His lips were on hers before Cain could even blink.

"Oh, John! You came." Tears streamed over the woman's face.

John pressed her head to his chest and stroked over her hair. "Always, my love. I'll always come back for you."

Cain rose. He was happy for John, but now it was time to find Faye. He turned to Baltimore who was now tied to the metal bed frame.

"Where's Abel?"

Baltimore spat. "I don't know."

Cain slashed his claws across Baltimore's face, leaving deep cuts. Blood seeped from them, filling the hut with the scent of vampire blood. "Try again. Where is he taking Faye?"

"I don't know."

"He's lying," Nicolette interrupted.

Cain spun his head to her. "What do you know?"

"He got a phone call a short while ago. I was already in the form of a rat, so he didn't think I could hear him."

Cain's heart rate accelerated. "What did he say?"

"I could only hear his side of the conversation. Abel must be somewhere in New Orleans."

"Where?"

Nicolette shook her head, regret in her eyes. "I don't know." She motioned to Baltimore. "He asked "which one?", but that's all I heard."

Cain felt his heart clench with fear for his mate. He snatched Baltimore by the throat. "Where is he keeping her?"

"Go to hell!"

"You first!"

Baltimore let out an evil laugh.

"Talk or I'm going to kill you!"

"You'll kill me anyway, even if I talk."

Cain stared at his adversary, but he knew Abel's most loyal follower knew the drill: once he'd divulged what he knew, either John or Cain would kill him.

"Fine, have it your way." He turned to Gabriel. "Use whatever methods you see fit to make him talk. Eddie will stay with you. The rest of us, let's go."

Cain looked around the room and spotted what he was looking for. He snatched Baltimore's cell phone from the table. Then he pulled his own phone out of his pocket and dialed Thomas's number. Scanguards' resident IT genius answered immediately.

"Thomas, have you been able to trace Abel's phone via satellite?"

"Not yet. He hasn't used it in the last hour."

"I'll make sure he does. Hold on." He put down his phone and started typing a text message on Baltimore's cell phone. "Let's see if you bite, little brother."

44

Faye slowly felt her consciousness returning. A bitter taste was still in her mouth and made her gag the moment she took her first conscious breath. With it, stale air filled her lungs and dust lined the inside of her nose.

Her eyes shot open and she reared up, but something jerked her back. Simultaneously, pain shot through her wrists. To her horror she realized that she lay on a large slab of stone, her wrists and ankles chained to it with silver, the only metal a vampire couldn't break. The contact with the toxic material made her skin burn. Blisters had already started forming around her wrists, though the skin on her ankles thankfully was protected by her jeans.

She looked around, turning her head as much as she could in her position, and perused her surroundings. It was dark, but her vampire vision had no problem figuring out where she was: in a crypt, chained to a ledger stone, a large flat stone placed above a grave.

Trying to calm herself, she fought to be rational. Abel was nowhere in sight, which most likely meant he'd left her here to rot. But she knew that Cain would be looking for her. She had to help him find her.

She collected her thoughts and sent a mental message to him. *Cain! Cain, help me.*

Almost instantly she felt warmth gather in her mind and a voice reply to her.

Faye, my love! You're alive!

She sighed a breath of relief. Cain had heard her.

I'm locked up.

Where are you?

In a crypt.

Do you know where?

She shook her head. *Abel knocked me out. I don't know where he brought me to.*

Can you read any of the names on the gravestones?

I'm chained to one. She looked around once more, focusing her eyes. *Oh, shit!*

What?

Her heart thundered and her palms felt clammy all of a sudden. *There are mirrors all around me.* She hadn't instantly noticed them, because she wasn't reflected in any of them, and no light was shining onto them.

Mirrors, what the hell?

She twisted on the slab. *Everywhere*, she confirmed.

Can you find any names at all? We have to know which cemetery you're at. There are too many in New Orleans.

Faye twisted her body, contorting it, trying to bend to the side so she could peek at the ledger stone beneath her. Her wrists burned from the silver, making her hiss in pain. But she didn't allow it to deter her from her mission. She had to find out where she was.

Faye! Please!

Tears shot to her eyes, but she swallowed them and shifted farther to the side, exposing a portion of the slab. She focused her eyes.

M, she thought. *A name starting with M.*

She sucked in a breath, twisting further. *MON.* She exhaled sharply. *MONT. That's all I can see.*

Then she relaxed back onto the slab and her eyes wandered up the wall to the ceiling. Her heart stopped.

"Oh, God, no!"

You have to hurry, Cain! You have to find me! There's a hole in the wall and another in the ceiling. When the sun comes up, it will shine right onto me.

And the mirrors would make absolutely sure that any ray entering the crypt would hit her, no matter at what angle it entered. The sun wouldn't have to be at its peak to do damage.

Oh, God!

"Well, hello, look who's awake." Abel's menacing voice came from behind her.

Faye twisted her head and saw him emerge from behind one of the mirrors. She made a mental note that the exit had to lie behind it.

The laugh that rolled over his lips chilled her to the bone and made her shiver. And the way he was dressed made him look like the devil. He was clad in Kevlar gear from top to bottom, his hands covered in dark leather gloves, his feet in heavy boots. In one hand he carried a motorcycle helmet with a polarized shield.

"Looks like the witch's brew is more potent when swallowed."

"Abel."

"Yes, Faye. It's me, but then you knew that all along, didn't you? You never trusted me."

He was right. Deep down she'd never been able to trust him, though until Cain's return he'd never done anything to warrant her hesitation to open up to him.

"Cain will kill you."

"I'd be disappointed if he didn't try. Now, let's see if Cain loves you more than his kingdom."

***

The partial name Faye had given him could only mean one thing. "She's at the Montague crypt. Our family's crypt. He has easy access to it."

Cain looked over his shoulder at Haven who sat in the back seat. Wes was driving. Blake was riding in the second SUV with John and Nicolette. They'd split up and driven toward different sections of New Orleans to cover as large an area as possible once they got word of Abel's position. But Thomas hadn't been able to pinpoint Abel's cell phone. He hadn't replied to the text message Cain had sent from Baltimore's phone, probably guessing that his minion had already been taken down.

"Where is that?" Haven asked.

"St. Louis Cemetery number 3. It's on Esplanade Drive, just south of City Park." He glanced at the dashboard's clock. "We have less than twenty minutes till sunrise. I'll drive, Wes!"

Cain reached for the steering wheel and motioned Wes to change seats with him. Through the opening between the two front seats Wesley squeezed into the back, while Cain jammed his foot onto the gas pedal and slid into the driver's seat. He knew this city best and, right now, every second counted. They had to reach Faye before the sun had a chance to shine into the crypt.

"Call John and have them meet us there. He knows the crypt. Tell him Abel knocked a hole into the ceiling and the wall and chained Faye to a grave right below it." The thought of what would happen to her if he didn't get to her in time sent a shudder through his body.

"Shit!" Haven cursed. "Fucking asshole." He pulled his phone out and called John. "John listen, we've got Faye's location. Meet us . . ."

Cain didn't listen to the rest of the conversation, because his own cell phone started ringing. He looked at the display. Abel, it said.

He answered it. "You—"

"Oh please, spare me the accusations. We have no time for that. You have about fifteen minutes to rescue your precious Faye, so let's get down to business."

Cain kicked the gas pedal down farther, accelerating the car to a speed of over eighty miles an hour on the almost deserted Lake Pontchartrain Causeway. To either side of the road was only water.

"What do you want?" he bit into the phone.

"You know what I want. My kingdom. It was always supposed to be mine. We agreed to it when we disposed of the old king."

Cain remembered all too well that this had been the plan. "The people didn't want you as their king. They chose me instead."

"Because you played the hero. But this time they don't get to choose. I'm going to be king. And you'll make sure of it. Or Faye will burn to death. Is that what you want?"

"You harm one hair on her head and I'll—"

"Yeah, yeah, yeah. Heard it all before. What are you trying to do, bore me to death?" An evil chuckle came through the line. "Now listen carefully. You'll pull all your men off the palace grounds instantly. That includes all members of your personal guard. Call me when it's done."

"You must be out of your mind! The Mississippians are still in the area. It would leave the palace undefended."

"But that's the whole point, isn't it? It's called killing two birds with one stone. Victor will get what's coming to him. And don't play any games, or I'll play games with your bride. I have somebody watching the palace to make sure you comply."

A click in the line confirmed that Abel had disconnected the call.

"Shit," Cain cursed. Why would his brother make the palace vulnerable to the attack of the Mississippians? He had to know that they would take over the moment the guards had left. But he couldn't worry about what Abel had meant with his cryptic remark about the leader of the Mississippi clan. Faye was more important than his kingdom.

"I heard it," Haven confirmed. "Do what he says. It'll buy us some time. How much longer to the cemetery?"

"Five minutes."

"I'll call Thomas," Haven said. "Wes, you'd better come up with some spell to help us out."

***

The cemetery still lay in darkness, but at the horizon Cain could already see the new day dawning. He jumped from the car.

"There should be protective gear in the back," he called out to Haven and opened the trunk. Haven rushed to his side and together they rifled through the items at their disposal: one dark jacket, one hoodie, and gloves.

"Shit." He looked at Haven. "You'll have to stay here. I need the jacket for Faye."

Cain pulled on the hoodie, snatched the jacket, and slipped the gloves on while already running into the cemetery, his eyes searching for John's SUV. But it hadn't arrived yet. Cain barreled down the main path. He hadn't been here in decades, but he remembered the location of his family crypt well.

The crypt, which looked like a small chapel from the outside, stood at the far end of the cemetery, its walls a good twelve feet high and surrounded by a cast iron gate to prevent vandals from defacing the stones.

Faye, I'm here.

Her response came a moment later. *Hurry, the sun, I can sense it rising.*

Every vampire had that same sense, a survival instinct. It sent a warning signal through Cain's body now, letting him know that in a moment the sun would breach the horizon and the first rays would turn night into day.

Watch out! Abel is close.

Faye's warning came just in time. The sound of a motorcycle's engine revving up came from behind the crypt. Cain's head whirled to it and he saw a dark figure on the bike, navigating through the tight path between the Montague crypt and the grave on its left. Cain charged into the path of the motorcycle, facing it head-on as the rider, whose face was hidden behind a helmet, tried to get past him.

Cain reached for the handlebar and jerked it to the side, making the bike lose its footing on the gravel beneath its wheels. While the bike's front wheel slammed against Cain's leg, pushing him to the ground, the biker hurtled toward him, landing on Cain's chest.

Despite the disguise, Cain could identify his brother's aura.

Cain blocked his brother's first strike with his forearm, then kicked him off and rolled to the side, jumping to his feet in the same movement. He whirled to face him, but Abel had jumped up just as quickly. He'd always been agile. Cain charged at him, tackling him and slamming him against the cast iron fence surrounding the crypt. The iron moaned under the impact, giving a little.

Abel grunted and fought back, his fists flying at Cain's unprotected face, knocking his head sideways and making his vertebrae crack audibly. Abel used the time this bought him to push himself away from the fence. But Cain caught himself quickly and landed an uppercut underneath Abel's chin, the only portion of his head that wasn't protected by his helmet.

Abel's head whipped back for only an instant, Cain's blow having done no damage. Furious, Cain aimed at his brother's neck, but the gloves impeded his claws from slicing into the part of Abel's flesh that was exposed. His upper body was protected too well. The heavy Kevlar vest was practically impenetrable.

Cain reached for the knife on his belt when a blow to his shoulder ripped him to the side. A ray of sun hit his face that instant and made him cry out in pain. Whirling back to Abel and turning his back to the rising sun, he finally gripped his knife and pulled it from its sheath. He aimed low.

While his knife drove into Abel's thigh, his brother ripped the hoodie off Cain's head, exposing it to the sun. He felt the heat as if somebody was aiming a flamethrower at him.

The scent of Abel's blood and Cain's burning hair mingled. Clenching his jaw, Cain's hand jerked up, trying to drive the knife underneath Abel's chin, but his brother's arm blocked him just before it reached its target.

Cain! The sun! Help me!

Faye's mental cry for help pierced his head.

"Nooooo!" he cried out.

A second later, Abel's fist knocked the knife from Cain's hand.

"Help me! Cain!" Faye's muffled cry now came from the crypt.

He had no choice. He had to save Faye. Abel knew it, too, if the evil laugh behind his helmet was anything to go by.

Killing his brother would have to wait. Cain freed himself from his brother's grip and raced past him, vaulting himself over the iron gate.

The lock on the crypt was broken. He pushed it open and charged into the interior. Light was already entering from the hole in the side of the building that faced east. It hit the many mirrors lined along the walls of the crypt.

"Faye!"

Faye lay on a stone slab in the middle of it, trying to twist away from the rays of the sun already hitting her. But the chains around her wrists and ankles prevented her from moving.

Her gaze shot to him. "Cain!" Tears streamed down her face and pain was evident in her features.

"Oh, God, no!"

Rushing toward her, he noticed to his horror that in his fight with Abel he'd lost the jacket he'd brought for her. He had nothing to cover her with. He pulled his dark hoodie off and threw it over her, covering her face and upper torso as best he could.

But the rays of the sun continued to shine onto her, hurting her. Just as the sun started to burn his own body. Yet he couldn't think of himself now. He had to rescue Faye.

"Hold on, baby!" he called out to her as he kicked his leg against one of the mirrors, shattering it into a thousand pieces.

"Cain!"

Her cries continued, the smell of burned flesh and hair becoming stronger now, as he aimed at the next mirror and smashed that one too. He felt his movements slow down as he destroyed the third mirror, but he couldn't give up. He would save Faye or die trying.

His next kick barely cracked the mirror. His strength was draining from him as more and more of his body covered with blisters and began to smolder. Recognizing that his own life was lost, only one thought counted now: he had to keep Faye alive long enough until his friends would arrive to help.

With his last strength, he ran to the center of the crypt and jumped onto her, covering her with his body to shelter her from the sun.

"I love you, Faye. I'll always love you."

Tears stung in his eyes and pain radiated down his spine as he took the full brunt of the sun's rays.

Darkness suddenly fell over the crypt, and he knew his end was coming. He would die in her arms.

"Cain," she sobbed.

He still felt her body beneath his, still heard her heartbeat, sensed her breathing. But he knew in a few moments he would turn to ash and she would have no further protection from the sun. Only one hope remained: that there was a heaven for vampires, and that they would meet there.

"Oh, fuck!" a male voice penetrated the haze in his mind.

Cain tried to focus on it, realizing he knew the voice.

"Cain! Fuck, you look like crap!"

Involuntarily, Cain lifted his head and turned in the direction of the voice. A blurry looking Blake came rushing toward him.

Was he delirious?

Then a hand touched his arm. "Easy, easy," Blake said. "We've got you. It's all good."

Cain's eyes adjusted, and he suddenly noticed that it was dark in the crypt. No sunlight was entering.

"What happened?" he choked out. Beneath him, Faye breathed heavily, and he quickly braced himself on his knees to take his weight off her, Blake helping him in his weakened state.

"Nicolette and I managed to throw a tarp over the holes. Wes helped with a spell 'cause the building was too high for us to reach the roof."

Looking up, Cain saw that indeed both holes, the one in the ceiling and the one in the wall opposite were covered with something dark. Relieved, he pulled on the hoodie covering Faye's face. Her skin was red and covered in burns, pink tears rimmed her eyes, but her eyes met his, and he knew then that everything would be all right.

"Cain," she murmured. "You came for me."

"Always."

Then she turned her head to Blake. "Thank you."

The door opened, and two more people entered: Nicolette and Wesley. They slammed the door shut behind them.

"You guys look like you need blood," Wes stated. "Way I see it, you've got three willing donors here. Take your pick."

Cain tried to sit up, but his entire body shook. Blake put his arm around him to steady him.

"Can you get some tools to get those chains off Faye?" Cain asked, knowing she was still in pain due to the continued contact of the silver with her wrists.

"Already on it," Wes confirmed. "John is driving the car through the main gate and bringing it closer. He'll bring a chain cutter."

Cain nodded. "And Abel?"

"We saw him drive away on the motorcycle. Haven is chasing him by car. But—"

The ringing of Cain's phone interrupted him. Cain pulled it from his pocket and looked at the display. He tapped it. "Thomas?"

"Is Faye safe?"

"Yes."

"Good, then I hope you don't mind that we'll defend your kingdom now."

"Are the Mississippians attacking?"

"Yes, but they're not only attacking us, they're also attacking their own leader: Victor."

Instantly Abel's words came back to Cain. "Oh, God, that's what Abel wanted."

"What?"

"Abel has the Mississippi guards in his pocket. You have to save Victor!"

45

Cain looked over the heads of his subjects and other guests that were assembled in the large ballroom of the palace and brought the glass of blood to his lips, taking a sip. A feeling of relief and happiness filled him as he watched his fellow vampires and the few humans—plus one witch—mingle and finally relax after the tense hours the night before.

Next to him, Victor, the king of the Mississippi clan set his empty glass on a table nearby. "I'm very grateful to you and your men for my life."

Cain looked at him, inclining his head by a fraction. "I'm glad Thomas was able to act so swiftly."

Victor shook his head. "I still can't believe it. My own men. Your brother managed to infiltrate my own king's guards and convince them to kill me."

"His greed for power had no bounds. He figured he could take both kingdoms in one swoop, deposing me by forcing me to withdraw the guards that were loyal to me, then letting you take the palace with your men, before your men killed you."

Victor frowned. "Do you think it was his plan all along when he invited me to come? He spoke about peace negotiations."

Cain scoffed. "My brother was never one for peace, though I do believe he'd planned things differently. From what John told me, I know that he was planning to pin my murder on you and your clan, thus inciting an open war . . ."

". . . during which my guards would have stabbed me in the back."

"Precisely," Cain concluded.

"So why didn't you follow Abel's command to withdraw all your men from the palace?"

"I did." He motioned to Thomas who stood in the crowd talking to Eddie and John. "But I'm afraid that some people just don't know how to execute a direct order."

Victor chuckled. "I'd call that insubordination."

"Do I hear insubordination?" Gabriel sidled up to them. "Not too long ago I knew somebody who couldn't take orders either."

Cain gave the Scanguards boss a sideways smile. "That's because that somebody isn't meant to follow orders but give them."

Victor nodded to Gabriel. "I hear you're the one who killed Baltimore. Guess you couldn't break him."

"Oh, we broke him. That's why Thomas took a few of the guards and hid in the palace with them. He knew something was gonna go down."

Though Gabriel didn't say it, Cain knew that Thomas had taken a few loyal guards and hidden in the tunnels with them to be ready to enter the palace again once he knew Faye was safe.

"Once we had all the information we needed from Baltimore, there was no reason to keep him alive," Gabriel added.

Cain turned to Victor. "Baltimore confirmed Abel's plan and how he was trying to manipulate you into a hostile action by letting you know that we were sheltering two of your clan members here." He took a deep breath. "Which brings me to an issue we need to discuss."

Victor raised his hand, interrupting him. "Before you go on, let me say this. I don't condone the defanging of vampires. It's beneath me."

"Then why did you do it?"

"If I may explain something first, please."

Cain nodded.

"My old king wasn't much better than yours. Many of us had had enough of him and his cruelties. So we decided to get rid of him. I was chosen to succeed him. But that didn't mean that the cruelties ended. There are still factions within our clan who follow in the old king's footsteps. As for the defanging of those two unfortunate individuals: It wasn't my doing. It appears that the guards that Abel turned over to his side took it upon themselves to butcher those two vampires."

Surprised at the revelation, Cain raised an eyebrow. "You're saying you didn't order this?"

Victor shook his head.

"Then why were you demanding I hand David and Kathryn over to you?"

"I needed them to tell me who performed this barbaric act on them. I needed to find the traitors in my kingdom. But I couldn't trust anybody, so I went along with the charade and called David and Kathryn traitors. I'm sorry I had to deceive you. I hope this won't stand between us when we negotiate for peace."

Cain set down his glass and offered his hand. "I look forward to our negotiations."

Victor shook his hand and bowed. "Likewise. Now, if you'll excuse me, I'd like to personally thank the man who saved my life."

Once Victor was out of earshot, Cain addressed Gabriel. "Anything new?"

With a regretful shake of his head, Gabriel said, "I'm sorry. We lost him. Abel knows the city better than Haven. Haven never had a chance at catching him."

Cain clenched his jaw, trying not to let this failure spoil his mood. "One day I'll get him and make him pay for what he did."

"If he values his life, he'll never cross your path again," Gabriel said and put his hand on Cain's forearm. "Try to forget what you can't change." He glanced to the side from where Faye was now approaching. "You have a wonderful life ahead of you. Don't let hate poison your happiness."

"I won't," he promised Gabriel and walked to Faye, opening his arms and wrapping her into an embrace. "My queen."

Faye looked ravishing in her long strapless red dress, the same dress she'd worn in his dream.

"My king," she responded, her lips only inches from his.

"I think it's time to leave."

Faye chuckled. "You can't leave your own welcome home party so soon. Your subjects came expressly to see you."

"I'm the king. I can leave whenever I want." He swept her up into his arms.

"Cain! Put me down. Everybody's looking."

Cain glanced at the crowd and noticed heads turning. "I don't care." It didn't matter what everybody thought of him taking his mate and carrying her out of the ballroom. All that mattered was that he wanted to be alone with her now.

They had both healed thanks to Blake's and Nicolette's blood, and now was the time to renew their love.

Cain kicked the door to his suite shut behind him and brought his lips to Faye's. "I had a dream."

"Yes?"

He carried her to the bed and stopped in front of it. "You were wearing this dress, but you wore nothing underneath."

A soft laugh rolled over her lips. "My love, you have a very wicked imagination."

"Do I?" He laid her down on the crisp sheets. "Or do I have a very wicked wife?"

Faye batted her eyelashes at him. "Maybe you should investigate that claim of yours."

Cain ripped his bow tie open and tossed it to the floor, then shrugged his dinner jacket off his shoulders. "Yeah, maybe I should," he answered teasingly. "Just as soon as I've gotten rid of my clothes."

Her eyes watched him as he freed himself from his shirt. "I've always loved you stripping for me."

Cain found himself smiling down at her as he opened the button to his pants and slid the zipper down. "Funny, in my dream I was the one saying that." He stepped out of his shoes and pulled his socks off, before dropping his pants.

Faye's lips parted on a breath while she let her eyes run over his nearly naked body. Cain dropped his gaze to his boxer briefs. The outline of his erection was clearly visible underneath the black fabric. Lifting his lids a fraction, he looked at her.

"Would you like me to take those off, too?"

Her eyes glowed with undisguised lust. "Don't be a tease. Show me what I want to see." Her hands reached for him. "Let me feel you."

Cain hooked his thumbs under his boxer briefs and pushed them down slowly, watching with delight how Faye's chest lifted and how her nipples hardened under the thin silk fabric of her dress.

Cool air wafted against his cock when he finally rid himself of the last piece of clothing and stood in front of her completely naked. His chest lifted with each breath, and his heart pumped more blood into his cock, making his eager appendage point upward, tilting toward his navel.

"Is that what you want, my insatiable queen?"

Faye opened her mouth wider. Fangs now peeked from her upper gums, slowly descending to their full length. He'd never seen a more erotic sight.

"Now show me if my dream was right," he demanded.

She stroked provocatively down her torso. Mid thigh she gathered the fabric in her hands and pulled it up higher, first revealing her calves, then her knees.

"More," he demanded, his voice now sounding hoarse.

She complied silently and pushed the fabric higher. Her bare thighs came into view. She spread them just a little, then inched the fabric over her hips, revealing the treasure beneath.

Cain's mouth went dry. Just like in his dream, she was bare. A dark nest of hair was all that guarded her sex. He lifted his head and connected with her gaze.

"Satisfied?" she murmured.

"In a moment both of us will be," he promised and gripped her dress.

She helped him strip her of it by sitting up, before pressing her flat back onto the bed. He moved over her and pushed her thighs farther apart with his knee to make space for himself.

When he felt her arms come around him and pull him to her, he knew the world was right again. Without a word, he adjusted his angle and thrust into her.

A moan came over her lips, bouncing against his.

"I nearly lost you. I've never been so scared in my entire life," Cain confessed and brushed his lips against hers.

"I was so scared when I lay there tied to that grave. But when I heard your voice in my head, it gave me strength." Her hand caressed his nape, making him shiver with pleasure.

"I'll keep you safe now, my love. Like I promised you a long time ago."

Cain pressed his lips to hers and kissed her. His hips started moving in synch with Faye's body, thrusting, then withdrawing, sliding in and out of her silken sheath, connecting with her. Their bond had saved them both. Without it he wouldn't have found her in time. It had made them stronger.

The fire between them would always burn brightly, just like it did now as their movements became more urgent, more demanding, and the need for ultimate intimacy was at its highest.

Cain severed his lips from hers and let his fangs emerge, while his cock drove into her with relentless thrusts and her thighs imprisoned him in her center. Faye's eyes glowed red, just like his. They were both driven by their most primal needs now. Only one thing could add to the pleasure already coursing through his body and rendering him boneless.

"Bite me!" he demanded and sank his fangs into her shoulder, offering her his neck.

The moment Faye's fangs drove into his flesh, Cain shuddered violently. A bolt as strong as a thousand lightning strikes charged through his body and into the tip of his cock. He exploded.

My love, my queen, my life.

A wave washed against him, and he knew it was Faye's orgasm that now crested.

My love, my king, my life, she responded.

She was all he would ever need. No matter what happened to his kingdom in the future, as long as he had Faye, he would be happy.

~ ~ ~

ABOUT THE AUTHOR

Tina Folsom was born in Germany and has been living in English speaking countries for over 25 years, the last 14 of them in San Francisco, where she's married to an American.

Tina has always been a bit of a globe trotter: after living in Lausanne, Switzerland, she briefly worked on a cruise ship in the Mediterranean, then lived a year in Munich, before moving to London. There, she became an accountant. But after 8 years she decided to move overseas.

In New York she studied drama at the American Academy of Dramatic Arts, then moved to Los Angeles a year later to pursue studies in screenwriting. This is also where she met her husband, who she followed to San Francisco three months after first meeting him.

In San Francisco, Tina worked as a tax accountant and even opened her own firm, then went into real estate, however, she missed writing. In 2008 she wrote her first romance and never looked back.

She's always loved vampires and decided that vampire and paranormal romance was her calling. She now has 32 novels in English and several dozens in other languages (Spanish, German, and French) and continues to write, as well as have her existing novels translated.

For more about Tina Folsom:
http://www.tinawritesromance.com
http://www.facebook.com/TinaFolsomFans
http://www.twitter.com/Tina_Folsom
You can also email her at tina@tinawritesromance.com

Lightning Source UK Ltd.
Milton Keynes UK
UKHW011043260319
339910UK00001B/416/P